WITNESSES FOR THE DEAD

 stories

WITNESSES FOR THE DEAD

||||||| STORIES |||||||

Edited by Gary Phillips and Gar Anthony Haywood

WITH CONTRIBUTIONS FROM:

Scott Adlerberg
Cara Black
Christopher Chambers
Sarah M. Chen
Aaron Philip Clark
Teresa Dovalpage
Tod Goldberg

Gar Anthony Haywood
Darrell James
Richie Narvaez
Gary Phillips
SJ Rozan
Alex Segura
Pamela Samuels Young

SOHO
CRIME

Published by
Soho Press, Inc.
227 W 17th Street
New York, NY 10011

Library of Congress Cataloging-in-Publication Data

Names: Phillips, Gary, editor. | Haywood, Gar Anthony, editor. |
Adlerberg, Scott, author. Title: Witnesses for the dead : stories / edited by
Gary Phillips and Gar Anthony Haywood ; with contributions from Scott
Adlerberg [and others]. Description: New York : Soho Press, Inc., 2022. Identifiers:
LCCN 2022011018

ISBN 978-1-64129-526-0
eISBN 978-1-64129-399-0

Subjects: LCSH: Short stories, American—21st century. | LCGFT: Short
stories. Classification: LCC PS648.S5 W565 2022
DDC 813/.0108—dc23/eng/20220401
LC record available at https://lccn.loc.gov/2022011018

Interior design by Janine Agro

Printed in the United States of America

10 9 8 7 6 5 4 3 2 1

In Memory of Lloyd Creary
Who lived for family and community and planted the
seed that became this book

TABLE OF CONTENTS

||||||||||||||||||||||||||||||||||||||||

INTRODUCTION

||||||||||||||||||||||||||

When former First Lady Nancy Reagan introduced the phrase "Just Say No" to young Americans as an approach to avoid crack cocaine in the early 1980s, no one could deny how catchy it was. And as a tactic in the War on Drugs, it sounded so simple and easily adopted. But just saying "no" to some things is often difficult, if not impossible, and the slogan's advice soon proved easier said than done.

Similarly, "See Something, Say Something" suffers from this same dichotomy: it sounds so easy to do and yet is quite often anything but. Aside from the natural reluctance many have to get involved in other peoples' business, reporting someone to the authorities over one infraction or another we just happened to witness feels something like only a snitch or a "rat" would do, to quote every film noir ever made. For in some cases, you can get yourself hurt or even killed for being a rat.

Luckily for all of us, there are heroes among us who, when they saw something, they said something. Despite the possible consequences for them. Darnella Frazier is one such hero.

Ms. Frazier at the time was a seventeen-year-old Black woman who, in recording George Floyd's death at the hands (or rather, left knee) of Minneapolis police officer Derek Chauvin in May of 2020, helped lead to Chauvin's eventual conviction on murder and manslaughter charges. People across the country, including Floyd's family, have applauded her bravery and quick thinking in the face of police pressure to leave the scene, which they say made the guilty verdict possible.

The stories in *Witnesses for the Dead* are inspired by Ms. Frazier's courage in choosing to make George Floyd's business her own. These tales are indeed about people driven, to lesser and greater degrees, to do the right thing, though what is "right" in some cases is purely subjective. The ideas some have about balancing the scales might give you, the ordinary, upright, pay-my-bills-on-time denizen, considerable pause.

There are characters populating these pages who, rather than simply observing a crime, take the initiative to see that the guilty are punished and the victims receive justice. In some stories, our "heroes" are drawn into perilous situations against their will, and must fight to survive just to ensure what they've witnessed will matter.

For the most part, the protagonists herein don't wear uniforms or carry a badge—they're ordinary people, sometimes shady people, who nonetheless take extraordinary steps to right a wrong. Given the choice between inaction and action, these men and women take the latter route, sometimes with great reluctance, and occasionally at great risk to themselves.

As the editors of this collection, we hope you'll find these stories entertaining as well as thought-provoking. You may not always find the actions of these characters "heroic," but you might admire their courage in the face of danger enough to find such courage yourself, should the need ever arise. Because you never know when you might stumble upon something dark and frightening that you weren't meant to see, and you'll have to decide what to do about it. Pretend it didn't happen or shine a light to answer an injustice?

When and if that time ever comes, we trust you'll let what Darnella Frazier did be your guide.

All royalties from this collection will be donated to the Alliance for Safe Traffic Stops.

Gary Phillips
Gar Anthony Haywood

DEATH AT THE SUNDIAL MOTEL

IIIIIIIIIIIIIIIIIIIIIIIII Aaron Philip Clark

The Sundial Motel was a relic on a dirt road. An old behemoth, it had forty rooms across six floors. It was the last stateside motel before reaching the Mexican border. When the property was converted into studio apartments rented by the week, it became affordable housing for those struggling to survive, many undocumented like Alma Henri and her son, Criston.

Ernesto spoke softly when he told Alma that Criston was dead. At first, the words struck her ears oddly, sounding like gibberish spoken through a funnel. It was as if she were listening to a song on a forty-five record, slowed, warped, the needle slipping out of the groove. But she knew this song—borne of her greatest fear, something that dwelled inside her, shone brighter each time Criston would venture out into the world. And it had been this way since he was seventeen when they came to the States. Now, he was dead at twenty, and Alma knew nothing except his body was lying in the street a few blocks from where she stood.

"I can take you to him," Ernesto said as they stood in Apartment 3. Though she was not tall, she towered over the boy, stoutly and bow-legged. The cheap floor lamp washed his face in gilded radiance while casting a grand shadow on the wall. "The police are there, so we'll need to be careful," he said. Alma knew what he meant. Like her, he was without papers, undocumented. The motel had become a haven for her and others who had escaped violence and famine in places stricken by death.

"All right," she said.

Ernesto looked to his mother as if to request permission to leave. Though Alma had seen the boy wander the Sundial's grounds and adjacent streets unsupervised at all hours, she thought it was a respectful gesture. Ernesto's mother was a frail woman sitting in a worn recliner. She was dressed in a hand-stitched frock of patchwork fabric and a knit cap because she had lost much of her hair in a fire. His mother nodded, and Ernesto got up from the bed's edge, drew air into his chest, and turned to Alma. "Follow me," He said.

Alma walked with Ernesto into the chilly San Ysidro night that carried dust on the wind. She was without her jacket but didn't feel cold. The boy led her down the sidewalk toward a cluster of red and blue lights in the distance. Her dreadlocks were wrapped in a scarf, and her once-white canvas sneakers were stained and threadbare. As they got closer to the commotion, each step felt like weights were anchored to her feet. When they were close enough to see the cordoned-off scene, the two stood under a bus stop's awning across the street. "There," Ernesto said, pointing to the skinny figure on the ground. An orphaned shoe was on the curb, and an arm stuck out underneath a sheet. A crushed gold watch still on the bloody wrist shimmered like a beacon in the dark. It felt like the arm had been reaching for something, for someone.

"Did you see what happened?" Alma asked, unable to cry. She had learned to stomach her pain, never showing it in front of Criston. Even in frightful moments, times she was certain they'd be sent back to Haiti, her face was stone. Fear had become a constant in her life, and it ruled her even now. Fear of deportation. Fear of not being able to protect her child. It was a feeling she had come to accept, just as she would now have to accept his loss.

"No, Miss Alma. I'm sorry."

"All right," she said. "Thank you." And with that, the boy left.

The night's air was all over her as she watched men and women with badges in uniforms and suits walk past her son's body as if it were no more significant than the hydrant feet from where he lay. An ambulance was parked, but its lights were off—there wasn't any need. The emergency had passed. The paramedics conversed with deputies, paper cups of hot liquid steaming in their hands. Their attention was on a howling man, who stood dressed in a tan jacket, jeans, and boots. The man's legs seemed weak, his torso a boulder affixed on two twigs. His laughter caused tremors that threatened his footing. He steadied himself with the aid of an officer's shoulder.

Alma grew up with drunks—piggish men—she recognized them by how they moved and spoke. The alcohol fouled their breath, got into their muscles and bones— seized their thoughts. Their bodies would confess what their mouths worked to hide. "I'm fine . . . I only had one," they'd say.

Alma shuddered at the thought of Criston dying in the street, taking his last breath without her there to comfort him. It was inexplicable. Mothers weren't supposed to bury their sons. She wondered how long Criston had been dead and what would happen to him next. Alma wanted to go to him, hug his thin body, tell him how much he was loved. It would surely mean her deportation, but what good was staying in the States now that her *pitit gason* was gone?

More deputies arrived in cruisers and SUVs, red and blue lights flashing. Alma had lived to avoid people in uniforms, especially the police, and now there were many standing near the pickup truck, shining flashlights against its front end. She didn't know the truck's model, but it looked American, with a long, wide body, and she could see the damage: a dented hood, cracked headlight, a broken side-view mirror.

Alma tasted a bitter taint in her throat. She coughed hard, nearly lost her balance. Then, vomited onto her shoes. The earth spun, and Criston's voice in her head was all she could hear. Not as a man, but as a tender boy, timid, holding onto her apron strings. The Lord told her he had a good heart and would grow to be a good man, and he was . . .

Unable to watch anymore, Alma left and returned to the Sundial. Her neighbors, many who knew Criston, stood with candles and prayed the rosary outside her apartment. Alma didn't speak to them as she opened the door, but she nodded appreciatively. She noticed the vomit had dried on her shoes as her feet crossed the threshold. Once inside, she collapsed to the floor and wept.

ALMA HAD ATTENDED WORSHIP services at St. Francis Church each week, but today everything felt different—foreign. She had never been in the priest's chambers. The room was paneled in mahogany, the carpet blood-red, and a dust-coated window offered the only measure of light. It rattled as the Santa Ana winds blew, whipping up the earth. Alma could see the brown billows sweeping across the empty desert and thought of her son. Criston loved the desert, though she didn't understand why. "It's so filthy," she'd tell him as he admired its scope. "It is what it is," he'd say without further explanation.

"Yes, that's my son," Alma said. She was sitting across from the priest, looking at an image of Criston's nude body on a metal table. The fact that it was on the priest's cell phone only made the process of identifying her son's remains all the more disheartening, which Alma didn't think was possible.

"The coroner will make arrangements with you. He will not ask about your status. Though I suggest you have the body brought here," the priest said. He had olive skin and was cloaked in a black cassock, fitted with a red sash around his waist. "You have my deepest condolences. May God bless you."

"How did they tell you he died, Father?"

"I was told a motorist struck him."

"And the driver?"

"I'm not certain."

"He's a man . . . I think he could be the police or a government official," she said.

The priest looked away as if he had heard something in the distance, but there was only silence. He turned to her slowly until their eyes met. "How do you know that?" he asked.

"I saw Criston in the street," she said. "And the truck that hit him and the man, I believe, was driving it. I didn't get close. I was afraid of what I'd do if I got close."

"That was wise," he said. "No reason to put yourself in jeopardy."

"Where can I bury my son?"

"We can have the funeral here at the church. All that's required is a simple donation."

"A fee?" Alma felt invisible, like the priest was looking through her. She wanted to scream.

"It will need to be a quick burial as we don't handle preserving the body."

"Where will he be kept?"

"The basement," he said. "It doesn't get very warm down there this time of year."

"The basement," Alma repeated. There was anger in her voice but also shame. The priest looked anxious, and she pressed on. "What about an investigation? Something should be done."

"Investigation into what, praytell?"

"He was hit. That isn't something that just happens."

"I understand it was an accident. A dark road, no side-walk. Perhaps he wandered into the traffic."

"My son never wandered," she said. "Especially not into someone's vehicle. The man who hit him was drunk, I know it."

"Miss Alma, I can't speak to any of that, but I would caution you not to make any allegations that could put you and those at the Sundial in danger. Your choices don't only impact you. Leave the matter to the police. If alcohol was involved, I'm sure the evidence will come to light." Alma nodded, though she felt sickened by each word he spoke. "It's best we mourn Criston and know that it was just his time. He's in the heavens now, with the Creator. It's where he was needed."

"But my son should be here with me!"

The priest reached for Alma's hand. She wanted to pull away but surrendered to his touch. No one had touched her since Criston hugged her the morning of his death. It was all the comfort she was awarded, even if it was out of pity. "You're familiar with the Book of Revelations?" he asked.

"I know the prophecies."

"Good," he said. "Then you know that everything must end. But what some won't tell you is that the prophecies in the book may have already come to pass."

"I don't understand."

"What if we exist after the destruction told in the text? A people born out of time. Living in limbo, waiting for God to turn off the lights."

"That carries no importance to me."

"What I'm trying to say is death isn't the end. It's a beginning. In the heavens is where we truly belong." He reached his arms above his head and shook them violently as if it were a ritual calling of haints. "He's up there, Miss Alma, and he's looking down on you, and he wants you to go on living."

"Stop," Alma said, slamming her fist on the priest's desk. "Your words are meaningless." She rubbed her temples and stood up from the chair with a sigh.

"Excuse me?"

"Save it for your sermons," she said. "My son was killed, and you want me to forget?"

"Please, Miss Alma . . ."

"Why can't you speak to the police for me?" she asked. "See if they checked the driver's blood . . ."

"It wouldn't do any good."

"Why?"

"Leave it, Miss Alma." The priest spoke sternly as if she were a child. "There are things about living in this country you still don't understand."

Alma didn't need to understand and knew when a man was hiding something. She snatched a letter opener from a small jar on the priest's desk and held it tightly in her palm, studying its tip, appreciating its heft.

"I know why God took my Criston," she said. "It was to punish me." Alma moved closer to the priest, and she laid her hand on his shoulder. "When I first came to this church, all I felt was guilt. Do you remember what I confessed to you?"

"I do," the priest said.

"You told me that I'd be forgiven," she said. "I know that's what you're supposed to say, but I didn't believe you. God's seen what I've done, looked into my heart, and he knows what I am."

"And what are you, Miss Alma?"

"Nothing good," she said. "In my village, they called me *destrikte . . .*"

"What is that?"

"Destroyer," she said, bringing the letter opener to the priest's throat and pressing its tip into the flaccid flesh, to the right of his Adam's apple. "Why don't the police come for us? Arrest us? Deport us?"

"If you want to continue living at the Sundial, be careful what you do next—"

She pricked him, producing a dollop of blood. It ran down the priest's neck until it reached his collar, spreading into the white fibers. "You are not the first man I've made bleed," she said.

"Please, think about what you're doing!"

"Tell me what arrangement you have with the police." She pressed the opener's point further into his neck. It was like jabbing a pen into an inflated balloon. She knew his neck would burst like an opened valve with a little more pressure.

"There is no arrangement!"

"Stop lying," she said, needling his neck more, twisting the blade's point until more blood trickled. Killing him would be easy as slaughtering a chicken and she imagined how undetectable his blood would look seeping into the red carpet.

The priest's eyes were locked on her's. Alma wondered what he saw in her brown pools with green halos. Perhaps the emptiness she felt? Hollowed and heartbroken now that Criston was gone. Could he see it? Somewhere behind her severe glare, that she didn't fear prison or death or purgatory? Damnation had already come to her.

"Okay, okay," he said, exasperated. "Apartment twenty-two. You'll find answers there." Blood slipped down the opener's edge to Alma's finger. It was warm and oily.

"What about it?" Alma asked, releasing the priest.

He coiled back into the chair. "Go, see for yourself. But once you do, you can never set foot in this church again. What I've told you could ruin everything."

"If what you've told me is anything but the truth, then God help you."

"Oh, Miss Alma," he said, removing his blood-stained collar. "The only thing left now is God."

WHEN ALMA RETURNED TO the Sundial, she didn't encounter anyone, though she could sense eyes on her peering from behind curtains. Most residents at the Sundial had mastered the art of minding their business. They rarely asked one another about who they had been in their home countries. Everyone had given up something—status, career, a family. They were transients hoping to one day become citizens of a country they knew little about but had placed all their hopes in. There was a common yearning to remember where they came from and hold onto tradition, beliefs, and pride for who they were, even if their worlds had changed.

Alma hadn't worked at the janitorial company that morning and was certain she had sacrificed her job, which had been her only personal source of income for a year. Alma was paid five dollars an hour to clean office buildings throughout San Diego County, and the company's owner, a man she knew only as Mr. Rattler, paid her cash each week. She didn't bother explaining to him she'd lost her son. Rattler rarely remembered her name and reminded the workers that they were replaceable.

A note was tacked on Alma's door from the motel's manager—a reminder that her rent would be due in three days. She would have to go into her and Criston's savings to pay it. No longer would she have what he made at the gas station to help with expenses. She ripped the note from the door, went inside, and sat on her bed.

If Criston were to have a tombstone, she considered what it would say—*Beloved Son, Shining Light*? Old photos and texts had become precious now; she read them and sobbed. When she came to the last message Criston had sent her, she read it aloud:

"On my way home. Picked up pain haïtien."

Alma loved bread and coffee at breakfast, and she could see him like a shimmer in the dark, coming home after his shift as a gas station attendant, bread tucked under his arm, delighted to serve it to her in the morning.

Alma didn't trust the priest and couldn't fathom what she'd find in Apartment 22. She removed a long wooden box under her bed, opened it, and pulled a blade from its sheath. Alma's reflection showed clearly in its metal. It was a *manchèt*, often called a machete in the States.

In Haiti, it had been Alma's weapon of choice. She preferred it over a gun or knife, though she had used both in her line of work. The *manchèt* was decades older than her, passed down through generations. It was a humble weapon with a handle wrapped in crocodile skin, long, curved, and sharp. It had been used in revolutions, helped secure schools for children, kept bandits at bay, protected the wealthy, and later cleared an escape path through the dense jungle when men came to take Criston's life.

She slipped the blade back into its leather sheath, tied its braided strap around her waist, put on a long coat that best hid the weapon, and left the apartment.

Apartment 22 was located at the rear of the motel and faced a parking lot. When night fell, the lot became the site of fights, drug use, sex in cars. She and Criston only ventured to the rear of the motel in daylight, usually to throw garbage into the roach-infested dumpster or pour frying oil into the dirt.

It was five minutes to 2 P.M. She stood at the foot of the stairs leading to Apartment 22. Many of the Sundial's residents would begin making lunch soon, and she anticipated the smells of plantains, chicken adobo, stewed corn, and beef braised in mole. It always astonished her that the most delectable smelling dishes were made on two-burner stoves and ovens that couldn't fit most roast pans. Alma climbed the stairs to the unit, and when she reached the door, she stood in front, unsure of what to do next. The window's curtain was drawn, and she couldn't hear anyone inside, despite the thin doors and single pane glass that made for cold, drafty nights. Alma felt uneasy and thought it best to watch and wait. She walked downstairs into the parking lot and waited near the dumpster. She debated returning to her apartment, believing 22 to be empty and the priest to have lied. Then she saw Ernesto carrying a grocery bag, walking from the front of the building. He went upstairs to

Apartment 22 and knocked. The door opened, and he entered.

Alma continued to wait near the dumpster. When the boy appeared, he headed downstairs. She moved quickly, meeting the boy as he came down the last few steps. When Ernesto saw Alma, he stopped. She crouched down until their eyes met and said, "Hello again."

"Hello," Ernesto said, standing meekly in a windbreaker a size too small.

"Can I ask what you were doing in that apartment?"

"I make deliveries," he said.

"Is that your job?"

"People pay me to bring them things."

"What people?"

"I should go," he said, moving away from Alma. "I have more deliveries."

"Wait, please? Can you tell me who you gave the food to?"

Ernesto was hesitant and looked up toward Apartment 22. "I shouldn't."

"I promise, you won't get in trouble," Alma said. "But if someone in there needs help, we should help them, right? Just like you helped me when you took me to see my son."

Ernesto nodded. "I bring food to the sick girl."

"A sick girl lives there?"

"Yes."

"Do you think I can see her?"

"Why?" he asked.

"If she's sick, I'd like to help."

"Were you a doctor?" he asked. "I mean before you came here?"

"No, but I've helped many girls before. Many of them were sick."

"You have medicine? Can you make her better?"

"I can try," she said.

"All right," he said, overcoming his hesitation. "I believe you, Miss Alma." She followed Ernesto upstairs to Apartment 22. The boy knocked twice. Alma stood out of view. When the door opened, a man's voice said, "What is it, boy? You forget something?"

Ernesto lowered his head, didn't speak. Alma nudged the boy aside and pushed her way into the apartment.

A withered man with wrinkled brown skin stood disheveled, holding his pants to his waist with one hand and an unlit cigarette in the other. He was missing most of his teeth, save for two that poked up from his bottom gum. It reminded Alma of the fence pickets orphaned in the sand after flooding demolished her childhood home in Haiti.

"Who are you?" he asked. A baggy sweatshirt swallowed up his frail limbs. "You need to leave." He glared as if trying to see through smoke, and Alma thought his vision might be poor. She noticed a girl asleep on the single bed. Heavy makeup was on her face: red lipstick layered to a thick sheen. The apartment smelled of jasmine; a large yellow candle burned on the stove.

She looked back at the doorway, and Ernesto was gone. The frail man looked as if he wanted to retaliate but did nothing. "Don't move," she said, walking to the corner of the room where a video camera was mounted to a tripod. It looked older than one Criston had bought at the Sunday Swap Meet last year. Instead of a slot for a memory card, there was a chamber where a tape would go.

"What's wrong with the girl?" she asked.

"She's ill, has a condition."

"Why do you need a camera?"

"Please, leave. You're going to make it bad for all of us.

No one comes into Apartment Twenty-two without permission. That's the rule."

"Whose rule?" she asked, but the man didn't answer. "Where's her family?"

"Who the hell are you to be asking about her family? I told you to leave."

"Careful, old man," she said, raising her fist. "Tell me, where are her people?"

He began to sulk, then answered, "Deported."

"To where?"

"I don't know," he said. "Honduras, I think. I just watch her, that's it—"

"And who told you to watch her?"

"I can't tell you that. Please, I beg you, leave before you make things worse."

"No," she said, looking at the sleeping girl.

"There's nothing you can do, leave her," he said. "You'll only ruin your life."

"Be more concerned with yourself," she said, pulling her coat back to reveal the *manchèt* on her hip.

"You don't have to hurt me. I'm nobody—"

"Tell me why she's here."

"He makes me do this," he cried.

"Who makes you?"

"Please," he begged, his hands steepled as if he were praying. "I don't know his name, but he'll send me back to Cebu. I can't go back."

"Why isn't she waking up?"

"It's the medicine," he said. "All I do is give her the medicine, but I never touch her."

"Show me."

"Here." The man took a prescription bottle from the kitchen counter and handed it to Alma. At least twenty capsules were filled with white powder. The label was removed. She presumed the drug was powerful enough to keep the girl heavily sedated for what could have been hours.

"When will this *man* be back?"

"After sundown," he said. Fear had strangled his vocal cords, and he sounded hoarse. "The boy brings dinner. Then he comes, and I can go home."

"She never goes out?" she asked, setting the bottle on the counter.

"Never," he said. "Your accent . . ." He searched Alma's face, leaning forward, glaring. "You're Haitian."

"What?"

"Yes, it's you. I heard about your boy."

"What do you know about it?"

"My wife died six months ago," he said, growing misty-eyed. "I'm very sorry."

"And did she approve of you watching this girl?"

"The job came after," he said. "My body is broken, can't work in the factory anymore. Needed money to live."

"So you became this man's watchdog?"

"He said I only had to sit with the girl during the day."

"How old is she?"

"I don't know . . . I don't ask questions," he said. "I rarely talk to her and only do what he tells me." He put the cigarette to his lips and dug inside his pocket.

Alma's hand moved to the *manchèt*. "Easy," she said, watching the man closely. His hand shook terribly as he pulled out a lighter, worked his thumb over the spool until it produced a small flame.

"Please, believe me, I tried to help her," he said, lighting the cigarette and taking a drag. "I swear I did, but she wouldn't listen. Told me it was better than living on the streets . . . better than dying in the desert."

"She's going to leave this place," Alma said. "You're going to help me."

"But you don't understand—"

"I'm not giving you a choice." She pulled the *manchèt* from the sheath and held it high. The man backed away. "Do you see her? She's not yet a woman, just made to look like one."

The man gazed at the sleeping girl. The cigarette was a dangling branch of ash. "What was I supposed to do?"

"That's between you and God. Now tell me about the man."

"He comes and goes. Doesn't talk too much," he said. "Pays me, and I leave."

"Don't lie to me," she said. "There must be something." Her patience was wearing thin; she brought the *manchèt* to his neck, and he trembled.

"Wait. Wait," he said, pumping his hands. "I have something."

"What?"

"In the recorder."

Alma pressed a button on the camera, and the chamber opened. Inside was a small tape; she feared what was on it.

"You record for him?"

"He makes me sometimes . . ." The man took a step forward and reached for the camera. "Do you want to see? Should I play it?"

She gripped his hand tightly, then yanked it away. He seemed surprised by her strength or perhaps the ease with which she moved. Grabbing the man came easy for her, as did many things that involved force.

"I'll do it," she said, pressing the play button. Time-code appeared over black on the small three-inch screen. Then, she saw the sleeping girl step into the frame. She was naked and small and climbed onto the bed. A man approached, only a white towel wrapped around his waist. His chest was specked gray and black, and his skin was blotchy and red. He was big, wide-shouldered, with a lapping belly. Alma recognized him instantly as the one who had killed her boy. He wrapped his arms around the girl, and she disappeared in his embrace.

"He has other tapes," he said in a husky whisper. "Many . . ."

"You should have given it to the police."

"The police? I would have been deported."

"Better than dying here."

"Dying?" he asked. "But I had no choice. I'm not a bad man—not like him."

Alma couldn't watch anymore. She stopped playing the tape, ejected it, and put it in her pocket. "You always have a choice," she said. Her heart was beating with ferocity. She knocked over the recorder and tripod. Pieces of plastic broke off onto the floor. The screen cracked, and the focus ring became dislodged from the housing. It was loud and violent, but the sleeping girl didn't wake.

"The man will come soon," he said. "He'll see the camera and want to know what happened."

"And then what?" she asked. "You think I should fear him?"

The man was silent.

"Those pills . . ." Alma snatched the pill bottle from the counter and rattled it. "You know what they are?"

"No," he said. "Makes the girl tired. She sleeps for hours."

Alma took off the cap and sniffed the capsules. They smelled metallic. "Leave before you join your wife."

He ashed his cigarette into the kitchen sink and moved

toward the door. Alma followed close behind him. He opened it. She took hold of his arm in the doorway and spun him to face her. Alma stared at him as she had stared at many men before. Under different circumstances, she would have pushed the man from the landing and watched him fall to the concrete, but that would bring unnecessary attention.

"Please," he said, more afraid than before. "I'll do whatever you want."

"Go back to your apartment. Not a word to anyone."

"Yes," he said. "But what are you going to do?"

Alma didn't respond and looked to the sun. It was resplendent and flooded the desert with golden light. It glowed against her skin, and she was reminded of Criston's smile and how it made her feel safe, loved.

"What about the tape?" the man asked. "What will you do with it?"

"I don't know."

"Give it to me," he said. "Please, let me make it right."

"How?"

"I'll find a way."

Alma looked skeptical. "Now you're fearless?"

"The others . . . I never believed they could help her, but you—"

"Others?"

"Some her family, some strangers," he said. "Everyone was sent back to their countries beaten—even crippled."

"Take it," Alma said, handing the man the tape. "Now, go." He put it into his pocket, hobbled down the stairs, and didn't look back.

ALMA WAITED BY THE dumpster. All she could think about was the girl in the apartment. Enslaved. Victimized.

It could have been Alma's fate in Haiti had it not been for her mother, who taught her how to wield a blade and where to put it if a man ever came for her. She had lost count of the men her *manchèt* had blessed, but she remembered how it felt when she dug its tip into their thighs, penciled their groins, tattooed her initials deep so they'd never forget.

It was sundown; Alma had waited hours. She was tired and hungry. When Ernesto returned, he was carrying containers of food and bottled water. She watched him go upstairs and knock on the door to Apartment 22. "Is that food for the girl?" Alma called to him from the bottom of the stairs.

"Yes," the boy said, arms working hard to manage the containers. "Tacos."

"You can put it down," she said, walking up the stairs. "Don't take it in just yet."

"Did you help her?" Ernesto asked with worry as he placed the container on the step. "Is she better?"

"I'm trying." Alma crouched next to the food and opened both containers, which held refried beans, rice, and what looked like beef and chicken tacos. "The door is unlocked," she said. "Take this food to her." She handed him one of the containers. "I will tend to the other." Ernesto went into the apartment with the container while Alma opened the meal she set aside for the man. She removed capsules from the pill bottle and began opening them, pouring the powder into the food.

Ernesto returned minutes later. "Is she awake?" Alma asked as she poured the last of the white powder from the capsules into the beans.

"Yes," he said. "She's eating now. Where's the old man?"

"Gone."

He studied Alma for a moment. "I know what you're going to do," he said. He reminded her of Criston, precocious and astute. "Will it kill him?"

Alma had poured at least ten capsules into the container, folding the powder into the rice and beans with a plastic knife. "I hope so," she said. The boy looked on as she continued to stir the drug into the food.

"Can I watch?" he asked.

Alma's heart was heavy. "Him die?"

"Yes."

"Have you ever seen someone die?"

"No," Ernesto said.

"It stays with you . . . something you can't forget."

"Even if they deserve it?"

"Stays longer when they deserve it." She was disturbed by the boy's request but more so by her calm delivery. Her hands were steady as she prepared the man's last meal. "You're just a boy," she said. "Best to keep being that."

Ernesto's foot was fidgety, like he was kicking imaginary dust. "I lied before, Miss Alma . . . I saw when Criston was hit."

She reached out her hand, and Ernesto took it. "I know," she said. "It's all right."

He pulled away, putting his hands into his pockets, and looked on with curiosity. Alma closed the food container. "You should go home," she said.

Before leaving, Ernesto asked, "Who are you, Miss Alma?"

Alma knew what the boy meant, but it was complicated. "I'm a mother."

"That makes you brave?"

"Maybe," she said.

"I don't like being afraid . . . I wish I could have helped her."

"You're helping her now," Alma said. The boy looked as if he were going to smile, then left.

ALMA STEPPED INTO THE apartment and set the man's food on the counter. She could see the girl better now. Her face told of the horror she was living. The drug had taken its toll: eyes drained of life, pain-filled.

"What are you doing in here?" the girl asked. "What do you want?"

"To help."

"Is that his food? Why do you have it?"

"I need him to eat it all," Alma said. "It's the only way you'll get out of here."

"What did you do to it?"

"The drug he's been giving you, I mixed it in."

"That will kill him, won't it?"

"Yes, I believe it will."

"Then what?" she asked, looking at the broken camera on the floor. "Where will I go?"

"You can come with me," she said. "I'm leaving this place."

"But I'm sick . . . he made me sick," the girl said. "I'm not good without the pills."

"I can get you to a doctor." Alma stood over the bed as the girl continued to eat. "And I can get us money."

"You'd do that?"

"Yes."

The girl looked at the alarm clock on the nightstand. "He comes soon, and he'll be drunk."

"All right."

"I have to get cleaned up. He gets angry if I don't smell good." The girl pushed the food aside and slowly scooted to the edge of the bed. She slipped her feet into beach

sandals and stretched her arms above her head. The over-
sized shirt looked more like a nightgown and poorly hid
the bruises on her arms and thighs.

"What's your name?" Alma asked.

"Carina."

"You?"

"Call me Alma. He'll need to eat everything, Carina—
every bit of it."

"He will. Always does." Carina went into the bathroom and began brushing her teeth.

"I'll be outside," Alma said. "It may take some time
before . . ."

Carina spat the white foam into the sink. "It's just one
more night," she said somberly. "Did the boy tell you
about me? Is that why you came?"

"No," Alma said. "I didn't know. If I did . . ."

"You would have been sent away like my family . . . he
deported everyone who tried to help me."

"He has that power?"

"Homeland Security," she said. "I've seen his badge."
Carina cupped water into her hands and drank. She
swished it around in her mouth. "He's here," she said
before spitting out the water. "That's his truck's engine."
A backfire followed a faint clamor. "You have to go."

Alma quickly walked to the door, then stopped short of
opening it. "I'll be back in an hour," she said.

"Okay," Carina said, spritzing her skin with cheap-
smelling perfume. "An hour."

As Alma walked downstairs, she saw the truck that had
hit Criston parked and the Homeland Security officer getting out. She was sure to keep out of sight, moving to the
other end of the landing, away from Apartment 22. She
peeped around the corner as he stumbled. As Carina had

predicted, he was drunk and dressed in jeans and a flannel shirt. He fiddled with his keys while slurring, muttering to himself. Alma watched him climb to the top of the stairs, taking bold, reckless steps, and thought—a just God would see that he tripped to the bottom, neck snapped. Then, she wouldn't have to take matters into her own hands. But as long as she could remember, justice came without divinity; rather, it took a woman's dedicated hand.

THE HOUR PASSED QUICKLY, and Alma found herself standing outside the door of Apartment 22. A woman and man were arguing in the parking lot near a rusted van. The air smelled of marijuana. The two were cursing, throwing beer bottles. She couldn't hear a sound from inside the apartment.

Alma knocked gently and waited with her hand on her *manchèt's* handle. She knocked again, slightly harder, and the door opened. Carina stood draped in a blanket. The color was gone from her face. Alma stepped into the apartment and saw the man sitting shirtless in a chair. He was a mass of pink flesh, bloated and greasy. Next to him was the empty container of food.

"She told me everything," he said, barely able to speak. "You're both dead." His breathing was wispy. Sweat poured from his brow, and his legs shook uncontrollably. He tried to stand but fell back into the chair.

"I wanted him to know," Carina said, holding the man's cell phone in one hand, "so he knew what was happening to him."

Alma picked up the man's pants at the foot of the bed. She dug into the pockets, removed his wallet, flipped it open to his driver's license. "Thadius Wayne Jackson," she said.

"I'm a cop . . ." Jackson coughed. "You did this to a cop."

"You were police . . . a murderer . . . and a rapist."

He coughed again, nearly fell from the chair. "Carina," he said. "Please, baby? I love you. Don't do this to me."

"Love?" Alma shook her head, remembering all the men in her village who had claimed love for women they brutalized.

Jackson's breathing worsened, along with the shaking. His face contorted into something horrid and *baby* became *bitch*. "You goddamn bitch!" he said, foaming at the mouth. Alma had seen men make these types of faces, working desperately to drown out fear with rage. She was certain those men like Jackson became seething beasts in the afterlife.

After Jackson had what Alma presumed was a seizure, he slipped from the chair onto the floor. There were more convulsions. Then his body was still, and Alma knew he was dead.

She found a bottle of bleach, filled the kitchen sink, and submerged Jackson's cell phone. Then, she and Carina left the apartment and walked to Alma's unit as if nothing had happened. Carina showered and changed into Criston's clothes: sweatpants and a T-shirt. As Carina slept in Criston's bed, Alma listened for sirens, wondering if anyone would find Jackson and care enough to call the police. But the night was quiet, and Alma soon fell asleep.

IN THE MORNING'S LIGHT and without makeup, Carina looked slightly younger than Criston. Alma served her bread and milk and watched as she devoured four loaves, stopping at the fifth when she began to feel ill. Alma knew it wasn't because she was full of bread, but her body was craving the drugs and her withdrawal would need to be managed. She served her a hearty black tea and Carina seemed to improve.

After breakfast, they packed the car with as much as it would fit, and she drove to St. Francis. She marched into the priest's chambers. "I want to see my son," she said. "Take me to his body."

"You can't barge in here," the priest said from behind his desk. "I told you never to come back."

"I went to Apartment Twenty-two." Alma looked to Carina as she stood wearing Criston's hoodie and pants; she had cuffed the legs so they fit better. "He kept her there drugged, but you knew that, didn't you?"

He stammered. "Of course not," he said. "This is terrible. We should call the police!"

"You know we can't do that . . . but that's why you sent me there, isn't it? You wanted to be rid of me. Maybe you hoped I'd be deported or worse?" In his eyes, Alma saw no shame or remorse. "How long have you owned the Sundial?" she asked.

"Oh, Miss Alma," he snickered. "I've misjudged you."

"I've known too many men like you," she said. "Unholy men that breathe to exploit and corrupt everything they touch."

Carina locked the door.

"Are you too blind to see that I'm the only reason you had a roof over your heads . . . the only reason *you* people can live safely in this country?"

"Safely? You preyed on us. Took our pennies to live in that slum, corrupted the gospel while letting a cop do whatever he wanted to a defenseless girl."

"What do you want?" he asked in a cold sweat.

"You're going to give us money," Alma said. "Enough

for us to get out of town, and tomorrow morning, my son will be buried in the church's cemetery, as promised."

"And if I don't?"

She pulled the *manchèt* from its sheath. "I pick up where I left off."

The priest touched his neck, feeling the scar left behind by Alma's last visit. He opened his desk drawer, removed a metal box. "I see now . . . you are the monster you confessed to being." He unlocked the box with a brass key. Inside, he took out a stack of bills. He handed them to Alma, and she put the money into her coat pocket. "This is all I can offer you. As for Criston's remains, they are in the basement. He'll be buried tomorrow as you wish, then I want the both of you gone from the Sundial and this town."

Alma and Carina followed the priest downstairs to the basement, where a makeshift coffin was surrounded by clutter: boxed paper goods and crates of wine.

"Leave when you're done," the priest said. "And God help you."

Alma ignored him and opened the coffin. She nearly collapsed at the sight of Criston. Carina came to her aid, took her hand, gripped it tight, and together they cried until Alma felt strong again. "That was his favorite sweatshirt," Alma said, running her hands down the arm of Carina's hoodie. It was stained with her tears.

"I'd like to know more about him," Carina said. "I feel like he saved my life . . ."

"Yes," Alma said, smiling. "I suppose in a way he did." She touched her son's hand. His skin felt like a thin sheet of wax, slightly moist.

"Can I ask you something?"

"All right."

"Why did you leave Haiti?"

Alma swallowed hard. "My son fell in love," she said, "with a boy who was very dear to him. But those in our village saw their love as unconsecrated."

"What happened?"

"The church condemned them, and Criston's lover was murdered. He was probably no older than you are now."

"I'm so sorry."

"That night we fled for America," she said, still looking at her son's body, wistfully. "Seems like all I've ever known is death."

Carina touched Alma's cheek and she flinched. "Maybe it doesn't have to be that way anymore?"

"I pray for something better," she said, resting her cheek in the girl's warm palm.

Outside the church, they stood shielding their eyes from the desert wind. A storm was forming in the distance. Dark clouds were closing in; the sun had disappeared. Alma remembered what the priest said about Revelations. For a moment, she wondered if he was right—had God come to turn off the lights? Then, she thought of her son, how his love made her worst days bearable—how he gave her hope and perhaps sent Carina to her so she could be a mother again, and she prayed for more time . . .

They got into the car and started down the road, driving away from St. Francis. Ahead of them, dust kicked up in the distance as police cars approached. Red and blue lights, blaring sirens. Carina took Alma's hand and looked at her, but Alma said nothing. When their eyes finally met, Carina said, "Thank you."

They continued to drive, Alma picking up speed, hand in hand into the storm . . .

THE GARDENER OF ROSES

Richie Narvaez ‖‖‖‖‖‖‖‖‖‖‖‖‖‖‖‖‖‖‖

FBI agents shot and killed the dangerous terrorist Edilberto Santos de la Mar today after he opened fire on them in front of his home in Hormigueros.

The militant leader was linked to a terrorist group known for many acts of violence committed between 1978 and 1998, the most notorious of which was the robbery of $7.2 million from a Wells Fargo depot in West Hartford, Connecticut. The group is likely also responsible for blowing up nine airplanes at a US military base in northern Puerto Rico in 1981.

Santos's wife was also killed in the standoff.

FBI Special-Agent-in-Charge Lambón Fraticelli was on the scene.

"We arrived and asked him to surrender. He refused. It was clear that he posed an imminent threat to our agents. When he came at us guns blazing, we had no choice."

Except that wasn't how it happened.

Nathalie Chiriboga turned away from the TV screen and pulled her jean jacket tightly around her. They had attacked first, without warning, *yesterday*. Why were they announcing it now—"shot and killed . . . today"? It didn't make sense. And the news had said nothing about Edilberto's beliefs, nothing about what he was fighting for. Wasn't that important? Why leave that out?

"The plane to San Juan will fly in fifty minutes!" yelled the airport attendant, a short man with dyed blonde hair. He was only four feet away from the passengers, seven people waiting in an area with only five seats. "Fifty minutes!" he yelled again. He was also the reservation agent, the air traffic controller, and bathroom attendant. She wondered if he would be the pilot, too.

Speaking of the bathroom, she needed to get in there to wash her pits. She had been on the move and sleeping out in the open, and she didn't want the other passengers to feel like they were stuck with a pig on the plane. But whoever was in there had been in there since she got to the airport. Maybe they'd been having a bad day, too, but she would bet they hadn't been running from the FBI for more than twenty-four hours.

Nathalie looked out the window again at the tarmac and the planes, a dozen of them, parked out there. Is that what you said about planes—*parked?* What she saw didn't give her a lot of faith. They were tiny things, looking more like her baby brother's toys than something a human being should risk her life getting into. But she had no choice. She had to be in San Juan that morning, or she might never make it off the island alive.

A little man in a cowboy hat to her right leaned almost on her shoulder and made little puffing noises as he snored. He reeked of cologne layered with cigarettes. The older lady next to her offered her another *pilone de ajonjolí,* the kind of candy they sell to tourists in airport shops, airports bigger than this tiny one in Mayagüez.

"No, *gracias.* I can't have too much candy," Nathalie

said, lying. She loved candy, but she hadn't eaten any-thing since yesterday morning—ham and eggs on *pan de agua* smeared with butter—and this lady had already fed her three of these lollipops. What Nathalie needed was a strong café con leche to get her through this morning.

"You sure? You look hungry, *mi'ja*," the lady said. She wore a bright red and yellow handkerchief around her neck and a wool coat, warm for September in Puerto Rico. But she smelled like skin lotion, like Nathalie's abuela.

"I'm sure. Thank you."

The man on the TV news repeated the fake news about Edilberto, but this time he added:

Also wanted for questioning in the attack is Nathalie Chiriboga, a college student who is likely involved with the terrorist organization.

Her eyes went wide, her shoulders stiffened, her armpits became waterfalls. She waited for someone to pull her out of the chair and shove her to the ground and shoot her.

"Are you nervous about the flight?" the lady with the candies said, with a big smile. "I take this every day to go to work. It's like my *subway*, you know?" She said the word "subway" like "soobway."

"Every day?" Nathalie mumbled.

The cowboy spoke up, his breath like an ashtray but his broken smile as warm as the Caribbean. "*Si*, the plane is much faster than driving. There's too much traffic. And everyone drives crazy. I never drive anymore when I don't have to. You're much safer on the plane. Don't you worry."

No one in the small room moved. No one seemed to care about the news. She was safe, here in this miniature, out-of-the way airport. No one was looking for her here. Her shoulders relaxed.

She considered asking the lady for another lollipop when the door of the bathroom opened and out walked a tall man putting away his flip phone. He wore a dark suit and dark shades and looked like he wanted to kick ass and not ask questions. *The FBI.* They had found her.

She was fucked.

"WHAT DO YOU THINK about revolution?" Edilberto Santos de la Mar wore jeans and an old denim shirt. His long, wavy hair was almost all white. They were in his garden, which was lined with roses.

"I don't know," Nathalie had said. "I don't believe in violence. So, I guess I don't believe in revolution."

"Lolita often talked about an ethical revolution, one with no shots, no violent retaliation."

"Lolita?"

"Lebrón. You should read about her. Real revolution comes from a thousand little decisions, a thousand little moments that build and build. Violence can move things forward, but it can just as easily move them back."

"I guess. I mean, I can see that. But if someone comes to harm me or my family, then I would fight."

"Great remedies are required to cure great evils. But our best defense is your mind. Remember what Pedro said. 'Young people have a duty to defend their country with weapons of knowledge.' You understand? That's the best time for true revolution. You're not stuck in the old ways. You're not stuck to tradition. You understand what I'm saying? Young people like you, they are always our great hope. When the time comes it will not be old men like me, someone whose fate has already been decided, who will change the world. It will be people your age, people like you."

She had shown up barely awake at his house at seven in the morning, the time her Titi Yolanda had insisted she go. Santos's wife, Alma, had answered the door. She had a kind smile, open and welcoming, but her eyes looked at Nathalie and then behind her with suspicion. Nathalie introduced herself first as a niece of their neighbor Jose Anthony Chiriboga, and then added breathlessly that she was a student at the University of Puerto Rico, that she had an assignment for her English class to interview a signifi-cant person, that she had mentioned the paper to her aunt who she was visiting over the weekend, and that her aunt had said a famous *independista* lived down the road and she should go talk to him.

"Yolanda called me and told me you were coming. You look just like her," Alma had said, letting her in but keep-ing an eye on the road and the trees in front of the house. "'Berto is in the backyard with his flowers. Do you want a little breakfast?"

"No, thank you." Nathalie said what her aunt told her to say, but she could see Alma was already moving toward the refrigerator.

"Go down the hall and to the right. You'll find him."

She noticed then that all the windows were covered with black cloth. On the walls were pictures of people in front of crowds, people she didn't know, and the Puerto Rican flag, so many Puerto Rican flags. And then, in the room just before the backyard, a rifle leaned against the wall.

She found Edilberto outside. She watched as he chose huge, drooping rose blooms, then cut them back.

"The shrubs are starting to go to sleep," he said, look-ing at her. "But if I sacrifice the fading ones like this, the rest stay awake a little longer. Hello."

"Hello." Nathalie introduced herself again.

Edilberto took off the gloves he wore. "Here," he said, handing her a poofy pink rose. "I understand you have questions."

"Yes. So, first of all, you are an *independista*. That means you want Puerto Rico to be independent, to stand on its own. But what I don't understand is what's wrong with statehood? I like the United States. I spent most of my life there, in Mount Holyoke."

"That explains your accent," he said.

"Sorry!"

"No, no, don't apologize. You're still Boricua even if you were born on the Moon. Now: Statehood! Why? The Unites States thinks all of this, these houses, all of this land and beauty belongs to them. They think our island is their island, to do with as they please. But statehood—statehood is just more money for their rich. And what will they give us in return? No more than paper towels."

She was taping him, but just in case she wrote down as much as she could.

After a while, Alma brought out breakfast, and they sat in the shade to eat. Nathalie placed the flower Edilberto had given her on the table. The morning air grew warm, scented with the perfume of roses.

Afterward, Alma had gone back inside, and Nathalie and Edilberto were still talking. She looked up from taking notes and noticed that something had changed. He looked at her and smiled. But his eyes were different now. Not unkind, but not seeing her anymore. They were focused on something else.

"Today of all days," he said.

"What?"

"Nathalie, do you know the *Grito de Lares*? You can look it up on your computer. Five hundred rebels against thousands of soldiers. We tried to throw off the Spanish yoke, much like we are trying to throw off the American one. Eight died, many were imprisoned, many died in prison. Today is the anniversary. I recorded a speech that will be on the radio later." His eyes moved to the left and then to the right. "You should listen to it."

"*Grito de Lares*," she repeated, writing it down. She had heard of it but didn't know the details. "What speech?"

"Pardon me, but it looks like you have picked a bad day to come visit."

"What? Oh my god, I'm so sorry, I—" She'd had more questions, but she felt embarrassed, like she had overstayed her welcome.

"No, no, no. You didn't know. Come inside."

Inside the house, he asked her to sit down in the living room. "But away from the windows," he said, then quickly added: "Because of the heat."

She went back down the hall, to the living room where Alma was watching a talk show.

"Where is my gardener? Still outside?"

"No, he told me to come inside but to stay away from the windows. Is something going on?"

Alma popped up. "Edilberto!"

"Coming," he said, emerging from the hallway wearing a bulletproof vest and carrying a rifle, the one Nathalie had seen tucked against the wall. It had seemed like a prop before, something from a movie. Now it seemed deadly.

Nathalie was confused. And starting to get scared. "Again, what's going on?"

"They found me," he said.

Alma put her hands to her heart. "Are you sure?"

"Wait a second! Who found you?"

"*Niña*, I'm sorry. It's the government. Their FBI. They've

surrounded the farm. They're behind every mango. You can still get out by the grave if you leave now."

"Oh god! The grave?! I don't understand."

"The 'grave' is a tunnel," said Alma. "He gave it a funny name. He thinks he's funny."

"But why do they want you? Are they going to arrest you?"

Edilberto shook his head and said, "No." Then he placed his hands on her shoulders. "I'm sorry we did not get to talk more, Nathalie. The corruptors in this world fear dissent, and they will always try to rip it from the earth. But the truth—the truth is always a thorn." He smiled, to himself really, a sad smile. "But now—"

The sound of insistent mechanical fluttering—they looked up at the ceiling. Something Nathalie had heard only in TV shows and movies: helicopters.

"It's a siege," Edilberto said. "Alma, take her out of here and get to safety."

"Old man, I'm not going anywhere."

"My love, you have to live. There has to be a witness."

"Old man," Alma said again, and as she went to hug him, something crashed into the room. It hit the black cloth covering the window and slid to the floor, thudding—a dark gray cylinder. "Cover your eyes!" Edilberto yelled.

Then there was an unbelievably loud *bang*, like a cherry bomb times a thousand. Nathalie couldn't see, couldn't focus. She heard stuff crashing, things breaking, Alma screaming. Then the firecracker sound of bullets.

THE DARK WAS ABSOLUTE in the narrow grave. Its walls were sandy, moist—and unpredictably loose.

"Move quickly, *mi amor*," Alma had said. "And don't worry about the spiders." Before Nathalie could ask another question, Alma added, "And when you get to the end—there is a cover there, it's metal—you wait. And listen. And when you hear nothing and see no one, lift the cover—it's heavy, so push. And then look for the electric tower and run to that. That will lead you to the road."

Nathalie was trying hard not to think of the spiders when something heavy, with legs like thick fingers, touched her bare ankle. Not knowing what it might do, not knowing how much anyone could hear her, she went still and, wanting to scream for her mother, shoved her face into the dirt and gritted her teeth. The heavy thing cleared one ankle and she knew it would get to her other one and it was taking forever.

There it was! She closed her eyes, her fists. And then it was gone.

Nathalie spit out soil and breathed again. She began scrambling forward, a very long way. When she got to the metal cover, she listened and waited. She peeked. Seeing no one, she squeezed out like a snake, the heavy lid pressing down on her shoulder, back, and legs. When she freed her last toes, it made a thick "Boof!" sound that made her flatten her face into the earth. She waited. The helicopters sounded far away. She raised her head—and saw the tower. On her knees she crawled toward it—and then ran.

She got to a road, which she recognized. Brushing dirt off her face and jeans, she walked toward where she was pretty sure her aunt and uncle lived. She followed the road for a half hour until she came to her aunt and uncle's street.

Two black SUVs were parked askew in their driveway. She watched from behind a tree. The men got back in their car. But only one of them drove away. The other sat in the SUV in the driveway. Watching. Were they watching for her?

She knew what they could do. She had no choice. She turned back, found her way to town. Across the street from the Basílica Menor Nuestra Señora de la Monserrate, directly in eyesight of the open-armed Jesuchristo, was a pay phone. Even though she was desperate, she was embarrassed to have to call her cousin Julia collect. She didn't get to finish her apology.

"Nathalie! Oh my god, you're okay. We didn't know if you were still in the house."

"You know what happened?"

"Yes, it's on the news. And Mami called me right away. She told them you were there. I'm so sorry. But she was worried about you."

"She told the FBI? Oh no! I don't know what to do. Where do I go?" Nathalie said. "I don't want them to get me."

"Tell me what happened."

"They started shooting through the windows. Without warning. Grenades and bullets. They hit Edilberto in the shoulder, and he was bleeding but he was still alive when Alma shoved me into this tunnel. I don't know what happened to her." She realized she was sobbing as she talked, that it was hard to breathe like she was still in the tunnel.

"Oh my god, you need to get here. My car is busted, of all days. Do you have money for a taxi?"

"Nothing. I left my money at Titi's. I'll walk it if I have to."

"You can't. It's too far. Aha, wait."

Nathalie heard her cousin typing.

"There is a tiny, tiny airport in Mayagüez, and I bet they won't expect you to go that way. They have flights from there to San Juan. I've taken it a few times. The flight is only half an hour, faster than if you take a taxi."

"But how much will that cost?"

"Don't worry. I'll call them and a ticket will be waiting for you, okay? Just get there as soon as you can."

"But how?"

"Hold on. I have a map. Aha, you need to find the Avenida Eugenio María de Hostos. It's the first big road out of town. From what I remember, when you get to the Chili's, you take a right and it's straight from there to the airport. You have to take a few turns, but you'll see the signs. Just keep the ocean on your left, okay?"

"Very funny. I hope I remember all that."

"You will. Listen, Nat, I have a friend who is a journalist. I will call her. You need to tell your story. That will protect you. But you have to get to San Juan."

"I'm scared, Julia. I'm afraid they're going to find me and shoot."

"I know you're scared. Just concentrate on getting here as fast as you can. Don't let anything get in your way."

"I won't."

"And, Nat, don't talk to anybody, okay? Seriously. You don't know who you can trust."

AVENIDA EUGENIO MARÍA DE Hostos was easy to find. It was the big road with so many tinted-windowed SUVs on it they were like a single black line crossing out that direction.

She would have to find another way to Mayagüez.

She turned back and found another road that seemed to vaguely go in the same direction. But soon she found no sign of people, no stores, no houses. Just the infinite amount of trees that covered the island.

She thought about going back to the main road. Maybe they had given up looking for her. How many hours had it been? Behind her, the road veered into the endless green—how many turns had she taken?

It started to get dark. It wasn't that late, but there were clouds moving in. September was the middle of the hurricane season in PR. She hadn't heard anything major was on its way. But you never knew with Mother Nature, did you?

She thought about what Edilberto had told her. Besides things she had heard of like "colonization" and "poverty," he had spoken of "forced migration," "social discrimination," "social oppression." It sounded so sad and confusing. Why wasn't anyone doing anything about these things? Edilberto had been fighting for the same things for decades, and he had said people had been doing the same for generations. Why had nothing changed?

She heard a car coming up, turned to look, then immediately regretted it. What if it was the FBI men come to hunt her down?

But it wasn't one of their hulking SUVs. It was just a car, a little blue thing. What would they think of her, some jibaro girl out in the middle of nowhere with night falling? If she were back in Massachusetts, the car would keep going. But since this was Puerto Rico, she knew what would happen next.

"*Buenos dias*. Are you all right?" A woman's voice.

Nathalie didn't look at her, wanted to ignore her, but did not want to be rude. "Yes, I'm all right. I live right there. I'm just walking down the road."

"Pardon me, but it looks like the road has been walking on you. There's nothing here for miles. I can give you a lift."

The woman was maybe in her thirties or forties, with tinted glasses and tinted red hair. She looked like a teacher, not the FBI.

Nathalie opened the car door, and the woman cleared containers and newspapers off the passenger seat onto the floor. Inside, the car smelled of spilled coffee and fried onions.

"It's never safe for a woman to be alone outside," the woman said. "That's true everywhere in the world. Trust me, I've been everywhere."

Nathalie nodded but kept her eyes on the road.

"So where are you going?" the woman said.

"I'm going up a little ways, to Mayagüez," she said, praying it was a "little ways" and she hadn't walked halfway to Ponce.

"This is Mayagüez," the woman said. "Where do you want to go? To the mall?" She laughed.

Ashamed of the way she looked, Nathalie hung her head and saw a gun strapped to the woman's ankle.

"Oh shit," she said, thinking they had found her, they could be dressed like normal. She opened the car door and jumped out. Even at the car's modest speed—it couldn't have been going more than ten miles an hour—the impact of Nathalie's fall hurt, and she sprawled and spun onto the side of the road.

The woman was yelling at her, "Wait! Come back! What's wrong?"

But Nathalie was up, running, almost hit by one, two cars, and then over a fence. In a few feet more, she was swallowed by the trees.

AT LAST NATHALIE CAME to an abandoned gas station on the side of the road. Concrete walls painted turquoise and orange. Concrete holes in the ground where the pumps used to be.

But there was a short wall in the back, next to the

locked bathroom door, and a collection of dried plants and soil in the corner of it. It was a warm night, and the corner looked comfortable enough. She was exhausted from walking on the road. She sat down, put her back against the hard wall. A million stars watched her from above. A million coquis sang. She started to worry about the million insects that might be around.

When she had started college, she was going to study to be a journalist. She had dreamed of interviewing Mariah Carey, Gwen Stefani, Alicia Keys, the biggest stars ever! Her English teacher had assigned the class to interview "someone of significance, a significant source," and Nathalie had freaked out. She didn't know anyone. Who would talk to her? She had no idea how to start. How was she ever going to be a real journalist like Nancy O'Dell or Leeza Gibbons?

But none of that mattered now. It wasn't the sound of the grenades or the bullets that still rang in her ears. What she remembered most was Alma's last words to her. "Go!" Alma had yelled, voice broken in pain, and Edilberto wounded on the floor in front of them, breathing rapidly. *"Survive!"*

Now, she worried she would linger awake for hours, staring at the sky, replaying thoughts of death. But before she fell into a deep, restless sleep, she remembered with regret that she had left behind the rose Edilberto had given her on the table in the garden.

IN THE MORNING NATHALIE felt like the thousands of insects she had slept with were still with her. She kept brushing them off. And she needed food. But at least she had found another road. This one looked better, with houses at least, a few barking dogs.

Six miles later she found the Chili's, took a few turns,

saw a worn sign that read "Eugenio María de Hostos Airport." There was a gate, no security, one tower, and one little building. She headed for that.

At a pay phone outside, she called her cousin collect, told her she was fine, and that she would be getting on the next flight.

She went to the ticket window and asked the blond agent if there was a ticket for her. He wore a red vest with a name tag that said "Carlo."

"What's your name?" he said.

She paused, thinking she should keep her name a secret, but she had no choice. "Nathalie Chiriboga."

"Yes, my darling, there's a ticket here for you. You missed the seven o'clock plane and the eight o'clock, but there is a nine o'clock plane."

"Okay, but it's nine oh-five now."

"The nine o'clock plane leaves at ten o'clock. You are very lucky there are still seats available."

Nathalie looked back and saw just a few people sitting and standing about the room.

"The plane is small. It can only fit nine passengers," the agent said.

"Oh."

"Yes, it can be very noisy and very bumpy."

"Oh."

"But don't worry. It's safe!"

She went to the bathroom door, but it was locked and someone inside with a deep voice said, "Occupied!" She went across the small room to the one chair that was available.

She put her backpack down and sat between a man in a cowboy hat reading *El Vocero* and an older woman in a wool coat.

Three lollipops later, the man in a cowboy hat slumped down and snored. The man on the TV news said her name. She froze, and then the FBI man emerged from the bathroom. She didn't trust anyone there, but this guy looked just like the men who had been in front of her aunt and uncle's house. She couldn't tell because of the shades he wore, but she was pretty sure he was looking straight at her. He stood to the side and flipped open his phone.

He might be calling headquarters about her, telling his bosses. Then they would be there in minutes. They would shoot her, leave her body to bleed out for a day like they must have done with Edilberto and Alma.

Nathalie reached down for her backpack. She had to get out of there. She would find another way to San Juan. She had gotten this far on her own.

She looked at the door and she was about to get up when she felt a jab in her ribs. The man in cowboy hat said quietly, "Young lady, this is a gun. Please do not move. We have a plane to catch."

"Who the hell are you?"

"Me? Just a retired sheriff. But I know trouble when I see it walk into a room."

"Bullshit. You've been waiting for me to show."

"No, in the name of God. I drove five minutes from Angustias. I'm on my way to San Juan to go to the casino. But you, you said your name to the attendant when you came in, and the news, they said your name, and me, I'm a smart cookie. I listen! When we get to San Juan, I can turn you over and probably get a reward. I could use the money."

"The plane to San Juan is now boarding!" yelled the airport attendant. "Please have your tickets ready."

IT WAS COOL, ALMOST chilly as they walked across the tarmac. The plane looked tinier than it had before, as if there was no way all of them would fit. Inside, there were five rows, and the pilot sat in the front one, on the left. The next two rows were single, but the cowboy steered Nathalie toward the last row, which had two seats. But people were already sitting there: the man she thought was FBI sat in one, and the lady with the candy in the other.

The cowboy said, "Pardon me, but my niece insists that I sit next to her. Do you mind if we take these seats?"

"Of course," the lady said, getting up.

Mr. Not FBI said nothing, but got up too.

Maneuvering around each other in the tiny space was an ordeal, but finally Nathalie sat in the back seat at the back of the plane, with the cowboy's gun in her side.

She was too tired, too hungry, too stinky to resist. She just wanted this over.

As if hearing her thoughts, the cowboy put his face close to hers and whispered with nicotine breath: "I'm sure the FBI will treat you fairly. I know people in the FBI. They only want what is good for the island."

"How do they know what that is, these men from the United States?"

"Ah, many of them are from right here. You are young. You don't understand. Someone like Santos will ruin this island. He will bring the United States down on all of us. We can't have rebels like that in our homeland. We had them before and it never worked. We're too weak. They got all the power. They got all the money, and we won't have even a penny if we cause them trouble."

He kept talking but the plane's motor sputtered to life with a deafening jolt.

The pilot—some guy in a T-shirt and leather jacket who

had just shown up, not the airport attendant—taxied the plane forward and then turned sharply to line up with the runway.

Nathalie closed her eyes as the plane picked up speed on the runway. It lifted once, twice, and then rose completely into the air. The ground fell away beneath her.

The plane banked and turned north. She would sleep. She would keep her eyes closed and she would sleep.

The plane rocked violently.

Nathalie's eyes flew open. She noticed dark clouds above the island reaching far into the Caribbean Sea.

The pilot said nothing to reassure the passengers, and none of them seemed disturbed. The cowboy stared dead ahead, but kept the gun at her ribs.

She decided she hated tiny planes. All planes should be gigantic, so that you would not have to see everything going on outside.

Out there, on the sea, a trio of boats hurried toward the island, and behind them dark clouds roiled in.

In that moment she decided she would not let this happen to her, no matter how tired or stinky she felt. She had a job to do, a story she had to tell to people who would listen.

The clouds grew darker. She waited. The sea seemed to shimmer and pulse. She waited.

And when it happened, when the plane bucked wildly again, she reached for the gun and pulled it forward, aiming it up and away from her face, toward the window. Not knowing what would happen, but too afraid not to do something.

The cowboy grunted, cursed her.

The Not FBI guy in the seat in front of her turned around.

"Some help, please," Nathalie yelled.

Not FBI grabbed the cowboy's arm, took his gun.

The lady with the candy peeked around her seat too. She turned around fully and hit the cowboy with her impressively sized purse. "How stupid! You could kill everyone."

"You don't understand," the cowboy said. "The FBI wants her. She was working with Edilberto Santos. She is a fugitive."

"That man they killed?" Not FBI said. "They killed his wife too."

"Yes, but he was a revolutionary. A terrorist."

"The one who stole the money," the candy lady said. "That's why they wanted him. For the money."

"I saw everything," Nathalie said. "They shot him. He was defending his wife. His wife—she helped me get away."

Nathalie finally broke. The pain of the last thirty-six hours released itself. The lady looked at her, saying she understood, and reached around to give her a tissue.

Not FBI man waved the man's gun and said, "Look. There are no bullets in this. Nothing."

The man in the cowboy hat lowered his head. "My wife doesn't let me carry bullets anymore."

HER LEGS WERE SHAKY as she stood up to exit the plane. The Not FBI man told her to get going, he would keep the cowboy busy.

Standing next to a blue car on the tarmac was her cousin Julia. Next to her was a familiar face—the woman with the gun. Nathalie froze.

"It's okay," Julia said. "This is Ida. She is a reporter."

"I was in the area where you were," Ida said. "It was only after I got home that your sister called, and I figured out it must have been you on the road. I'm sorry if I scared you."

"The gun?"

"The world is not kind to journalists, even less so if you're a woman."

Nathalie collapsed into her cousin's open arms and held her tightly. They got into the car and took a roundabout road out of the airport.

"What now?" she said.

"We clean you up and get you some food," Julia said.

"No. I mean, yes. But also: What about Edilberto and Alma? What's our next step?"

"The government says their men followed procedure," said Ida. "But if they had, Santos and his wife would be alive. So now you tell me what you saw, in your own words, and we tell as many people as we can."

"Like a thorn, then," Nathalie said. "We'll show them the thorn."

ENVY |||||||||

Christopher Chambers |

It's for nights like this one Arthur feels vindicated going into hock to Apex Heating and Cooling . . . ten thousand dollars at twenty-one percent APR. All so Mama and Baby may rest, cool, comfortable. Indeed, with no moonlight providing sharp edges to a formless sky, the air's like a black oven: baking, palpable. Heavy in the lungs, sickly sweet to the tongue. Most folks on the block have no central air, relying instead on laboring, gasping, sputtering window units that give the neighborhood a weird hum as Arthur trundles across the still-hot concrete, Baby struggling to keep up after each sniff of a street sign, tug on the Day-Glo orange lead.

Ahead up at the corner, as the 24 Uptown rumbles away from a bus shelter festooned with swap-meet posters and marred by gang tags, Arthur spies a group of men. He squints through his glasses and sees they are young by their dress, hair, manner . . . and now he discerns a creole of Spanish and English. The shop where they congregate, lit garishly in Christmas-color neon: "Pipes-Papers-Tobacco." Arthur sneers, "Damn shame," looks down at Baby, who noses around the holes and frayed rubber straps of Arthur's scuffed black Crocs.

The spot was okay before the city legalized marijuana.

Passable convenience store owned by indifferent people who Mama said were "from the Horn of Africa so Africans nonetheless and we in the Diaspora must show them respect." Arthur abided despite their vacant looks behind the bulletproof glass.

That kid, who was not from the Horn of Africa— Neil? He worked there sweeping up, stocking—was at least polite to Mama, delivering items when she could no longer walk. Neil did it right. Head down, mouth shut. He's in college, in Pennsylvania. Probably now on summer break in a toney internship downtown! Arthur nods to himself as Baby lets loose a strain of pee onto the curb. Yes, Neil did it right, and now can move away from his father. Floyd or Roy? Lives around the corner, a super in that six-unit brick tenement. Jerk with the part pit, part boxer named Tyson, who never barks at Baby. Just leers, whining hungrily.

"Ah, the old market . . . Baby, you'd have dug it," Arthur announces to the skittering animal. Yes, long ago, when a young and gangly Arthur delivered meat for Mr. Silverstein, the butcher and former owner. Mama'd get the best cuts for dinner, deli stuff for lunch, sausage for breakfast. Arthur grins, sighs—recalling the glass counters brimming with raw beef and lamb shanks, glistening livers and other organs, pig and poultry parts. That smell, too . . . and the crunch of the sawdust underfoot. These supermarkets with their bleach odor, or the yuppie gourmet-whole-trader-food crap with the fair-trade coffee—what are they compared to the timber and taste of real blood on the floor back in the day, dripping from the cleavers and chopping blocks?

"Yeah, we're all antiseptic now, Little Dog . . . but back then people respected each other, they had pride . . . and all of us could walk these streets without whitefolks having to move in to get the police to care."

With a high-pitched yelp from Baby signaling her desire to go home, new memories occlude and salt Arthur's sweet visions of Silverstein's market. Boys stealing his deliveries, calling him soft, a sellout, a nerd.

And the girls, yes, them. Lounging or bobbing on their stoops and porches in the barely there tube-tops covering pendulous boobs, cutoff jeans restraining thighs and buttocks. Oh, those ridiculous braids, rows and puffs. The giggling at Arthur's blood-stained Silverstein's apron over a starched collared shirt and ill-fitting dungarees.

One of those "chippies," as Mama labelled them, was Sylvia Green. "Bean Pole" was what she called Arthur. And it stuck.

Arthur searches a protrusion of hairy belly fat emerging between his tee shirt and shorts. "Bean Pole . . . if only," he muses, recalling the moniker. And as the fellows on the corner curse and tussle he whispers, "I don't think so." With a grunt he scoops up Baby. "They mock us, Little Dog."

Baby whimpers, squirms.

Across the boulevard, it's dark even with occasional headlights and the green, then red pallor of the traffic light. The glow's diffused by the leaves of a massive gingko tree on the corner. Before each burning sunset, the little green fans cool the pavement. At night, however, the destination's the least nasty choice between Scylla and Charybdis . . .

. . . until Arthur walks right into Cat, lolling and loitering in the shadows at the gingko's huge trunk.

In the meager light Arthur, now cradling Baby like a baby, makes out Cat's wink and smirk to his single cohort, whom Arthur had never seen on this block, ever, yet is a bizarre copy of Cat. As a car's headlight flash illuminates the pair, Arthur notes the same stubble on their chins, made white by dark skin. Same sweat-yellowed white tank tops—Arthur tries not call them "wife-beaters" given the terrible connotative meaning—billowy nylon ballin' shorts, black wave caps with ties falling down their necks like the pigtails of the intricate 19th Century "Chinamen" painting on Mama's teacups in the curio, which nobody was to mess with. Why would grown-ass men dress in such a way, as children? No self-respect and home training, Mama'd say, particularly about Cat, who'd tax Arthur's meat deliveries like a stagecoach robber or highwayman.

Look at him now, Arthur scoffs inwardly, still a loser . . . peacocks for new generations of chippies yet so old his nickname dates him. His government name's "Morris" so he was tagged "Cat" for Morris, the tabby cat that pitched pet food back when there was no Facebook or Instagram, and just three TV networks.

"S'up, Bean Pole," Cat greets, his eyes strangely aglow, like a cat's. His tone and accompanying snicker belie how inapt Arthur's nickname has become—given Arthur's middle-age girth.

"Cat . . ." Arthur mumbles, head down. He doesn't want any trouble from dudes born from jump to fight. As old as he is, Cat flexes impressively, while Arthur laments each morning in the shower-fogged mirror how his tits have grown. "Baby had a touch of the trots, walking her late." When Arthur catches a craned neck and frown, he corrects his cultural vocabulary. "I mean . . . the bubblies, the shits."

"His mama feedin' the mutt crab cakes," Cat jokes to his companion.

"Aw, Cat . . . y-you know my . . . my mother can't afford crab cakes. Not since I got furloughed. Got an email saying they might be bringing us back after Labor Day, full pay. Got bills and all . . ."

No reply from Cat, though the feline eyes narrow, dim.

"Well, have a good night, fellas . . ." Arthur cheeses, praying they'll grant him leave.

They don't.

"Hold up, Bean."

"Um . . . y-yes?"

"You jus' missed her."

"Huh?"

"Don't clown me, Bean," Cat huffs. "That white bitch . . . you just missed her, bruv."

After a swallow of something cold, hoppy-smelling from a green long-neck bottle, Cat's retainer clarifies, "Yo' pinktoe, nigga. Girl who can't even toss a nigga—an original resident a this damn 'hood, not no carpetbagger—a hello, huh? Who this bitch think she is?"

Arthur purses his lips as if they're glued. His thighs tremble. Baby's growling now.

"See?" Cat adds, teasing the little poof's comic menace. "Even the dog know this fool's game."

"That girl, um . . . she's . . . she's cordial to me. Lives up the block. Has a very nice dog named 'Norman.'"

"On who, Bean? I know you, man. You ain't said shit . . ."

"Ha! Dig it, Cat, this muv prolly heard her say 'Good boy, Norman . . . fetch, Norman,' while he in the window beatin' his meat an' he mama snorin' fronta *Real Housewives* and shit!"

Ungluing his lips, all Arthur can offer is, "Mama likes Brit shows on PBS. *Midsomer. Death in Paradise* . . ."

The reference flies over their heads, yet Cat snorts, "That lil' pooch a yours ain't no ways catchin' up wid-dat pale leggy bitch and her suburbs-picket-fence dog. But g'won, Bean, she down to that lot what used to be Laqui-ta's house . . . excuse me . . . the 'Community Garden' be by now. Run ya fat ass down an' you might atch up wid her . . ."

Finally given leave, Arthur quickly moves into the real darkness cut only by porch lights. As he clutches Baby tighter, he calls over his shoulder. "Karen. That's her name."

Laughter sprays from the shadows shrouding the gingko, mocking Arthur's silly defiance. "*Karen*? For real? Karen . . . *oh Karen, don't let these Blacks scare thee an' thou an' shit . . .*" Yet in a second the mirth ends, and a hard and harsh prompt halts Arthur and turns him all the way around. "Ain't you forgettin' someffin' nigga? Bean . . . I'm talkin' to you!"

"Y-Yeah."

"Today Silvia Brown's birff-day. Ten years she be gone, none her peoples still know where she be. Twelve don't give a fuck, FBI, CIA, NAAC-damn-P, no one say shit. Thas' my first kiss, my first feel'a jelly."

"I'm sorry."

"Artie . . . Bean . . . I know yo' mushmouth ass was sweet on her. So you need to show her respect."

As Baby whines, Arthur returns to the gingko; he's offered whatever foul liquid the cohort's been guzzling. Maybe the alcohol's killed the creepy-crawlies on the bot-tle, but Cat insists he give a full swallow.

"To Greenie," he snorts.

The cohort shouts, "We love you baby, swallowed by these streets. Drink, muv."

And the stuff almost shoots out of Arthur's nostrils . . .

"Now get the fuck outta here," Cat orders. "Missy *Karen's* waitin' on ya."

Arthur hurries into the alternating splotches of dark and of light created by the lines of streetlamps. "Bastards," he curses to Baby, now crying and yelping, and yet Arthur won't release her. "If I wasn't a pussy, I'd kill them with Daddy's revolver, I swear."

Finally, he feels the hot trickle of Baby's urine on his belly, tee shirt. He drops the dog and Baby shrieks as she hits the concrete. She circles, limping a bit and Arthur's eyes narrow, like Cat's did. Not quite a predator's stare, yet cold, uncaring. A deep breath, exhale and heavy swallow help Arthur dispel his hatred for that damn poof with legs; he falls to his knees, strokes the little animal.

"I'm . . . I'm sorry . . . I'm sorry, Baby. Little Dog, look at me, piss all over me. I'm a mess . . ."

And from across the street, from one of those islands of light, Arthur hears something that fills him full of dread . . .

"Hey . . . *hi*! Are you okay?"

She cut her hair. That brick-colored ponytail that reminded Arthur of the swaying tail of her dog . . . a setter or retriever? It was in a bob, parted on the side. He didn't like it.

He'd been honored by a rare daylight sighting a few weeks prior, just after July Fourth. The A-5 Crosstown. She must have been coming from some magical job she got upon graduation, given the animated conversation she was having on the other end of her ear buds. Arthur strained to listen and then had her evening all hashed out: home, walk and feed Norman, shower and doll up into a sundress—but nothing that'll make her look trashy—meet the posse at the usual watering hole and hopefully that young man who works for the bank will be by.

What a lucky young man he'd be, as she was face and shoulders-full of intriguing coral freckles except where the summer sun tinted the flesh orangey brown, and the freckles darkened to a transparent cocoa, with one layer, offset, on the other. Long pale legs, again like Mama's porcelain. Toes peeking from her sandals that day on the bus were painted red as a newly washed fire engine from the old Seventeen Hook and Ladder, now a coffee shop. At least it wasn't blue, or childish yellow varnish like these chippies still do to themselves on the block . . . marred underneath by crust or fungus. Arthur recalls Mama's feet. They're bad. He has to get the nurse's aide back and that's more money on top of the new Apex bill . . .

"I-I'm fine. Just . . . grabbing a spare poop bag."

Baby gives a high-pitched bark; the larger dog's sitting on its haunches. Glum, staring.

"Hey, I've seen your dog," the young lady declares cheerily, almost sing-songy. "With the very nice older lady who sits on her stoop . . . you're in number sixty-three, right?"

Nice lady? *Mama?* "Um . . . y-yes."

With a gasp and giggle she answers, "Oh my Gawd!" She slaps her own thigh, almost bare due to the rise of her shorts. Arthur follows every undulation of the meat. Lord, her skin's so pink even that gesture leaves a red mark. "I'm in number fifty-eight down the street. Been there a whole year and I never . . . well . . . look, I wasn't raised with bad manners so I apologize. I'm Karen. This is Norman."

"No . . . you're fine . . ." His mouth is so dry he coughs, swallows, to finish his sentence. "This is Baby. Mama . . . my mother . . . is Mrs. Arthur G. Banks, Senior. Geraldine."

"And so you're Arthur G. Banks, Junior," she gushes.

"Oh, yeah . . . me." He wants to kick himself because he can't think of any small talk; he's certain he's too weak to will himself across the street. He's crying inwardly, for she must have a sense, a pheromone talent that he's touched, messy, a pussy . . . there with dog piss on his potbelly.

She shrugs, smiles. The brush-off's nigh. "Well, Arthur G. Banks, Junior, let me get going. It's icky hot and these noseeums . . . Jeez. They are eating me alive and here I thought they went to bed at night like the skeeters, huh?"

"Yep."

"So nice to meet you, then. See you around. Norman, be good and say g'night to Baby."

She tugs the lead and continues down the street. If this is her usual late route, then she'll double back once she reaches Tenth, near the basketball courts.

Arthur follows, parallel, forcing Baby into a hard skitter yet not rapid enough so Norman'll hear the jangle of her tags on her faux-gem collar. Indeed, but for an occasional car and one sweaty, heavy-breathed cop on a bike, the street belongs to Arthur and Karen and Baby and Norman.

The girl's speaking *loud* on her phone, hands free. The cops tell women to do that, as Arthur'd seen on one of those true crime shows Mama hates watching with him. See, the old message was stay off your mobile phone so you aren't distracted, as if women were kudu stalked by lions. Yet women are people, not prey, and the cops are right: if someone with evil intentions knows you're on the phone, they'll be less likely to jump you, tear you apart if there's a digital witness listening in.

Still, it attracts attention from ignorant bastards like Cat.

There's Tenth, and the courts. The tower floodlight

bathes the rims and painted keys but the gates are typically padlocked after nine, much to the disgust of the teens around here. Matter of fact, that was the last time Arthur saw Neil. Bunch of boys forced him off the court, took his ball. Neil's in college so why associate with these pygmies, these Bushmen, going nowhere?

Arthur's contemplating that look on Neil's face that day. He'd seen it before, in a mirror many times. Bloody snot streaming from nostrils, Mama banging on the door, demanding to know what's wrong, warning he better not be playing with his pee-pee in there . . . so come out an' eat your supper . . . don't mind those silly delinquents . . . if your daddy was alive they'd be sorry . . .

A blunt and scary word from the opposite side of the street jerks Arthur from the foggy memory.

"*Please!*"

It's a male voice.

There's a throaty bark from Norman, and loud talk from Karen, "Hey, BFF, I-I gotta go home. Creepy stuff. Later."

In the meager light Karen turns tail, whips Norman around on the lead, hurries back up the block. Arthur reaches for Baby, clamps his hand around her snout to stifle her growls.

There . . . glinting off the beam coming from the court's tower floodlights. It's not a flashlight, or the glow from a mobile phone. Arthur tracks Karen: good—to the next pool of light. Yes, zig-zag across the street, in front of me . . . *attagirl*. Get back on your phone!

Still, no sight of any figure in pursuit. Not even a sound other than Arthur's own heavy breaths and pounding pulse, and Baby's anxious panting.

She halts ahead for the false refuge of a narrow, unaiding

slat or crease of light skeeting from a single bulb in a basement apartment alcove.

And now Norman's barking, furiously. Tips a trash can over into the alcove steps.

She shouts, "I'm calling the police, asshole!"

Porch and window lights snap on from the house above the apartment. *There* . . .

. . . short pants, a male . . . lanky like Arthur used to be, yet taller. An arm's extended, almost in a pleading gesture.

"Please, Miss," Arthur hears again. This time the voice competes with an AC window unit's buzz.

"Who the hell's out there?" comes a disembodied voice from that same window.

Arthur looks up; shadows move beyond the panes and sash but nobody comes to investigate . . . rescue?

Arthur looks down. There's that glint.

And now Arthur beholds a macabre dance, as if Karen and this figure whirl in football game slow motion. He lunges. She's twisting away, hand to her face, the other tight on the lead. No, don't do that, Arthur's mind pleads. Let go . . . It's keeping Norman from attacking the attacker and in an instant two humans and a dog are bound up in the lead's coil . . .

. . . until the glint disappears into Karen's ribs.

She screams for her mother. The glint disappears into Karen again as she falls. And then again. And again, as she's prone, as she's silent but for a mere hiss of her lungs.

Arthur's mouth is open to scream yet nothing comes out but spittle. His feet are stapled to the pavement. His body quakes.

Coward. Pussy. He hears the words in his head as loud and venomous as when he was a boy, then a teen, then a young man, taunted by the Cats of the block, tempted and teased by the Sylvia Greens.

Yet not even Norman comes to her aid. He freezes, like a statue of a loyal dog. Perhaps with the same terrible shock that cements Arthur's body to the ground, robs him of a voice.

The other figure groans, however, as if wounded himself. Takes off into the darkness. Norman responds—still on his rump, trembling—with a sick, low-pitch combination of a howl and growl.

Arthur drops Baby, and both move to the upended trash cans.

Karen's on her back, eyes aflutter.

A black puddle behind her expands and fills cracks in the sidewalk. It's warm to Arthur's touch when Baby starts to lap at it and Arthur yanks her back . . .

"M-Miss? *Karen*?" he stammers, hoarse, eyes flooding. "*Evil*. So evil . . ."

Voices are in the doorways as more lights pop on.

Arthur mouths the word "Help" but it's no more than a coarse whisper. He could drop to the pavement, perhaps comfort her till EMTs arrive? Talk to her, keep her from sinking away.

He knows the cops will grill him. How could this happen with you a few feet away? There are kids out chasing city lightning bugs, idiots laying about porches and stoops and in window ledges and fire escapes lit up, cheap brew and fortified wine and gobbling hot-sauced fried crap from take-out or burnt on the hibachi—and you didn't call for help?

Ask *these* people for help, Arthur posits. *These* people . . . they gossip, they're cruel and stupid . . . they'd stand around and she'd still just die. "And they'll swear it was us, Little Dog," Arthur frets. "That *we* killed her."

He hears a heaved breath from Karen. Her body shakes, her eyes roll up toward Heaven away from Arthur's gaze. God has made the decision for him. There is nothing he can do. Nothing he could do. He tucks Baby like a football, whimper or no, backs into the darkness like a vampire would, to hide.

But there, in drops just where his toes meet the light, lies what would look like a feeding vampire's leavings.

Slinking along the curb, he spots more blood in the glow of the ever-expanding bloom of house lights alerted to the evil at their front doorsteps. Arthur doesn't care about them anymore. He's like a hound, on a trail of it, scenting direction, detour. It's like he was back at Silverstein's butcher shop, tracking the blood on the market floor. Wiping and washing. He grew to be an expert on blood . . . how it changed color as the oxygen waned, coagulation began. How the iron scent gave way to copper.

What seizes Arthur next is neither fear of a murderer, or vengeance for the murdered. It is cold, naked obsession. Caring nothing for the shouts and shrieks of neighbors on this hot summer night, Arthur follows the droplets, spatters and smears. Soaked clothing, saturated shoes, a bloody weapon—who would be so similarly uncaring of the gore of guilt? Or perhaps . . . perhaps *uncaring* is the wrong feeling, the inapt flavor, Arthur muses. Perhaps this killer's obsession is the kill itself, rather than avoiding a reckoning?

And so Arthur, hugging Baby to his breast, follows a fresh trail down to Tenth, around the courts. He's almost back up to the boulevard in a perfect "U" shape.

Almost, indeed . . . back to Arthur's own block.

"I know what I must do, Baby," he finally confesses. "You think Mama will forgive me? She always has for stupid things I've done. But *this* . . . aw, Little Dog . . . that poor girl. That poor, poor girl. This is evil."

In reply, the animal's suddenly no longer stiff like Norman, but barky, agitated. He releases her and she runs as fast as her little feet can carry her, lead trailing behind her on the sidewalk, to the mailbox on the corner. There, Baby sniffs, growls . . . then whimpers anew. Begs to be held but Arthur refuses. He bends instead to pick up the source of that awful glint, gingerly between two fingers . . .

. . . a knife blade, like Silverstein's butcher tools for trimming fat and viscera, prying off silverskin for the perfect brisket.

Baby whirls around the mailbox as if in a fit, tiny red tongue trailing. Then halts. Looks up, panting. As does Arthur, equally breathless, just when the wail of sirens a few blocks over hits his ears.

In front of them is a six-unit tenement, rigged and ringed with rusty fire escapes and dotted with AC units, all trailing water. And on the second level egress terrace is a young man. Sobbing. Moaning. Blood soaking his chest, shirtsleeves . . . and the stuff seems black as ink in the ambient light.

Arthur remembers being very small and hearing his father rant about the changing nature of the neighborhood, decades before the "pilgrims"—as he called whites—moved in. A bad class of people, desperate, ignorant. Mama would nod, repeat this long after he died. "*Male prohibutum,*" she recalled him saying in a weird dead tongue of which he was fond. They shoot each other over a lost game of dice or a petty insult, one less gram of weed. Yet still, it was *male prohibutum.* They weren't evil. Evil, he said, would come with the rot that they bring. "*Male in se,*" he'd proselytize. "Evil for evil's sake."

And that's when Baby barks, and the figure above wheezes from the fire escape. "It was you. You saw me?"

Arthur stays mute a single second that seems like half a minute, then mutters, "*Neil* . . . aw shit . . . what happened?"

"Just . . . just don't tell my dad."

"Neil, what did you do?"

"My dad's with some friends, at some club . . ."

"Neil, listen to me." Arthur pauses to scan the street for interlopers, the windows of Neil's building for backlit eavesdroppers. "I-I don't care about your father. I need to know if—"

Neil cuts him off again with the same train of gibberish. "I-I was supposed . . . supposed t-to walk Tyson . . . and . . . and she walked her dog . . . and she wouldn't let me apologize . . . for Tyson messing with her dog, I swear."

"*My God.*"

"God doesn't care. God didn't save Tyson. He'd follow me around, tore up my shoes . . . *he shit in my room.* Your dog shit in your room? Damn . . . he bled as much as *her.*"

Arthur shakes his head. He's not quaking, his eyes are dry. "Listen," he says, calm, no stammer. "I witnessed you kill a human being . . . with a knife you hadn't the good sense to get rid of, like it was no big deal." He can hear Neil sobbing. "Come down. Lemme talk to you, lemme help you. We'll get . . . coffee at the place the rich people hang, before it closes. My treat." When he makes out the tearful head shake from side to side he presses, "What happened to you, huh? You're in school, you're smart. A good boy . . ."

"*A good boy?*" Neil suddenly cries—yes, uncaring if anyone can hear or see him. "I'm already going to Hell. I mean, can you go to Hell for killing a dog, thinking about killing your dad? This . . . thing . . . tonight. Her. This means no stop in Purgatory, Arthur. Straight to the devil."

"Only the devil knows, not me. But you must tell me . . . why her? Why *her*, Neil?"

At first Neil doesn't answer. And oddly, his face brightens. "You think . . . you think her hair that's down around her . . . *you know* . . . is as red as on her head? I imagined so."

Arthur clenches his eyelids shut. To hell indeed with coffee at the swanky new whitefolks' diner. If he was strong like Cat, he could coax Neil down, offering a shoulder to cry on as the bait. Then he'd choke him out. Avenge this girl. Trade horror for horror. Send him where he belongs. And it'll send a message to all the miscreants, all the petty predators on the block like Cat! Bean Pole, he's not to be fucked with. He's death, staring you down.

But Arthur knows himself. Too well.

He opens his eyes.

He smiles.

"I imagined it, too, Neil. *Red*, like apples. Wet."

"Yeah?" He sees Neil give a strange grin, as if he and Arthur are comrades. The grin dissolves into a pained grimace. "Wait . . . r-really?" Yes, as if he and Arthur are comrades . . .

"So what was it like, plunging that blade into her?" Arthur says, just loud enough for Neil and no one else.

Still grimacing, Neil mumbles, "Like . . . like she was *mine*, like it was a w-weapon *and* my dick . . . all at once . . . and I was stronger . . . than anyone on earth."

For a second, Arthurs swears his shorts are tinged with electricity. He sighs, almost coos in pleasure, then corrects Neil. "Well, I'd like to think of her . . . as *mine* first."

"You . . . you mad at me—at what I did? You gonna testify, as a witness?"

"Nope."

"What about my dad? Will . . . will you help me . . . talk to him, square all this with him? He's gonna be sore . . . *aw shit*, worse than ever. He's bad, Arthur. To my mother, and me. Lord you don't know . . . how bad."

"Yep."

As Neil tries to wipe the blood from his face, Arthur picks up the knife, this time by the handle. He grips it tight and holds it behind his back. Baby retreats under the mailbox, crying. She's seen Arthur's eyes narrow, go cold. But she's never seen them go hollow before.

"Arthur," Neil begins, meekly. "You know . . . m-my dad . . . he doesn't like you. Says your mother's crazy . . . says you might be a faggot like he says I'm a faggot."

"Really?"

"He told me once . . . he wanted to tell the cops something, but your mother gave some money not to. He says . . . says he saw you a long, long time ago, *bothering* some woman. She yelled at you to stop and you grabbed her hair. Couple days later, she disappeared."

Arthur nods. "Sylvia Green. She was mean. Not like my . . . *our* . . . Karen. Karen was nice."

"Uh-uh. I told her about school, my major."

Arthur gives Neil a wide smile, so wide it's easy to make out even at night . . . this hot, stinking night. Neil scampers to the latch and hook holding the fire escape ladder off the pavement.

"Neil, you wanna hear more about Sylvia Green?"

"I guess."

"Good, unlatch the ladder, come down. Because I'm so anxious to hear more about our Karen, you lucky fella. *So anxious . . .*"

STAR WITNESS

ⅰⅰⅰⅰⅰⅰ Darrell James

The detention center had become a brooding mass of humanity. Living beings, crammed tightly together—more tightly still, as others arrived. Inside the rudely constructed chain-link enclosure, beneath the highway overpass, men, women, children, young and old huddled, competing with one another for some small piece of bare ground on which to sit or lie. Black ribbons, woven through the chain links to a height above their heads, prevented the prying eyes of the public from seeing in, prevented the detainees from seeing out. Flood lamps, above, substituted for the lack of the natural light inside the compound.

Because the ground was cold, ten-year-old Dia Alvarez lay across her mother's lap, her mother sitting with her back against the chain links. Dia shivered against the cold night air and snuggled tighter into her mother's embrace. She had been coughing, sometimes uncontrollably, for days. Her mother said her forehead felt hot to the touch, afire with fever. She tried to remain quiet, as her mother had instructed, so as not to attract attention.

They had begun their arduous journey weeks, perhaps months, earlier—Dia had lost track—leaving from the church Iglesia de la Inmaculada Concepción. Father Vega had provided last minute instructions to the group, introductions to the four young guides who would see them safely across the desert, protect them from coyotes and the many other dangers along their way. He had then said a quick prayer and blessed them. He kissed Dia on the head and covertly passed a cell phone into her mother's hands. "One number programmed into the phone," he whispered, "should you encounter trouble at the US border." Lastly, he'd ushered them from the church, bidding, "*¡Vaya con Dios!*"

Mile after mile of endless desert followed, rugged canyons, small towns where they could gain momentary relief and restock supplies. Then, on the move again, to arrive at the US border in the dead of night—tired, hungry, and some, like Dia, sick with fever and exhaustion.

Dia remembered being buoyed by relief, by hope, as they plodded their last remaining steps through the sandy wash, crawling under the double strands of barbed wire to see an official-looking sign that warned, rather than welcomed, them to the land of opportunity.

That starlit night . . .

Then, the sudden blare of flood lights. Moments of chaos. Running. Shouting. Weapons glinting. Name-calling—names Dia knew to be aimed at her.

"Do what they tell you. *¿Si?*" her mother had said.

"*¡Vámonos!*" the authorities had told them. "Get in the van!"

Now, they were here, caged, in the chill and damp of the night, days later. *Waiting. Waiting.*

THIS NIGHT, DIA AWOKE to the sound of voices, cutting over the roar of traffic on the overpass above.

Guards!

She recognized the voices from nights before, when the

men would arrive, two of them, to take one or another of the young women away for a while.

Tonight, Dia moved to try to see what was happening, but her mother drew her tighter, covering Dia's eyes with her hand and curling them both into a tight ball, as if desperately trying to make them small. *Make them disappear.* Dia managed a glimpse, again, in the direction of the men, despite her mother's efforts to shield her.

They were across the compound, moving through the crowd, stepping over sleeping bodies, poking, prodding at others with their night sticks, kicking others aside with mal-indifference, inspecting, closely, now and again, the women and young girls, as if looking to select just the right cut of meat for a meal, making their way in Dia and her mother's direction.

At one moment, the guards seemed interested in a teenage girl. Dia's mother seized on the momentary distraction to rise on hands and knees and crawl, urging Dia to crawl ahead of her toward the portable toilets that were lined against the chain link fencing. She pushed Dia inside one of the johns, just as Dia heard one of the men call, "You!"

Dia's mother froze, Dia crammed into a corner of the toilet.

"Yes, you, Chiquita!"

Her mother reached quickly down the front of her own jeans and withdrew the cell phone Dia had all but forgotten. She remembered Father Vega saying, "One number should you need help."

Her mother shoved the phone deep into the folds of Dia's clothing, whispering, "¡Don't let them find this, *niña*!"

"¡Mami!"

"Shushhhh!" Her mother quickly clamped a hand over Dia's mouth, silencing her. "¡*Tranquila, pequeña*!" She then quickly withdrew, slamming the toilet door, leaving Dia alone in the dark with only the devilish smells about her.

Dia clutched tightly to the cell phone, drawing odd comfort from its presence. She swallowed down the rising terror and quickly locked the door.

"You! Up!" she heard. She pictured the short one, hand on the heel of his gun, keeping watch on the crowd as the big man dragged her mother to her feet. She heard her mother's defiance: "*¡Alto! ¡No! ¡Bastardo!*"

"Let's go, bitch. You need to get properly processed."

She pictured her mother struggling vainly against an iron grip.

"*¡Vámonos, zorra!*"

There was additional scuffling, then all was quiet beyond the door again.

Dia sat in darkness for long minutes, her hands, her body, trembling. Then noise from behind the toilets, at a distance outside the caged enclosure.

Dia got to her feet. Dim light came through a small peephole that had been punched through the back wall of the john. Climbing to stand on the toilet seat, Dia put one eye to the hole. From her vantage, she could look out onto a construction yard that ran the distance from the back of the compound to the hillside far away. In the dim glare from streetlights on the overpass, she saw her mother being dragged forcibly, against her protestations, toward a construction shack across the way.

Dia stifled a cry, her right eye, wide and unflinching, pressed against the hole.

Now the two men, together, were forcing her mother inside the shack, when she heard the big man roar in agony. In that moment, her mother broke free of their grasp. Emitting a hellish scream, she fled across the construction yard toward the road leading out.

"¡*Puta*!" The bigger man spat, a hand to his face, the other hand quickly drawing his gun and firing two shots in her mother's direction.

The roar of a truck overhead drowned the sound of the gunfire, but Dia saw the muzzle flash in the dim light. She squelched a sound, her breath caught in her throat.

"Goddammit, Stitch!" she heard the shorter guard yell.

"Shut up, Charlie! My face! Look at my goddamn face, the fucking whore!"

"¡Mami!!!" Dia cried, unable to hold back any longer, her mother downed, somewhere on the road, no longer visible to her through the peephole.

Her cry drew the attention of both men.

Out of reflex, Dia withdrew from the peep hole and flattened herself against the side wall of the toilet. She emitted a whimper and wiped her eyes to clear her tears. She remained frozen for a long moment, silence falling all about her. Dia couldn't calm the shaking in her body, prevent the tears from streaming down her cheeks. She pictured what might come next, the men bursting back into the compound, throwing-open the doors of the Porta-Johns, one at a time, until she was quickly discovered. She waited, holding her breath.

Nothing happened.

In the dark of the toilet, Dia ventured another look through the peephole. The two guards were still standing in the dim light, their eyes scanning the back of the compound and the toilets where she remained hidden.

"What do you think?" the short guard said, the highway quiet for a time. "I thought I heard something."

The bigger guard continued to survey the compound.

Finally, he holstered his weapon and wiped the blood from his face. "Let's just get the bitch out of here."

Dia watched as the two men crossed from her view and were gone.

The night beyond the compound fell silent again. Dia climbed down to crouch on the floor of the toilet, sobbing her grief into the vile odors.

Long minutes passed, until she finally pulled herself to her feet and emerged from the toilet, banging the door back on its hinges.

Some of the migrants glanced up at her, surprised by her abrupt appearance. Others remained unmoved. All seemingly unaware of the gunshots amid the roar of truck traffic overhead.

Dia felt numb, unable to move. "¡Mami!" she whimpered, until a hunched old woman came forward to comfort her.

Dia allowed herself to be engulfed by the woman's nurturing embrace.

Only then did she let her tears flow.

TWO-THIRTY IN THE MORNING, Bill Daniels awoke to a phone ringing in his ear. He blinked himself into consciousness and lifted his head from the desk where he'd fallen asleep at his work.

"Can you get that?" his wife, Marta, said.

Daniels turned a foggy gaze to her. She was still typing away on the computer at the desk adjacent to his. She threw a nod, without missing a keystroke, toward the phone that continued to ring.

Daniels cleared his throat and ran a hand through his thinning hair, drawing a clean comb-over front to back. He answered the call. "Daniels."

There was momentary silence where he considered hanging up. Instead, he said, *"Hola. Háblame."* And waited, gazing at the front door to the small office he shared with his wife, seeing their signage in reverse through the glass: *Immigration Advocates, Daniels and Cabrera, Attorneys at Law.*

"¡Ayúdame!" a tiny voice said.

"¿Perdón?" he said, not sure he had heard it correctly.

"My mami, they took her." The voice was that of a young girl, he believed, tentative, coming to him through tears, perhaps.

"You speak English. Who are you? How did you get my number?"

There was no response, but he could tell the girl was still on the line.

"Can you tell me your name? *¿Como se llama?*"

"Dia," the girl said.

"Where are you, Dia?"

The girl hesitated a response.

"It's okay," Daniels said, sensing her apprehension. "You can talk to me. Look around, tell me what you see."

"People," the girl said.

"People? Do you know these people?"

There was hesitation, then, "No."

There were no other sounds or voices coming through on the call. Daniels snapped his fingers to get his wife's attention. He motioned to her to join him on the call, and waited as she picked up.

"What are the people doing?" he said into the phone now.

"Sleeping. Some are awake, just sitting."

"And someone took your mother?"

"Help me," the girl said again.

"I want to help you. I will. I promise, I will. Just tell me where you are."

"I don't know . . . a cage."

Daniels and his wife shared a knowing look, concern knitting both their brows.

"Are you in the United States?" Daniels asked.

"Oh, for God's sake," Marta said to her husband. Into the phone she said, "Dia, my name is Marta. It's okay, sweetheart. You and your mother were picked up by Border Patrol, is that right?"

The girl was sniffling into the phone. Daniels let his wife run with it.

"Can you tell me what happened, sweetie?""

A sudden flood of anguish poured from the girl now. "My mami! They took her! They shot her!"

Marta's voice became constricted. "Tell me . . . tell me where to find you? I'll come to you now. I promise."

There was hesitation on the line again, voices were now coming from the background.

"How can I find you?"

"I have to go," the girl said.

"Wait, just tell me . . ."

The phone line went dead.

"Dia . . . ?"

"She's gone," Daniels said.

Marta listened with hope that the girl would come back on the line. Then she settled the receiver back into its cradle.

Daniels leaned back in his chair and pondered the situation. "What do you think?"

"I think she's in trouble, God dammit! She's alone. She's scared! And she believes her mother has been shot. She's traumatized, Bill!"

"Yeah, well, they've been separating these kids from parents routinely." He tried playing devil's advocate.

"Not at gunpoint!" Marta shot back.

Daniels nodded. He was struggling with the image of the girl, too. "How'd she come by a phone? How did she get our number?"

Marta gave her husband that look that he knew all too well. *Really?* "I think you probably know," she said.

Daniels did know. It could only have come from his friend and confidant in Guatemala, Father Emilio Vega— the good man using his church to assist migrants with their arduous and dangerous journey to the US and freedom. Daniels called and, not surprisingly, found Emilio still awake too.

ON THE DRIVE HOME, Daniels briefed Marta on his call with Father Vega.

"Emilio confirmed he had given the mother a cell phone with our number in it. Anica Alvarez is the young mother. Her daughter is Dia. The two are very special to him. He worries for them and wanted the mother to have someone to contact when she got across the border. He thought of us. He's deeply concerned that it was Dia who called and not the mother."

"Does he know when they might have reached the US?" Marta asked.

"Emilio didn't know for sure," Daniels said. "Recently, he believed. It takes months to get here. There are a multitude of delays and contingencies. But said they would have crossed somewhere near Agua Prieta, if they had stuck to the plan.

"We could assume, I guess," Marta said, "that they were initially detained together. Perhaps just the two of them, or possibly with others from their group. It's hard to say what happened when they reached the border. If it was recent, and if they crossed near Naco, they would have been taken first to the only temporary holding compound in the area, under the overpass on Highway Eighty, before being transferred to one of any number of formal processing centers."

"Border Patrol's only supposed to hold them there for no more than twenty-four hours," Daniels said.

"Yeah, right, if you believe the media," Marta said. "Some have been detained for weeks without due process. And, if she is there, we won't find her by name. They're not registered or recorded at the temporary facilities. They're simply rounded up like stray dogs and tossed in a cage."

"It's a long shot," Daniels said. "But maybe our only shot."

"Yes," Marta said, still, imagining the girl—*God!*—frightened and alone in that place. "I've got court in the morning. And I need sleep."

"I've got it," Daniels said. "I'll head to the compound first thing, see what I can find out. It's all we can do."

IT WAS GOING ON 7 A.M. now. Daniels was sitting on the edge of the bed still in his boxers and T-shirt. He'd had little sleep. Marta was up as well, in the bathroom in her nightgown, getting ready for her court appearance. Daniels was talking to her through the open door.

"I know not to expect much help when I get to the compound," Daniels said. "I'll be inquiring about an unregistered minor, one I've never seen, and one that may or may not have already been moved."

Marta came out of the bathroom to finish dressing.

"So, you understand," she said. "I can't rest until we find her. I'll catch up with you when I'm clear of court."

Daniels watched as Marta dressed. He admired her dedication, the depth of passion she had for immigrants like herself.

Marta slipped into her shoes, touched at her hair briefly in the mirror, then was out the door, saying, "Let me know as soon as you can."

Daniels remained sitting on the edge of the bed for a time, his heart heavy, considering what options he had, if any. Then, resigning himself to the day, he rose and began to dress.

ON THE DRIVE SOUTH, Daniels thought about his wife. How she, herself, had once made the trek across the border. How she'd told of her abuse at the hands of the coyotes, her abuse at the hands of US Border Patrol. About other things she was unwilling to tell even him. She had survived to be deported.

Daniels met her serving drinks behind the bar at a resort in Puerto Peñasco. God, she was beautiful then; beautiful now. After they married, she moved into his house in the old barrio district of Tucson, finished her law degree at the university and joined him in the firm. That had been her immigration story, twelve years ago. Another story was unfolding today . . .

DANIELS ARRIVED AROUND NOON at the Highway 80 overpass, a grand curving bridge across the Agua Fria wash. Finding an off-ramp, he followed a gravel road down into the wash and back along and below the highway to come to what appeared to be an ADOT maintenance yard—a small shack with various pieces of highway maintenance equipment littered about the hard-pack that surrounded it.

The detention compound itself was across from the shack, directly under the overpass. It was a sizable, black-ened chain-link cage that carried neither identification nor promise. There were perhaps a half-dozen white vehicles, mostly SUVs, parked haphazardly on this side of the enclo-sure, all with the familiar green and brown *Immigration and Naturalization, US Border Patrol* emblem on the door panels.

Daniels drew his car to a stop between the maintenance yard and the compound. He killed the engine and took a moment to survey what lay before him. From where he was parked, he could see the girth and depth of the chain link enclosure, but nothing of the inside of the compound nor the people detained there.

Was the little girl, Dia, alone among them?

Daniels wanted to find out.

He slid out of the car and crossed around to the oppo-site side of the compound where he found an entrance gate. A pair of Border Patrol agents stood guard at the entrance—one female, one male.

Another small group of agents was gathered nearby, chatting idly. All were armed with steely black handguns. A pair of agents in the group had automatic assault weap-ons slung from their shoulders, forearms resting on the stocks.

Daniels approached the gate, dressed in his suit, tie loosened about his neck.

The male agent at the gate—Ross, according to his nametag—moved his hand to rest it casually on the heel of his weapon. "This is a restricted area, sir."

"Hi," Daniels said, offering his business card. Ross

looked it over briefly then passed it to his partner—Fuentes, her nametag read—who glanced at it and passed it back to Daniels.

"We can't help you," Ross said.

"Agent Ross," Daniels said, "maybe not. But I'm trying to find a young girl, nine or ten years old. She could have been picked up at the border in recent days. I want to find out if she's being held here."

Ross and Fuentes exchanged a quick look. "Like I said, we can't help you. These people here," Ross said, thumbing Daniels's attention toward the compound, "they're all still waiting for in-processing. Besides, we don't hold unaccompanied minors. They're taken elsewhere."

"How do I go about finding this girl?"

"Well, like I said, we can't help you. You'll have to file a formal request with the main processing center in Sierra Vista."

"I have reason to believe that the girl's mother may have been taken away without the girl."

Ross shrugged. "Yeah, well, you'll have to take that up with Sierra Vista too."

Daniels could see from the set of their eyes, the steel in their stance, that there would be no softening of their position on the matter. "Okay, thanks anyway," Daniels said, tucking his business card into his breast pocket, and turning away.

"You have yourself a nice day," Agent Ross said to his back, a condescending edge to his voice.

CHARLIE SIZEMORE WAITED TO catch his partner's eye before giving him a nod to direct him away from the others. He had been only half participating in the idle chatter of the other agents, listening with one ear more intently to the man who had approached the gate to inquire about one of the detainees. Something about a young girl . . . maybe a girl who had been separated from her mother . . . maybe alone in the compound. He couldn't help but think about the night before, the incident with the woman still weighing heavily on him.

"Did you hear that, Stitch?" he said, when he had his partner alone. "That guy at the gate? We need to find out who he is. Maybe find out about this girl he's looking for."

Donald "Stitch" Lassiter turned a concerned look toward the two guards at the gate and called out to them. "Hey, Ross! What was that all about?" Making it sound casual, as if only a passing interest.

Agent Ross gave him a shrug. "Just some guy looking for a young girl. He's an immigration attorney from Tucson. No big deal."

Stitch threw him a nod, a feigned smile in acknowledgement.

"A fucking attorney!" Charlie said beneath his breath. "I knew no good was going to come of this!"

"Get ahold of yourself, Chazbro. It doesn't have to be about us."

"Stitch, I'm all in for a little bit of fun with some of these good-looking bitches. You know that, man. But, Jesus Christ, I didn't sign on for killing one of 'em." He was working to keep his voice down against his rising fears.

"You saw what she did to me," Stitch said, turning a cheek to Charlie to show him the still-red, raw claw marks down the side of his face. He'd been explaining them away all morning with a joke about his crazy-ass girlfriend.

"I still think we should have buried her," Charlie said. "'Stead of just tossing her out there among the cactus. My God!" His eyes were on the ground, not able to look at Stitch when he spoke.

"And dig through six feet of hard desert caliche? Fuck that! Ain't nobody gonna give a shit about one more illegal found dead in the desert. Happens all the time. Now get a grip on yourself. We dug the bullets out, ain't nothing to tie her back to us." Stitch slapped a hand to the nape of Charlie's neck and gave him a playful shake. "We got this, *amigo*! Right?"

Charlie watched Stitch saunter off. Could the girl this attorney mentioned have witnessed what happened? And if she had, could the attorney have somehow found this out? Charlie couldn't see how.

Still, he didn't feel right with any of it.

ON HIS WAY BACK to the office, Daniels stopped by the Cochise County Sheriff's office to talk to Sheriff Tom McClellan. Daniels had known McClellan since they were kids, running the streets together on Tucson's south side, and they were still good friends. He found Tom at his desk, piles of paperwork in front of him. Tom waved him inside.

"Well, look what the coyotes dug up. You must want something," Tom said. "Only time I see you these days."

"Sad but true," Daniels said. "We need to have that beer together we talked about the last time I saw you."

"And the time before that, and the time before . . . So, what's up? You look a bit troubled, everything okay with you and Marta?"

Daniels realized he was wringing his hands. "What?

. . . Yeah, sure, we're great." He stilled his hands and said, "No, it's this young girl I got a call from. Maybe ten years old. Said they . . . said it like that . . . 'they' . . . had taken her mother. She pleaded with me to help her. I believe she may be being held at that temporary Border Patrol compound under the overpass. You know the one."

Tom nodded. "Yeah, and we all know how they're handling it from there."

"I know," Daniels said. "It's in the hands of the feds. But, here's the thing. It was two-thirty in the morning, Tom. A ten-year-old girl. And she claims she saw her mother shot. I just want to get into that camp and see if she's there and talk to her."

"She had a cell phone?"

"Yeah, I'm assuming the mother managed to smuggle it into the compound."

"Did you try calling the number back?"

"No!" Daniels said. "I'm afraid it might give her away. I tried texting the number but got no reply. I went to the compound this morning, but the agents there weren't any help. All dead ends. I was hoping maybe you could help get me in there. Use some of that Cochise County clout you're so damned well known for."

"These days, not as much as you think, friend. Besides, that's the federal government. I have no say in what they're up to."

Daniels nodded, reluctantly. "I guess. I just thought maybe . . ."

Tom came out from behind his desk. "Maybe the girl will call back. Let me know how you make out."

Daniels rose to shake his hand. "Thanks anyway, buddy. We still need to have that beer."

"Sooner than later," Tom said, and walked Daniels to the door.

BACK IN TUCSON, DANIELS said, "The Border Patrol was no help, as expected. I tried Tom McClellan, he couldn't do anything either."

It was late afternoon now, and he and Marta were back in the office together again.

"Blue by a different color," Marta said. She was behind her desk, her chin propped on her elbows.

"The news on my phone said the body of a Jane Doe was found in the desert, south of the compound. No evidence to directly tie her to Dia."

Marta sat up straight. "Seriously, Bill? You really need more convincing?"

"Not me, babe. But it will take more evidence and more charm than I have to get inside that compound." Daniels crossed to the refrigerator and took out a can of beer, popped the top, and joined her, plopping down in his chair behind his desk. "I've tried the camp. I've tried the Sherriff's Department. I even made calls to the Border Patrol in both Sierra Vista and the offices out on Ajo Way. No one's willing to help."

"I sucked in court this morning," Marta said. "I can't get my mind off her. I just have this feeling she may be in mortal danger."

They sat in silent contemplation for a while, Marta head-in-hand again; Daniels swigging his beer. Finally, Marta said, "Maybe I can get inside there."

"I don't see how," Daniels said. He lowered his beer to look at her. "Wait! What are you thinking?"

Marta gave him a slight shrug.

"No! That's crazy! You've been there before."

"It's not crazy *because* I've been there before. Besides, it may be the only way. Of course, I would have to trust you to get me out. Or maybe you'd rather leave me there." She gave him a coy smile.

Daniels shook his head, but sipped his beer in contemplation. "It's too dangerous."

"I know the way. I know the language. I know the drill. I've never shied away from danger before. You know that."

Was there any other way to find the girl? Daniels couldn't think of one.

Daniels said nothing more, knowing that once Marta made up her mind about something, there was no changing it.

Privately, they sat quiet, each in their own way, pondering the details of what was to come. And waiting for the sun to drop beyond the Tucson Mountains to the west.

CHARLIE COULDN'T HELP HIMSELF. The panic he was feeling had been growing throughout the afternoon, putting his nerves on edge and making him want to scream. Should he chance taking a walk through the compound, see what he could see? But then, maybe risk the girl recognizing him—that is, if there was a girl and if she'd seen anything. Maybe he could just let it go, trust what Stitch believed about the migrants having no power, no incentive, to cause trouble for them. He ground on the decision, pulling at the stubble on his chin, remembering the night before and the muffled cry that both he and Stitch had believed they might have heard. It seemed he could hear it now more clearly—"*¡Mami!*"

Goddamn!

He continued agonizing, working himself up, until he

couldn't stand it anymore. Do something—*something!*—he told himself.

Charlie made his way to the gate that led into the compound. The same two guards were still on duty. "Alma . . . Pete . . ." he said as greeting.

"Hey," Alma Fuentes said, somewhat deferential. Ross gave him a nod.

"I've been asked to get a current headcount of our detainees." Not waiting for acknowledgement, Charlie strolled on past and made his way inside.

He covered his nose with his sleeve, never having gotten used to the smell of humankind packed shoulder-to-shoulder.

He scanned the crowd, then moved off among them, feigning the process of counting, searching the faces, not knowing who or what he was looking for, but specifically inspecting the young girls, seeing what, if anything, he might detect.

It was more difficult than Charlie imagined. The boys he could scan past. Ignore the teenagers, ignore the toddlers. Still, there were dozens of young girls in the age range he was looking for. Hell, too goddamn many of them. Charlie was starting to lose hope, but moved on through the crowd, searching the faces of the adolescent girls who looked back at him with mostly dead eyes. Then . . .

He spotted a girl across the compound, near the toilets, holding close to an old lady. The woman was watching him closely—maybe a little too closely—as he made his way through the crowd. The girl was curled up at the woman's feet, clutching the woman's leg, keeping her eyes diverted. Intentionally, it seemed to Charlie.

He approached the old woman, keeping his eye on her

until he was directly in front of them. Only then did he turn his eyes to the girl. "Kid!" he said. "¡*Niña*!"

She refused to look at him.

Charlie turned his gaze on the old woman. "¿*Está ella contigo?*" he said.

"*Yo soy su abuela,*" she replied.

"You're her grandmother?"

"*Sí.* Grandmother," the old woman said.

Charlie could tell by her eyes she was lying. He turned his gaze back to the girl.

"What's your name, girl? ¿*Como se llama?*"

She said nothing, still refusing to look at him.

"¡*Háblame!*" Charlie reached down, grabbed the girl by the wrist, and jerked her to her feet. An object slipped from her jacket and clattered to the ground at Charlie's feet.

"Well, well! What have we here?" Charlie shoved the girl aside and bent to pick up the object. "A cell phone? How's a little degenerate like you come to have a cell phone? You know how to use this?" He turned the phone in his hand, looking it over. "Of course you do. All you little rats are using phones these days. I think I'll just have to keep this one."

The girl grabbed for it; Charlie slapped her hand away.

"¡*Por favor!*" the old woman said, imploring his mercy, placing herself between Charlie and the girl.

"Huh-uh, now, Abuela!" He studied the girl intently. "I found this little piece," he said, speaking more or less to the old woman. "But the question now is what am I going to do with her?"

Charlie glanced back across the compound at the guards outside. They were still at their posts, indifferent to his presence inside the compound. The detainees turned their eyes away as Charlie moved his gaze across them. He directed his attention back to the girl and the old lady.

"I'm going to have to deal with you for sure. Maybe both of you," he said. "But, for now, it's going to have to wait."

Charley took one more look at the girl. "Don't go anywhere," he said with a sneer, enjoying the irony of his little joke. Then, slipping the cell phone into his pocket, he turned back toward the exit. Other detainees challenged him with their eyes, but diverted their gaze, submissively, one by one, as he made his way through and out.

DANIELS DROVE HIS WIFE to the Naco border crossing, showing their passports and IDs to the agents manning the port of entry. Then, waved on, they crossed into Mexico.

It was past nightfall, the desert under a dim white glow of starlight. About a quarter-mile down the highway, Daniels pulled the car off into the desert and killed the lights.

It was a bold and dangerous plan for Marta to make her way back across the border on foot, along the same San Pedro River wash where hundreds of other migrants had gone before.

Daniels could see the transformation in his wife's eyes, changed from the confident, experienced attorney, as she had been in the office, to a woman who had already previously lived far too much of what she might be facing now.

"You don't have to do this," Daniels said, taking her hand.

"Would you like to trade places?"

"I don't think it will work that way."

"Exactly," Marta said.

Daniels nodded reluctantly, and collected Marta's purse and wallet, confirming she had no other identification on her. The image of the Jane Doe found dead in the desert flashed before his eyes, but he pushed that image aside as he pulled a backpack from the back seat and handed it to Marta—the pack stuffed with the barest of partially used travel essentials.

Marta opened the car door to step out. She paused momentarily to give her husband an adoring look. With a sigh, she said, "You're a good man. Wish me luck, *amigo. ¿Si?*"

"I've got your back. Call me on the girl's phone when you locate her. If I don't hear from you in, oh, say, ten years, I'll come looking for you." He smiled and gave her a kiss on the cheek.

He prayed it would all go well.

Marta slid out of the car. Daniels watched her go, aching for her safety, as she crossed off into the desert on foot and disappeared into the starlit night.

Daniels waited, pondering the secrets of the night, then put the car in reverse and started to back out . . .

His phone suddenly rang, causing him to stop.

Daniels checked the call; it was the girl's number calling. "*Hola,*" he answered quickly.

"Who's this?" a male voice said.

Daniels checked his phone again, making sure he hadn't misread the number. He said, "This is Bill Daniels, I'm an attorney. Who are you? How'd you get this number?"

"Purely by accident," the man said. "I wanted to apologize for my daughter, she called you by mistake last night. The girl's just got a vivid imagination. Likes to make prank calls. You know kids these days. Them and their phones, huh."

"It didn't sound like a prank," Daniels said.

"Well, no need to worry. You have a good evening."

The call went dead before Daniels could probe further.

Daniels's heart lay wedged in his throat. He wasn't buying the shit the man was selling. He desperately scanned the desert for Marta, hoping to spot her and stop her before she completely escaped his reach.

It was too late; she was nowhere to be seen.

Daniels slammed a fist into the dash. He put his head in his hands and tried to think. He was sending Marta into imminent danger. Whoever had made this last call had found the girl, found the phone. Was the girl still in the compound? Had she come to harm? What would Marta be facing on the other side of the border?

Myriad questions.

Daniels didn't want to consider the answers. He threw the car back into gear and spun the tires getting out of there. He had to get back across the border. *Now!* And get to the compound. Where he prayed to God Marta would be taken.

MARTA WAS PICKED UP within minutes of crossing the border, having tripped a motion detector that summoned the patrols. She was tossed unceremoniously into the back of a van with two other detainees, a father and his teenage son. The agents' heavy-handed treatment of her and the apathy shown toward the other two reminded Marta of her previous journey across the border, and affirmed her belief that nothing much had changed, along the border, in all these years. They were transported immediately to the chain link compound under the Highway 80 overpass, given a box meal and a drink, and pushed inside with the hordes of others—Marta feeling a sense of relief to have, at least, found herself in the same compound as she believed the girl to be. She handed her boxed meal over to the father and son who had arrived with her, then took a moment to survey her surroundings, before beginning her search, wading through the crowd of migrants, inspecting the faces of the young girls as she went. "Dia . . . ?" she asked, as she made her way through. "Dia Alvarez? . . Dia?"

Marta continued on, querying the migrants as she went.

At last, she came upon an elderly woman with a young girl curled at her feet, the girl clutching at the older woman's leg. The girl stood, hearing her name, but still shielded herself behind the older woman's skirts.

"You're Dia?" Marta asked again.

The girl nodded, shyly. She was like an innocent little kitten, wrapped in the old woman's knitted shawl.

Marta threw a quick glance over her shoulder to the guards out front.

"I'm Marta. I promised I would come for you. Remember?"

CHARLIE AND STITCH MET up at a pull-off down the highway from the compound, Charlie sliding into the passenger seat of Stitch's car to talk to him. "Man, the shit is about to hit the fan!"

Charlie showed Stitch the phone and told him how he had called the only number in it. "I took the phone off some little bitch in the compound, a girl just like the one the guy was asking about. Guess who answered the phone, huh? Same fucking attorney, that's who! The girl has been talking to him! We gotta do something!"

Stitch seemed to ponder the problem, his brow knitted.

"Alright," he finally said. "But, if the girl goes away, you know, disappears, then what's the lawyer got? Nothing! A fucking figment of his imagination. The girl hasn't been registered yet. She technically doesn't exist. But we gotta do it now, tonight! You never know when another batch of them will be hauled over to Sierra Vista for processing. We can't let that happen."

"Fuck! Right?" Charlie said.

"We'll leave my car, take your Patrol vehicle," Stitch said. "It's about thirty minutes 'til our shift starts at the gate. Act like nothing unusual, same as always. Right?"

"Right!" Charlie said, feeling a touch of hopefulness now that Stitch was here.

They piled out of Stitch's car and into Charlie's Border Patrol vehicle and headed north on the highway toward the compound. They arrived just minutes before their shift, suiting up in the parking area in uniform jackets, caps, and side arms. Stitch slung an automatic assault weapon across his shoulder.

A different set of guards from the ones earlier in the day was manning the gate. It was a few minutes before 11 P.M. Darkness had fully descended upon the surrounding desert, only the glare of the bright flood lights bringing life to the area around the compound.

"We've got it!" Stitch said, approaching the guards, giving them a cheery smile. "Time for you cowpokes to get along on home."

The guards gave him a tired look, weary of any manufactured cheer. One of the guards unslung his weapon and gave Stitch a fist bump on his way out.

The other guard said, "All's quiet. Three more newbies picked up earlier, is all. They've been fed. You should have a quiet night. Maybe I should volunteer for graveyard, next time."

"Yeah, it's a real fucking joy," Stitch said, as Charlie took up his position at the gate.

They played it cool for a while, manning the entrance, appearing dutiful, until the relieved guards were well out onto the highway and on their way home.

"Let's just give it a few minutes," Stitch said. "Make sure everything is peachy keen. Then we'll do this together."

DANIELS HAD MADE IT back across the border and was speeding north, up Highway 80 as fast as he could manage. He called his friend Tom McClellan on the way and told him what had transpired, told him about Marta potentially being inside the compound and how he'd gotten a call from a man who was now in possession of the very same cell phone that the girl he was looking for had called him from earlier. "I'm not forgetting, Tom, about a Jane Doe found in the desert, nor the girl saying her mother had been shot."

"You and Marta are damned fools," McClellan said. "But all right. I'll grab a deputy and intercept you along the highway."

He did. And together they convoyed their way, fast, toward the Highway 80 compound.

MARTA WAS SLOWLY GAINING the girl's trust by simply talking to her, asking her about their journey, about Father Vega and her home in Guatemala. Now, she believed she could address the more pressing issue: what had happened to her mother, and why she believed she needed help.

"You came here with your mother, Dia?"

"Yes," the girl said, shyly.

"And you called the number in the cell phone that Father Vega gave you?"

Dia nodded. "He gave it to Mami."

"And your mother gave it to you?"

Dia nodded again. "When the men took her."

"You saw them take her."

"Yes. From the toilet."

"The toilet? You were in the toilet when they took your mother?"

"Mami put me in there. That's when she gave me the phone, and said 'don't let anyone take it.' Then, the men took her and hurt her."

"You saw them hurt her?"

"Through the hole. I saw them, out there," Dia said, pointing to the area outside the compound, behind the row of toilets.

Marta's heart was breaking for the girl. It was becoming obvious this tender little child had witnessed the abduction and possibly the brutal murder of her mother. And she had survived, thank God, with the nurturing comfort of the elderly woman.

"You were very brave to make a phone call. You talked to my husband, do you remember?"

Dia nodded.

"And you asked him to help, and he did. He sent me to help you."

The girl had remained huddled close to the old woman. But now she shrugged off the shawl to put her arms around Marta's neck.

Marta held onto her for a long moment, then drew her back to speak to her face-to-face. It was time to call her husband and get them the hell out of there.

"Do you have the cell phone, Dia?"

"One of the men took it. One of the men who took my mother."

Marta felt a chill run up her spine. She wasn't prepared for the perpetrators discovering the girl and learning she had witnessed their crime. This had not been in the plan.

"Dia, listen to me. You say you saw the men who took your mother and you could identify them if you saw them again?"

"Yes, I saw them."

"Do you know who they are?"

Dia had been holding Marta's gaze with her own, but now her attention shifted to the entrance.

"It was them!" Dia said, lifting her arm to point across Marta's shoulder.

Marta turned to see two Border Patrol agents pushing into the compound through the gated entrance. They were not the same two guards as had ushered her into the compound earlier. Both were armed. The larger one had an assault rifle slung across his shoulder. They were coming her way, their attention already focused on Dia.

Marta drew Dia behind her for protection and stood her ground.

"Step away from the girl. She's coming with us," the larger man said.

"She's not going anywhere with you. And nowhere without me."

"This doesn't concern you."

"I think it does. I know everything."

"You don't know shit! And what's a damn kid know about anything? What's she been telling you?"

"Dia, do you know these men?"

Dia lifted her eyes boldly to the men. "Stitch," she said, pointing a finger at the big man. "And Charlie," she said again, pointing now at the smaller man.

"Goddamn, Stitch!" Charlie cried. "She even knows our names!"

"Shut up, Chazbro!" Stitch said through clenched teeth.

"Seems like she knows quite a bit," Marta said. "And I'm not one of your migrant detainees that you can easily pass off. I'm an American citizen, an attorney from Tucson, and my husband will be arriving to get us out of here any minute now."

"Oh, well, don't worry. You'll be coming with us too." Stitch reached for Marta.

Marta slapped his hand away.

"Gonna be like that, huh?"

Stitch used the muzzle of the assault rifle to slap Marta up-side the head. She cried out in pain.

The other detainees had been passive until now. With the violence against Marta, the nearest male detainees came to their feet, fists clenched. Others reacted, joining in, crowding forward in a show of solidarity.

"Nuh-uh!" Stitch barked, waving them back with the muzzle of the weapon.

Many stood firm, a few of the males ventured a step forward.

Stitch raised the muzzle and fired off a quick burst. It backed them off a step.

"Now, go!" he said, to Marta, pointing her toward the door. "Bring the girl with you. You too, grandma. ¡*Vámonos*!"

Marta hesitated, touching the side of her scalp and feeling the wet sticky presence of blood. Stitch gave her a shove to get her going, using the assault rifle to wave a path through the throng of migrants, who now scrambled to make way.

They were marched roughly, out through the gated entrance and across the hardpack toward a Border Patrol vehicle parked nearby. The one called Charlie ran ahead to get the doors open to receive them.

Marta tried to think. *What to do? What to do?* She was leading Dia by one hand and the elderly woman by the other. If the three of them got inside the agents' vehicle, she knew they would never be seen or heard from again.

As they reached the car, Marta handed the old woman off to Stitch.

Then, as he was occupied with getting the woman folded into the back seat, Marta released Dia and set her free. "Run!" she cried. "¡*Corre!*"

Dia didn't hesitate. She fled, streaking across the parking pad toward the road.

"Stop her!" Stitch yelled, his hands encumbered by the old woman.

Charlie drew his gun and took aim at the fleeing girl.

Marta launched herself at him, pitching him back against the side of the vehicle, as his gun discharged an errant round toward the sky.

Charlie shoved Marta to the ground and turned his weapon on her now.

Before he could finish her, sirens suddenly wailed as cars came flooding into the yard. Flashing blue and red lights from a patrol car scraped the hardpack. Stitch shoved the old woman to the ground. He raced around to the driver's side of the car in an attempt to flee. Marta came to her feet and slammed the car door shut before he could reach it. She put her back against it, defiantly blocking his way.

The cars came skidding to a stop. McClellan and his deputy piled out, guns drawn. "Drop your weapon!" McClellan commanded, his own handgun leveled on Stitch. "Drop it! Hands in the air! Do it! Do it now!"

"You've got no jurisdiction here, Sheriff!" Stitch called. Charlie looked unsure.

"Maybe not, but I'm not going to let you drive away. Drop your weapons or I'll drop you where you stand. Higher powers than you can sort it out over your dead bodies."

Charlie gave in. He laid his gun on the ground and raised his hands above his head.

Stitch hesitated, his eyes searching for a way out, only to finally throw his hands up, letting the assault rifle slip to the ground with a clatter. "All right!" he said.

Marta turned her attention to the road. Her husband Bill was out of his car. He had scooped Dia up in her flight and now had her in his arms, carrying her back toward the scene, cooing in her ear.

Marta ran to them, throwing her arms around them. "Am I ever glad to see you!"

"And am I ever glad to see you! And you!" he said, patting Dia on the head. "You're a brave little girl, you know that?"

Dia tucked her face against his shoulder.

Red and blue lights circled the parking pad, as the deputy collected weapons and held their new detainees at bay. Sheriff McClellan was on the radio contacting border authorities.

Marta clung tightly to her husband taking Dia's hand in hers. "You're safe now," she said. "We're taking you home with us. These men will never be able to hurt you, or anyone, again."

Marta leaned in to give her a kiss on the cheek, already mentally preparing for the fights they would have to wage in the immigration courts on Dia's behalf, and in the criminal courts to seek justice for her mother. And know-ing—*knowing!* . . .

Dia Alvarez was going to make a star witness.

CODE NAME PÉNÉLOPE |

Cara Black ||||||||||||||||||||||| |

1941—Le Marais, Paris

Late for work—again—Odette Pilpoul hurried around the corner and stumbled into someone. A man. In the warm May morning he felt all hard edges and his bony elbow grazed her shoulder.

Surprised, she backed up. Could hardly move and found herself wedged between him and the wall.

"*Excusez-moi*, monsieur."

This man, she realized, was one in a long line shuffling down the sidewalk with their arms clasped behind their heads. They filed from the barracks, a former convent in the Marais. Screams reverberated off the limestone walls to rue de Béarn.

What scene from hell was this?

Prisoners? Yet he, like the others, wore street clothes, his shabby suitcase tied with string to his belt.

He peered around then whispered in a low hiss. "Police are rounding up foreign Jews. Warn others."

Alarmed, she wanted to ask more but he'd gone. Lost among the others. Now, she could see Parisian policeman marching the men onto a bus with blacked out windows.

Others? How could she warn others?

From inside the gate open to the barracks yard another piercing scream and dull thuds erupted. Before her eyes a *guardian de la paix*, one of those police adjuncts, kicked a man on the ground. She knew him. Delarue, the stocky brute, kicking a thin man with black wiry hair.

It turned her stomach. The poor man was shielding his face with bloodied hands. Now he was moaning and trying to curl into a ball. Still Delarue rained more kicks on him.

She felt the acute sting of injustice; kicking a man when he was down was a new low, even for the Parisian police. She should stay away from trouble. Wasn't she the bread-winner with a toddler and a husband missing in the war?

But this ripped her insides.

"What's going on here?" she managed.

The red-faced Delarue looked up, panting, and leered at her.

"Official business."

"Kicking a man when he's down?"

The man wasn't moving now.

"Get out. This area's restricted."

She glanced around, noticing this had become the Gendarmerie Nationale post.

"You should take this man to the hospital," she said.

"Scum like this? A thief? Not your business." He looked about to come at her with his raised fists. Stupid to argue with a bully. "Maybe I'll deport you, too, for obstructing police work."

Two policeman appeared and pulled her away.

Her stomach clenched.

"Madame, leave right now. You've seen nothing, *compris*? Heard nothing."

Liars. Thugs. Nazi pawns.

She made herself nod. Move her feet. And seethed inside. This wouldn't go away, she'd make sure of that.

She wouldn't have witnessed this if she hadn't been late. Her mornings got complicated dropping Jean-Marc at the *crèche*, and getting from the left bank over here to the right bank and her new job in the Marais. With all the German checkpoints, the bus lines rerouted and the Metro operating subject to power outages, it was a wonder she'd made it at all. The supposed shortcut led her to witness a brutal beating by a 'guardian of the peace.'

Shaken, she ran all the way down the narrow streets to the third *arrondissement's* Mairie, the town hall. As the *secretaire adjointe generale*, a job she'd taken a government test for and at which she'd become a *fonctionnaire*, her position was really just the general dogsbody.

She had a stack of files waiting on her desk. Inherited from the last *adjointe*. They could wait a few minutes longer. She ran up the marble stairs to her boss's office.

"Monsieur Lamarck, do you know of the police roundup happening on rue de Béarn right now?"

Paul Lamarck, the pencil-pushing fossil from the 19th century, smoothed his goatee. White-haired and a veteran of the last war, he resembled Maréchal Petain, the doddering hero who ran the government in Vichy—a Hitler puppet. Lamarck ran the department when he wasn't at his mother's bedside or his club.

"Police actions taken in our district are not in our purview, Madame Pilpoul," Lamarck said. He stood and plucked a dead frond from the small palm tree on his desk. "Not in this department's realm."

"So you do know, monsieur."

Pause. Dust motes danced in the slants of sunbeams. Something her little Jean-Marc loved to try and catch.

"The question is how do you, Madame Pilpoul."

"The streets are still public, *non*?" she said. "The passing world and I witnessed police brutality in broad daylight."

Surely he could understand the implications? The miscarriage of justice by a *guardian de la paix*.

He coughed. A raspy rumble in his throat. He didn't look well.

"We serve citizens in our *quartier* by providing services according to our mandate."

As if she didn't know that? But he was a politician and spoke *le langue du bois*—common parlance for officials who said in reality nothing at all.

"Monsieur, this was a round-up of foreign-born men. How can this be legal?"

"The Germans give instructions and our police cooperate," he said. "We're not under Vichy law where Maréchal Petain governs our country."

Was that better? He'd tried to weasel out of an answer.

"But you must alert Monsieur le Maire, the Mayor," she said. "He can stop this violence and investigate . . ."

"That's not up for discussion, Madame Pilpoul." He sat down. Wheezed. His skin looked gray. "You were given your duties upon your appointment. Understood?"

Issuing ration cards, birth certificates, IDs, the valuable *carte de sejour* were included in her administrative duties. Since the man who'd done her job was drafted to work in Germany, it fell on her shoulders. All of it.

Her boss Lamarck oversaw the bureaucracy and rarely checked it, as she'd discovered.

She nodded. "*Oui*, monsieur."

The police commissioner knocked on the open office door.

"Excuse me, am I disturbing you?"

"Come in, Commissaire." He turned to Odette. "That's all, Madame Pilpoul."

"*Mais non*, I believe she's the person I'm here to see."

A chill rippled up her neck.

Had someone pointed her out after she'd spoken up? Or followed her from the Gendarmerie's barracks and informed? She imagined the Commissaire would warn her off.

Or had he come to arrest her? Had the *gardien de la paix* trumped up some charge?

Her fingers picked at her jacket hem. The old Chanel she'd refurbished to complement her position at the Mairie.

She needed this job. No one else would put food on the table if she didn't.

"*A votre servis*, Commissaire," she said, aiming for a look she hoped came across as professional. Neutral and expressionless.

Her heart pounded inside her chest.

Could he see the perspiration forming on her brow? How the muscle pulsed in her neck?

"Our police actions require your assistance," said the Commissaire, "specifically in compiling lists of the quarters residents. The foreigners who apply for a *carte de sejour.*"

That was her job. But did they want to deport more foreign-born Jews?

Lamarck kept his gaze neutral. Would he berate her in front of the Commissaire?

"Of course, Commissaire. I'll furnish you the requisite forms. We require a formal request, then Madame Pilpoul will process and compile the information according to your needs."

She masked her shock by turning to the wall and pulling a requisition form from the office shelf.

"Please fill out a requisition form and Monsieur Lamarck will forward it to me for fulfillment," she said. "As per our mandate, *non*, Monsieur Lamarck?"

In the late afternoon, Odette held Jean-Marc's chubby hand in hers, trying to concentrate on his patter, as the peach sky was illuminated by the fading rays of the sun. Along the way posters advertised STO, the labor service in Germany, showing smiling men in the fields. Propaganda posters no one believed filled the billboards. The milk man clattered by on the cobbles, pulling his wagon full of glass milk bottles jiggling in their wire crates. Rumor was his cart and horse had been requisitioned by the Luftwaffe, who'd also requisitioned the local *lycée*.

Maiwenn, her Breton maid and part of the family, hopefully had found more than turnips today. Their ration cards only bought so much and the supplies dwindled fast. Last week poor Maewenn waited hours for their allotted ration of two hundred grams of meat which ran out before she reached the front of the line.

A familiar voice whispered to her as she opened the grilled gate of her apartment building. "Odette, *c'est moi.*"

Behind the gooseberry hedge at the building's side service stairs, she saw black hair.

"Laure?"

"Shhh . . . can you let me in the back?"

"But why are you hiding? What's the matter?"

"What's not the matter?" A troubled sigh came from the bushes. "Please, can you help me?"

Whenever a voice whispered from the bushes it spelt trouble. But she'd lived down the street from Laure in Bordeaux and they'd walked to school together.

"*Attends.*"

By the time Odette sat Jean-Marc at the kitchen table

with a piece of day-old bread soaked in milk and a tiny dollop of chocolate she saved for emergencies, Maewenn had returned with a smile.

"Half-bag of potatoes from the garden patch on the Champs de Mars," said Maewenn, pride in her voice. "I bargained him down, too."

Odette couldn't do what she did without Maewenn.

"*Merci*," she said. "You're a wonder, Maewenn."

Rationing tightened their belts and everyone dealt on the black market if they could. Whenever they could. Ration cards meant little if there was no food or charcoal for heat in the shops.

"Back in Brittany during the Great War, my father did the same. But that was for fish and oysters."

"Maewenn, we might have a guest."

With that, Odette hurtled down the back service stairs. The dark narrow staircase railing was made of rusted metal and wound past landings piled with garbage. She passed the coal chute and storage to open the door which scraped on its hinges.

It wasn't just Laure there waiting for her, but her husband, Remy Arditi, as well; he was leaning heavily on his wife's shoulder and his face was pale. "We've got to hide, Odette," Laure said. "Remy's afraid he'll be enlisted for the STO. I am, too. My name was on a list."

Odette stifled a gasp. "They take women, too?"

Laure nodded.

"Come in," said Odette.

Inside the tradesman's entrance filled with empty burlap sacks for coal, she put her finger to her mouth. She looked around, checked for any resident on the back stairs, then whispered, "Servants come down here any time."

Remy looked exhausted in the dim light.

"*Excusez-moi*, Odette, but can we stay for one night?" Laure pleaded. "We've got to rest. Please? Remy's not well."

"Of course, but I've got a nosey concierge and neighbors so you'll be my relatives from Bordeaux, alright?"

"Thank you so much," she said. "It means the world to us."

Odette's uncle or relatives from Bordeaux wouldn't tramp up the back stairs to evade notice from the concierge at the entrance, but she'd figure out how to explain that discrepancy later.

She shouldered Laure's heavy bag and whispered.

"Try to walk softly to the third floor."

Remy tripped, stumbling onto a garbage bin. She caught his arm before he could fall and by the time they reached her floor, she realized Remy was more ill than had appeared.

Maewenn had put the potatoes on to boil. Scents of chervil came from the board as she chopped and added spring onions. A heavenly scent of butter wafted along with the pungent odor of frying lardons.

Where had Maewenn come up with this gourmet feast? Potatoes with herbs, butter and pork bits?

Maewenn smiled at the couple.

"I heard we were having a guest . . . guests. It's not like this every night."

Thank God for Maewenn. She was tall and ungainly and often broke things, but her heart was gold. Jean-Marc loved her.

Odette winked at Maewenn.

After she'd taken them to her guest room, her *chambre des amis*, of which there were several in this apartment of her husband's family, she told them to take off their shoes and pad in their socks all the time. Also to keep voices low.

Back in the kitchen Jean-Marc banged his spoon.

"More, Maman."

She wished she had more.

"Later, *ma puce.*"

Jean-Marc started to cry.

"Ah, but that's why we will start a game. We'll play the pretend game, remember that? When Papa went away we pretended he was on a work trip?"

Jean-Marc's teary wail continued.

"Remember when we play this and you win, you get chocolate. *Maman* finds chocolate for the winner. Unless I win, then it's for me."

Jean-Marc shook his head, a sulky look in his eyes. But his tears had dried and he grabbed her hand.

"I want to play pretend."

"*Oui, mon cheri!* We pretend my friends who just came are my cousins. Your cousins, too, and they come from grand-maman's house. Easy, *non?*"

Maewenn looked troubled at the prospect of having to cook for this many mouths. Odette caught Maewenn's eye. "Tonight only, Maewenn."

But that night turned into two, then five. Remy's leg wound festered instead of healing and suppurated into a deep infection. He could barely walk. Odette daren't call a doctor, even the pediatrician she trusted for Jean-Marc's care. A man she'd known for years.

You never knew who'd denounce you—a grocer, the concierge in the building, a curious neighbor who coveted your apartment, something that had actually happened in the building next door. A family of Jews, the cultured and friendly Albrechts, were last seen piling their belongings into a horse cart. It was like the Middle Ages these days: full of witch hunts.

But this couldn't last.

Keeping up the pretense wore on her. Shredded her patience.

She could only keep Laure and her husband here for so long, yet Remy couldn't walk and they had nowhere else to go. And Jean-Marc had become attached to Laure, who played games with him endlessly and about whom he chattered all the time. Odette's nerves shattered more every day.

She had to keep Jean-Marc safe.

And poor Remy, who couldn't walk, much less defend himself.

Right now she had to take stock. Think. Her husband, Pierre, was gone, his whereabouts unknown like so many in the war. He'd be either dead, in a work camp or escaped.

Conditions were getting worse every day. Daily life in Paris was a constant struggle. She thought long and hard.

This time Pierre wasn't here to help her. She needed to make decisions affecting her work, her friends and Jean-Marc on her own. A tough thing to shoulder.

Still, she wasn't totally helpless against the Germans. There was something she could do.

But it meant sending Jean-Marc to safety with Maewenn. Could she live with that? Keep doing work at the Mairie to save her friends and others like them? She decided she could. She must.

If she didn't help, who would?

SHE HELPED MAEWENN AND Jean-Marc into the crowded train at Montparnasse station. He'd burst into tears when Odette said she had to stay and work.

"I'll send you a telegram in two weeks, three at most, when you can return, okay, *ma puce*?"

She hugged Jean-Marc tight. Blinked back her tears. Wouldn't let herself cry.

Maewenn took Jean-Marc's hand and smiled.

"Hear that, Maman's sending us to my house," she said. "You'll love our goats, their fresh warm milk and the fishing boats."

Odette pulled out the half-bar of German *Milchchocolat* for which she'd bartered two pairs of woolen socks, and handed it to Jean-Marc.

"I won, Maman," he said, a smile replacing his tears.

"Bien sûr, ma puce."

HER HEART SKIPPED AS the train puffed out and away in clouds of steam. Was this the right course to take? Yet every moment here could bring a round-up. Even if she wasn't Jewish, had only married one, she could be on a list.

Jean-Marc would be an orphan.

It hurt to send Jean-Marc to the country, but he'd be safe there. She trusted Maewenn to care for him with her life.

And what better protection for him? How would anyone tell the boy was half-Jewish if he was living with Breton fisherman and stinking of oysters?

As she walked back in the chill wind of an uncommonly cold June afternoon she realized she was thinking like a victim. A victim who had the luxury of care for her child, a paid job, an apartment and food rations.

Her position was better than so many.

And she'd decided, hadn't she? As her British English teacher at the *lycée* used to say, *in for a penny, in for a pound*—when people make a decision that means no going back.

She worked at the Mairie and had power at her fingertips. She could control the lists, couldn't she, since she compiled them for the municipality and the police?

Going back to her apartment, she saw Laure waiting at the corner. Odette sensed something had come up. A raid? Remy's condition having worsened? If it wasn't one thing these days, it was another even worse.

Laure stuck her arm in hers. "Let's walk on the Champs de Mars, I want you to meet some people."

"What's wrong, Laure?"

"Please don't hate me for asking another favor. It's a lot, I know."

They walked in the brisk air, under the leafy plane trees forming a green canopy. The grassy areas had been turned into vegetable plots: runner beans, turnips, potatoes.

"Remy's parents had to leave Bordeaux. They're here."

She spotted Remy's parents, whom she'd known from Laure and Remy's wedding, seated on a nearby bench. A lovely couple—he a stage actor and she a makeup artist in the theatre. Down to earth, grounded, yet looking regal in some way despite their bags at their feet.

"He can't perform in the theatre, he was dismissed. Her also because of their affiliations with me."

Odette doubted it was just that. No doubt the work of someone jealous or unhappy with Remy's parents' success, or greedy for his role in the theatre. The Occupation made it easy for denunciations—anything with a suggestion of smoke merited investigation.

At least she knew her concierge had the afternoon off and wouldn't return until tonight.

After greeting Laure's in-laws, she offered to help them.

She liked them. What else could she do—leave these older people on the bench and say *fend for yourself*?

"You're welcome to stay *chez moi* as my relatives. Yet it's only temporary, you understand?"

They both nodded.

"We must keep alert. Vigilant at all times. Keep noises in the day to a minimum." She looked around as if to check the weather and saw no watchers. If they were there, she had no idea. "Wait ten minutes."

Again, Odette met them behind the gooseberry hedge that shielded the service door.

Remy, his leg up at the kitchen table, kissed his parents and handed Odette a telegram.

"This came for you."

Her throat went dry. She feared the worst. Her husband, Pierre, missing in action. Killed.

She prolonged the moment before she opened it. In that moment, Pierre was still alive, they had a life together and he was laughing here in the kitchen like he had the last time she saw him.

"Don't forget me, you two," he'd said, kissing Jean-Marc and her. His warm arms, the hint of tobacco in his beard and the musky scent of him after making love enveloped her.

"Sit down, Odette," said Remy. "You look shaken."

Brought back to the present, she sat down, taking a glass of water Remy passed her. Drank. Made herself open the telegram.

Instead of the news she'd expected, the message was from the Mairie, summoning her back to work. Immediately.

What could have made her boss send an expensive telegram? The only thing she could imagine it being was an emergency.

"We'll have to sort out this situation," said Remy's

mother Cecile. "We're adding to your burden, so I'll clean and cook."

Right now, the last thing on Odette's mind was how to feed five people on two people's rations.

"*Merci.*"

ODETTE PULLED HER BICYCLE from under the stairs. A flat tire. By the time she'd sealed a hole with her last rubber patch and pumped air into the tire, she was sweating under her wool jacket.

Still, her bike should get her there faster than the Metro.

In the marble-floored lobby of the Mairie she met a stretcher with Lamarck, her boss, lying on it. He lay unconscious, hooked up to an IV, his face grey. Within minutes he was carried out to the arriving ambulance.

This would mean changes.

Lamarck supervised her and, while he hadn't approved her speaking up, he'd accepted her work. If his replacement took a closer look at it she'd have trouble. She didn't wish Lamarck ill and yet, until he was replaced, she could take advantage of this situation.

At his desk she opened the drawer and found the keys she'd seen him use for the forms from Imprimerie Nationale. There was a paper shortage these days and the printers had to use old blank official forms for birth certificates that required 18 to be scratched out and 19 substituted for the current century.

Here in the drawer were Lamarck's official stamps and seals.

"What are you doing in here?" said the Commissaire.

She jumped. Hopefully Lamarck's desk plant screened her alarm.

"*Moi?*" She slid the stamp, its pad and the official seal into her bag. And felt surprised when it all fit. She clipped the bag shut.

Since when had she become so adept at thievery?

"*Mais* Monsieur le Commissaire, I'm the adjoint general and under instructions to finish Monsieur Lamarck's work today."

He nodded, unsure.

"This work's administrative, part of my duties and sanctioned by Monsieur Lamarck," she said, picking up a report from Lamarck's desk as she walked around it, hopefully businesslike and neutral. "Of course, I'm ready to assume more responsibilities as needed."

"Isn't there a replacement?"

Keep him talking.

"Please ask the mayor, I received a telegram to come here and assume temporary duties. You can see for yourself." She lifted the telegram from her pocket and showed him.

He couldn't argue with that. She realized he felt stymied. No doubt he didn't feel comfortable working with a woman and anticipated her being a thorn in his side.

Not her problem.

"If you'll excuse me," she said.

"*Et alors*, Monsieur Lamarck was supposed to forward the lists. I requested them days ago."

She kept her gaze blank.

"Concerning which lists, monsieur? It will help me locate them if you can specify more."

She'd held the file up. A random file from Lamarck's desk, but the Commissaire didn't know it. Now it would be easy to blame Lamarck and his illness for a further holdup.

"We're conducting police actions, that's all you need to know," he said, regaining some of his bluster.

"*Bien sûr.* I'll take care of this, monsieur."

1941—Le Marais, a week later

A LIGHT DISTILLED FROM thin sunbeams brightened the dark wood in Odette's office and puddled on the floor. She culled the lists, hidden in her desk drawer, and added the men who were dead, missing, and on enforced labor in Germany. Now she had a formula for composing the lists the Commissaire requested. For the others, about forty men she couldn't knock off the list, she'd send an anonymous warning to leave. But how?

After some moments of thought, she knew. Didn't she have an actor in her house? She'd ask Remy's father.

Her mind went to the man she'd seen kicked on the ground earlier, the one she suspected had been beaten to death by the fat lout Delarue. He disgraced the police. He had to be stopped. He had to pay.

She'd discovered the first lists of the men who'd been rounded up and gone to the busses. She searched for the man she'd seen beaten. Without his name it seemed fruitless.

Finally she thought to search by date.

Found it.

Police action conducted at the Kommandantur's orders. Destination Drancy 180 men.

Followed by their names. But there were only 179 listed.

Did that mean the man she'd seen had been beaten so severely that he didn't make it? That he'd been beaten to death?

What happened to him?

The assaulted man's family should know. She discovered his name. Moises Ducray. No death certificate had been issued.

What had happened to him?

Over the next week, Remy's father, wearing a priest's cassock, visited the Jewish households to warn them. He told them rounds-ups were happening and to leave or hide. This spread throughout the *quartier*. For once Odette felt as if she'd done something right and honored what the man in the street with his hands over his head had said.

Warn others.

Odette began "forgetting" to stamp J for JUIF on identity papers, misplacing a deportation list when she could. Erasing, neglecting and otherwise sabotaging countless small exclusionary administrative details in the records.

PEOPLE ONLY KNEW HER as the *secretaire generale* at the town hall, the smiling *fonctionnaire* in the Marais. Not as the woman who forgot to add their names to the lists requested by the Milice and Gestapo, obtained ration coupons and false identification cards and hid downed RAF aviators and a Jewish family in her apartment.

Who could have thought a young mother, wife of a soldier, wearing her best pre-war wool dress and grandmother's pearls, acted as intermediary between Résistance networks to sabotage the Occupier every day? On the surface she appeared to admire Maréchal Petain and follow the Vichy government. She'd actually done so until 1941.

Father Cécil, at Eglise Saint Francis Xavier, the church behind Les Invalides, was key to her work. To him she was Pénélope.

Her administrative job was the perfect cover. Otherwise she couldn't have done her real work.

No one suspected her.

Careful, she was so careful.

The most successful operations are those carried out in plain sight.

&

To the memory of the real Odette Pilpoul, Résistant

THE KILLING AT JOSHUA LAKE |

Scott Adlerberg |||||||||||||||||||||||||||||||| |

I guess you could say I got caught up in a murder investigation because I'm a squatter. Or I was a squatter. I'm not anymore, but it took some doing to get where I am now.

What put me in a position to do what I did? I have to thank the pandemic. My life change happened during that period of lockdowns and isolation, though when the virus' spread peaked, I had no plans to transform my existence. I made my move hoping at first for nothing more than open air and contact with nature. But as the saying goes, "When opportunity's there, you have to grab it." Or something like that. I couldn't have expected a worldwide crisis, intersecting with a family's meltdown, to play out to my benefit.

And yet, as even my ex would admit, it did.

She calls me lucky, but I think it's more accurate to say I have balls and smarts. The Crenshaw siblings themselves would concede that, much as they must hate me. I can only imagine the words they use to describe me when they're communicating in private. A single Black guy going against the rich and white. A man whose list of assets you could write on a Post-it Note versus the scions of a powerhouse. Who's the favorite there in any sort of struggle? The answer's obvious, and that knowledge must add to the Crenshaws' rancor.

What happened? Well, that spring, as I had for years, I was running my car service company in Port Chester, New York. I owned the fleet, seven cars, and would drive customers myself. We catered to the affluent Westchester towns nearby—Rye, Scarsdale, Mamaroneck—and to upscale Greenwich across the state line in Connecticut. Since launching, I had grown my clientele base, which consisted mainly of corporate and entrepreneurial people who required rides to and from appointments in New York City and between their homes and the local airports when they went on work-related trips. My passengers liked me and could rely on my professionalism and reliability, and though I worked nine- and ten-hour days, my income was steady. It would never lift me into the top tax bracket but suited me just fine. I could pay without sweating for my one-bedroom apartment in Yonkers. After our divorce, I had repaid the start-up loan my ex gave me, and as she said, I'd surprised her. I'd exceeded her expectations for me. Perhaps if I'd shown that drive and initiative when we were married . . . But so be it. I could stand on my own two feet and had built something solid. The services I offered to people were modest, but they did satisfy a niche. I figured I could do what I was doing till I decided to sell or disband the business.

Then the pandemic struck.

For those who lived through it, I'm sure I can do without detailing the ways the outbreak hurt the economy. In my case, it killed what I had going. Under lockdown, nobody needed a car service to taxi them to and from airports. Nobody went to meetings in the city. Overnight, and I mean that literally, my car fleet had no one to take anywhere, and I had to tell my drivers to sit tight because soon things would return to normal. A month passed, then

two, then three, until it became clear that I might be looking at a long-term situation. I told my drivers to find other
work if they could, and I put myself on a strict budget that
would allow me to eat and pay my rent and keep the various streaming services that provided my daily lockdown
entertainment. At the rate I calculated, with the help of
unemployment payments, I could go on this way without
working for months. I hunkered down, yet another human
being alone in his apartment while the world dealt with a
fucking virus, but as time went by, I grew more and more
restless. Binge-watching I tired of and social media, with
its share of vitriol, its pseudo experts and crackpot theo-
rists, I went to rarely. The summer came on and I wanted
a change, a release. Doldrums engulfed me, my medicine
for that, tequila and orange juice. But out of the tedium, I
don't know from where, inspiration hit. I got an idea that
I felt was too good not to pursue.

I'd heard news stories about the people who were leaving New York City for their country houses upstate. It
seemed these people with their superior means were hoping to ride out the pandemic away from the city's garbage
piles and rising crime. In the green and bucolic Catskills,
they wouldn't have to hear the constant sound of ambulance sirens or deal with the homeless folks, increasing
in number, many of them with mental health issues, on
their streets. Home sales in the Hudson Valley, I'd read,
were booming. Count on a specific type of person to flee
their town when conditions become a little unpleasant.
I shook my head thinking about these people and their
privilege, but I realized I could do the same thing they did
even though I neither owned a country house nor had the
money to buy one. And actually, in Yonkers, right next
to the city, you could hardly claim the apocalypse had

descended upon us. But everything was closed and dead and depressing, and I was spending twenty-two or twenty-three hours a day inside. Other than for groceries, I'd leave my apartment for a brisk walk or a spin on my bike, that was about it. Since childhood, I've loved the outdoors and doing things like hiking, and I knew where I could go on my limited budget to find accommodations for a summer in the country.

It had been called Joshua Lake, when it operated as a successful resort decades ago. I'd come upon it years back when camping nearby; a bicycle ride along the country trails had taken me up a curvy road that led past a faded sign marking the grounds. Bungalows in disrepair, tennis courts with cracks and decaying nets, a volleyball court overgrown with weeds, two pools without water. The lake, which had been named after its original owner, had a green-blue color that was lovely, and I could hear bird cries and insects buzzing in the woods all around. The road through the place went over a stream and up a hill to what had once been the central hotel building, and it was here that the current owner, Robert Crenshaw, lived, in his withdrawal from the world. You can pretty much do what you want when you're as wealthy as him. I'd read up on the man after my ride that day, wondering why that one big building at the former resort was maintained. And on subsequent camping trips, during rides on that road, I'd daydreamed about how fun it might be to stay in one of the bungalows, if only for a night or two. I suppose it's the kid in me, the urge to explore a deserted space, like an old insane asylum or amusement park. A stay at the defunct vacation spot would be similar. I'd be trespassing, obviously, staying on what was now private land, but I thought I could do it unseen. The property, if you included the wooded portion, was vast. I had merely to not flaunt my presence, and Robert Crenshaw would never know I was there.

I drove upstate, stopping for supplies on the way. Dusk was falling, the fireflies busy, when I reached my destination, and the bungalows far down the hill from Crenshaw's residence looked like ruins in the twilight. I chose a cabin decrepit but intact, with a door that functioned, screens in the windows, and no roof holes I could see, and I carried my bike inside. As night fell, I unloaded my backpack, and I began to make myself at home. I swept and disinfected and I pumped up my mattress. I laid out my bedroll and put my camping stove on the kitchen counter. For a head I dug a hole in the woods behind the cabin, and that was where I found a spot to park my car as well, out of view from the road.

I enjoyed myself. During the day, I went for hikes or took bike rides around the area, and at night I'd chill with a book on my Kindle and the cannabis edibles I'd brought. It felt great to get away from TV. None of the bungalow's electric sockets worked, but I had my car to charge whatever I needed to charge, like my phone. I had everything for my stay except a place to wash—forget about the unit's shower—but I quickly realized I could use the lake on the grounds.

In reality, if I'm being honest, "lake's" a misnomer. What I'm talking about, when it comes to its size, is a pond. A large pond encircled by grass and trees, halfway up the hill to Crenshaw's residence. I ventured there one night, wearing a T-shirt and shorts, and thought that if I dipped in late, after midnight, no one would notice. The pond didn't have algae on it, and I knew, since it fed a stream dribbling off somewhere, that it couldn't be stagnant. Illicit nocturnal bathing had a ring to it, and I smiled, tickled by the image, but it didn't take a week for me to find out that the weirdo Crenshaw, a man who could've fixed up his property's pools or built a new one carved from gold, liked to use the pond, too. I'd gone in once and returned the next night, soap, a towel, and a flashlight with me, and as I left the road and approached the water, trotting along, I heard a splash and a cry of joy, an adult diving in with the zest of a child.

What the fuck?

If someone from his previous life had seen him then, a fellow banker, let's say, what would they have thought of Robert Crenshaw? As chairman and CEO, he had overseen the expansion of the bank he ran, and over time, he'd made a fortune. He was well-known for his natty dressing and sharp tongue. Around New York City, where he lived, he had won praise for his philanthropy, substantial donations to the Bronx Zoo and Central Park. His most famous non-business act had been the funding of Tiny Island, an artificial island park in the Hudson River, accessible by footbridge from Manhattan. His gift to those who like "a spot of green," as he called it, Tiny Island had drawn countless pedestrians since its completion, and Crenshaw had done interviews about it and promoted it with a much remarked upon modesty. Then, after buying all the acreage at Joshua Lake, he had stepped down from his job and begun his life as a country recluse. He was finished with the financial arena, he said.

But the man I'd seen on the news from time to time in tailored suits, who'd used a chauffeur and wined and dined with Wall Street chiefs, looked to me bone-pale and as lean as a fasting monk. The Internet had told me he was seventy-five, but he swam with a smoothness that belied his age. I'd crouched nearby, transfixed, careful to keep myself hidden in the moonlight, and I must have been squatting there fifteen minutes before he came back out onto the bank, stark naked. He had white hair to his shoulders and a wild beard and mustache, someone who clearly didn't give a goddamn about a respectable appearance anymore. Instead of re-dressing, he picked his clothes up off the ground and put them under his arm, and the last I saw him on that occasion, he was walking away and back up the hill to his gleaming residence.

I cleaned myself that night, and nights after. But no matter how late I'd come to the pond, I'd scout it from a distance first to make sure Crenshaw wasn't there. He swam more nights than not, but I couldn't predict when his swims would be. They followed no set schedule except that he never took a plunge, that I knew of, during the day. Maybe he disliked the sunlight. When I went in, it was after I'd seen him swim and depart or so deep into the pre-dawn hours that I felt confident I'd be undisturbed. I didn't sing or kick up water or create undue noise, and I thought I could continue with my baths for as long as I remained discreet.

I was wrong. Crenshaw may have abandoned his workaday life and public duties, may have gone Howard Hughes on the world, but he hadn't lost his alertness and marbles.

I had gone for a hike on a humid day and made my way to the pond that night as usual. I laid my towel and clothing on the bank. The water's coldness hit me with the bracing effect it always did, and I dove beneath the surface and snaked around to let my body acclimate. I was feeling at ease and applying liquid soap to my chest when a noise on the hill leading up to Crenshaw's residence caught my attention. Somebody had cleared his throat and after that, I heard a click. I froze in the water and looked up.

Standing in the dark were two figures, one wide-shouldered, one a beanstalk. The thin person was Crenshaw, clothed, and the massive guy someone I hadn't seen before. He was aiming a gun at me with two hands, and in how he stood and his perfect stillness, he had the look of a man who knew what he was doing with a firearm.

A bodyguard? A servant with military skills? Who could know what the rich had access to for staff? Perhaps Crenshaw had been keeping this guy in a cage, like a pit bull.

Crenshaw's the one who spoke.

"Don't try to run away," he said. "Carl here won't miss."

I'D NEVER IN MY life had a gun pointed at me. Seeing it made my heart pound so hard, my chest hurt, and I had to restrain myself from taking off, or diving under the water at least.

I held up my hands palms out to them.

"You speak English?" Crenshaw said.

"I'm from New York City," I said. Did he think I came from another country? "Don't shoot. Lemme get out of the water."

"Go ahead."

I kept my movements slow and deliberate, and asked whether I could get dressed.

"Hold it."

The muscleman, his gun still aimed at me, descended the hill and kneeled by my clothes. He used his free hand to pat through my shirt, pants, towel, and sneakers. Crenshaw had switched on a flashlight, which he trained on me.

"Nothing here," the muscleman said.

"No camera? No phone?"

"Nada."

"Put your clothes on," Crenshaw said.

He had a voice that rasped, but he spoke with authority, someone to whom giving orders, after years of doing it, came naturally.

I dried myself in a flash and threw on everything, my pulse hammering away. They could shoot me in the head and dump my body in the woods, bury me there, and who would know? I hadn't told anyone I was coming to this place. What was Crenshaw thinking as he looked at me? That some derelict had turned up on his land, some Black vagrant with the gall to coopt his personal pond for washing? If they shot me point blank and reported the incident to the cops, nothing would happen to them. That was certain. Crenshaw could concoct any story he wanted and what local DA wouldn't take his word for what he claimed had occurred? That I'd been so dumb as to be conspicuous . . .

"Let's go," Crenshaw said. "Walk up the hill, and Carl here will be behind you."

INSIDE, AT A BAR with stools, in what had been the guest gathering place for the Joshua Lake main hotel, Crenshaw treated me with a surprising hospitality. He dismissed Carl, who opened a door and vanished into a room, and slid behind the bar himself.

"Take a seat."

I obliged him.

I could stare at myself in the wall-length mirror behind the bar yet saw nothing else, no bottles, that one could tap to drink from.

Crenshaw reached into the well.

"Tonic water with lemon okay?"

"You have anything else?" I asked. "Tequila? Beer?"

"You drink tequila straight?"

"I can. But generally, I have it with orange juice."

"I see," Crenshaw said. "Interesting. But no. I have nothing alcoholic."

"You don't drink, if I may ask?"

"Don't touch the crap. Never have."

I recalled reading that about him, that he didn't drink or smoke, and I said I would take a seltzer with lemon.

"Tonic water," he said. "Not seltzer."

Whatever. Had he been like this in business, a pain in the ass? *Probably*, I thought.

"Yes," I said. "Tonic water."

He made the two drinks in tall glasses, with ice, and put mine before me on a napkin. No straw. He sipped from his while I contemplated mine, several feet between us for safety.

"Want to tell me who you are?" he said. "I'm curious. And what it is you're doing here?"

I told him my name and gave him a candid answer to explain my presence on his land. I saw no point or advantage in lying and didn't excuse myself for anything, though I didn't flaunt defiance either, or rudeness.

"It's a shitstorm out there," he said. "No question."

He had a lined face with sandpapery skin, a grimness to his mouth. But his eyes shone with something you might have called amusement.

"No one sent you here?"

"Sent me?" I said. "No."

"No one's paying you?"

"To squat on your land?"

"Not to squat only, no."

"Then for what?"

He let that sit, staring at me while he raised his glass and drank, and I waited for him to fill the silence. I felt oddly relaxed talking to this millionaire, but part of that sensation, I had to admit, came from his lack of hostility. The man was not what I'd envisioned he'd be.

"You like the outdoors then, huh?" he said.

"I do," I said. "If I could afford a house in the country . . . "

"Carl," he said, and in no time at all the guy with the chest bulging under his shirt appeared from behind the door he'd gone through. He was wearing a mask and handed me one. Had he been listening to me and Crenshaw?

"Walk him back to the bungalow he took. If it looks okay, no weapons—"

"I don't have any weapons," I said.

"If it looks all right," Crenshaw said, "you can come back here and turn off the lights. I'm turning in."

I FACED NO REPERCUSSIONS after that night, no threats. Neither Crenshaw nor Carl ordered me to leave. I slept in the bungalow and went out and about unbothered during the day, though the bodyguard instructed me not to come swimming in the pond anymore till after 2 A.M.

"Mr. Crenshaw doesn't want to see anyone, you included, when he goes for his swim. And he likes to go late. He doesn't want to risk running into you there. But if you want to go in after him, or start your day with a bath there, when he's sleeping, he says you're welcome to."

I was amazed, but I wondered if his willingness to let me enjoy myself on his land stemmed from the same impulse that had spurred his construction of Tiny Island. Was he letting me use his personal "spot of green" in the same spirit he'd provided that man-made park to the public? As super wealthy people go, he didn't seem half bad. Or racist. My being Black hadn't appeared to faze or upset him in the least. He'd acted as though he couldn't care less what color I was. He'd listened to my reasons for escaping the New York metro area during this stifling lockdown period, and he'd nodded as if he understood my rationale for coming to squat in a natural environment. I could very well have lived at Joshua Lake all summer if no one had interfered, but interfere, and worse, others did, and those others happened to be Robert Crenshaw's own children.

I'M NOT GONNA LIE. I've always been a nosy mother-fucker. I had that quality as a kid and I retained it into adulthood. I could indulge it on an everyday basis when driving passengers in my car, asking them questions about their work and lives. It's astonishing how much people share about themselves with those they feel comfortable with, as my regular customers felt with me. I was like their bartender, with no booze involved. Of course, none of this applied to Crenshaw, a private person if ever there was one, and besides, he didn't know me from Adam. Letting me camp in a ramshackle bungalow on his land didn't mean he'd ask me into his life. But now that I'd made his acquaintance, I couldn't resist the temptation to get to know him better. What did he do with all his time? On his entire spread with its acres and acres of woods, nobody lived but him and, apparently, his bodyguard Carl. No pets even, from what I'd seen. On some days, in the after-noon, I'd walk up the road that went uphill past the pond, and I'd go into the woods behind his residence to watch the place for a while. I could set myself up not far behind it, close to the woods' tree line. It had an antiquated look, early 1960s resort architecture, lots of glass, but Crenshaw kept it up well. He'd updated the inside, the part I'd seen anyway during my discussion with him. He was a man who'd bought a swath of land all of which, apart from the house, was undeveloped. Nature and dilapidation—that's what he owned. As for his routine, which I took in from my spot, he would emerge each day around three in his pajamas, and he'd sit on the huge rear veranda, covered by an awning. After oatmeal, he'd drink coffee for hours and work at a table on his laptop. Was he doing business? Not retired? Occasionally, his bodyguard brought him a sandwich wrap or a bowl of ice cream. That was it. He had no visitors. Until, one afternoon, people did come over, and it was evident Crenshaw hadn't invited either of them.

Preceded by Carl, they walked through the sliding glass door that opened from the house onto the veranda. Carl apologized to Crenshaw, saying they'd arrived without warning and insisted on seeing him. A man and a woman, he in his early forties, she in her mid- to late thirties, both fit and tanned and not bad-looking for a couple of blondish WASPs. Their clothes were top of the line summer casual, as if they were at a country club. The first thing Crenshaw said from his chair was, "How nice," with unmistakable sarcasm, and he followed that by standing up and growling, "I told you not to waste your time coming."

I couldn't have been more than fifty feet off from them. With the surroundings so quiet I could hear Crenshaw and his visitors well, and I had myself a spot where I could sit with my back against a tree. That they both called him "Dad" told me who they were, and a heated conversation among the three that broke out right away suggested they were picking up an argument in progress, a dispute long-running. Crenshaw had waved Carl off, telling him to go back inside, and he offered his kids no coffee or water or anything.

"If you're going to stand here and scream," Crenshaw said.

"We're not screaming, Dad," the brother said.

"Yes, you are. Put your masks on. Or are you trying to kill me that way, by spitting the virus on me?"

"Nobody's trying to kill you, Dad."

"Can you prove that?"

"Don't be ridiculous."

"Prove you're not."

"How can we prove we're not trying to kill you?"

"Tell me how my death wouldn't be to your advantage."

"Dad!" The sister was speaking. "Can we drop the subject? There's enough dying going on as it is."

"And mine wouldn't help you get what you want?"

By now, on one knee, hands steady, I had my phone out of my pocket, and I'd pressed the red dot to video record. Not that I was one of these people whose first instinct when confronted by drama was to whip out a smartphone and record what was happening, but in this instance, as I watched these rich people go at it, I felt I should. I didn't want violence to occur and didn't truly expect that it would, but you never knew considering how they were talking. And on the lighter side, insensitive though it may have been to think, I kind of liked seeing these one-percenters fighting. Dysfunction among people with money, conflict over stuff no one but people this well-off could quarrel about. And I had a ringside seat for the action! It reminded me of a television series I'd been watching, with offspring battling patriarch over the direction the family's business ventures should take, but—and here was the undeniable pleasure—for real.

The gist of this disagreement revolved around the Joshua Lake land. According to the siblings, their father had promised to let them develop most of it, a pledge he'd reneged on. They could accept that he intended to keep living at his residence, but all the woods and other acreage was going to waste.

"You two are a broken record," Crenshaw said.

"Because you don't listen," his daughter said. Her voice was high, her face flushed. "There'll be plenty of space for you here."

"I'm not sharing where I live with a new bullshit New Age resort."

"Just you and your friends the trees, is that it?"

"That's it," Crenshaw said. "My trees, my pond, no people. Not everything needs to be . . . developed. What a disgusting word."

The siblings exchanged looks; I could tell they had heard this pronouncement before. The brother let out a sigh and threw up his hands in resignation.

"It's a pity, Dad. Really is."

"For you, maybe."

"For all of us."

"And don't count on getting this place when I go," Crenshaw said. "Maybe I'll leave it to a nature conservancy. To bird sanctuary people. Who knows?"

Carl reappeared through the sliding doors, and he signaled to the siblings with a thumb jerking motion.

"Time to go. He's getting upset."

"*He* is?" said the brother.

"I'll walk you to your car."

No hugs or kisses were given, no affection shown

between the father and his children, and they went off as requested with Carl, anger in their strides.

Crenshaw sat down at his table. I lingered, eager to hear what he might say to Carl afterwards, but when the guy came marching back, all Crenshaw did was ask for tea.

"Chamomile with lemon. I need to de-stress after those assholes."

The whole afternoon and into the evening I couldn't get my mind off the clash I'd seen. I sided with Crenshaw Senior against his children on the matter of destroying the nature here, not that anyone had asked me. If he'd said he would turn the land over to them for a project and then reversed himself, tough on them. The environment would benefit.

I cooked a steak on my camping stove and ate it with a salad. I read, I downed an edible, I dozed. Come 2 A.M. I grabbed my soap and towel, and I walked by starlight to the pond, anticipating my dip. The clothes on the bank gave me a shock; Crenshaw hadn't left anything behind after his swims before. I scanned the water looking for him, thinking he may have swum later than usual, and I shouted his name.

"Mr. Crenshaw? Mr. Crenshaw?"

Nothing. Nor did I see Carl, though that made sense. Crenshaw had brought him to the pond on the night he accosted me but otherwise came for his swims by himself. Had he gone in but dashed back up to the house naked for something urgent? A phone call? That was conceivable, but my back hairs were tingling.

I waded in, cautious on my feet, on tiptoe, as if the bottom, soft mud, had pebbles. I didn't bump into anything and kept on going till I was up to my chest, and finally I submerged myself, eyes partly open. The below-surface darkness enveloped me and I did my underwater breast-stroke. I rose, breathed, dove again, and this time, as I moved my arms and legs, I saw the outline of an object below me. I let out a gasp, air bubbles rising to the surface, and forced myself to go lower. I touched it. Skinny, white, and face down, it confirmed the premonition I'd had a moment earlier.

Crenshaw, no mistaking it, was dead.

I DRESSED AND RAN up the hill. Light shone from a window or two in Crenshaw's residence. The poor man, despite his swimming prowess, had somehow drowned. He must have, I thought, but if he had, when tonight had that been? Carl should've noticed him missing and got his ass to the pond to check on him.

The old hotel lobby door was unlocked and I found the bodyguard sitting inside on a couch. He had on jeans and a black T-shirt and was watching a wall-mounted TV, highlights of the sports day.

"You look wet."

"I—"

"I told you not to go swimming when he's there."

"Mr. Crenshaw's dead."

"What?"

"He's in the water. I came straight here to tell you."

An unreadable face, then a smirk. My lungs, every breath, felt heavy.

"Were you waiting for me?" I said.

Carl reached behind his back, under his shirt, and took out his handgun.

"Don't you fucking move," he said. "I'm calling the police."

I MADE NO EFFORT to flee or talk while we sat waiting for the cops. I had no doubt that if I ran, this guy would shoot me and have a story for them. And why wouldn't they believe the supposedly loyal employee of a rich white dead man? In the police's eyes and the public's, I'd be no more than a ne'er-do-well who'd been encroaching on Crenshaw's property. I could hear the remarks folks would spew, and I wouldn't be around to respond:

"See how these people behave. They take, take, take. He couldn't stay where he belongs, in his rathole in Yonkers. Not him. So entitled, the piece of shit."

No one would know that Crenshaw had said I could stay on his land and use it.

My guess was that the siblings had felt out Carl some time ago. Whatever Crenshaw was paying him, they'd topped it. The argument I'd seen had been their last-ditch attempt to persuade their father to let them develop the land. When that had failed, they'd determined to get rid of him, and Carl had told them about me and how, if he killed the old man, drowning him in the pond, they could blame it on me. My presence at Joshua Lake had become fortuitous for them, something they could exploit. Carl's smirk told me that.

Calmness was crucial, keeping a level head. I knew I'd done nothing wrong, but I had no alibi. Whenever Carl—it had to have been him—had murdered Crenshaw, I'd been alone in my bungalow, eating or reading or nodding off.

Two police officers arrived in a single car, that's all. Carl had his story ready, and when the cops told me to lie on the floor, hands behind my back, I did. The older one, middle-aged with a belly, yanked me upwards to my feet, and the younger one hurried down toward the pond. Their car lights were flashing and their radios crackling, and I figured they were somewhat stunned themselves, small town law enforcement dealing with a murder of this magnitude, at two-thirty in the morning. I imagined it would take them a little while to get the technical help they needed to retrieve Crenshaw's body from the pond and process the scene.

I endured hours of sitting in the back of a squad car, a ride to a station house, and more time sitting alone in a cell. I was polite to a fault but succinct when I spoke. At last, they got to questioning me, the pudgy chief and his sidekick, in a dully lit room that had no windows, and I told them they were making a mistake.

"Let's talk and we'll see," the chief said.

"I don't have much I can tell you," I said.

"Is that so?"

"That's so."

"You could tell us what you did," the chief said.

Had they interviewed Carl first, listened to his lies? In everything I related, I stuck to the facts, admitting my initial squatting on the land but denying that I had killed Crenshaw.

"The man was gracious to me."

"Robert Crenshaw?" The chief grinned, his teeth yellowish. "And why would he be gracious to you?"

"We shared a love of nature."

"You bonded over that, did you?"

"Bond might be a strong word, but yeah. Basically."

"You spoke to him about this?"

"Once. I explained why I was on his land, and he was cool with it. Believe me, I was surprised myself."

"I'll bet."

Five hours? Six? Seven? I lost track of time in that miserable room, but the cops' persistence didn't wear me down. They spoke in circles, repeating their questions over and over, all but declaring, as Carl had alleged, that I had committed murder.

"Why would I do that?" I said. "Enlighten me. I had no reason to."

"You enlighten us," the chief said.

"There's nothing to say. I didn't do it."

"How 'bout you go over everything again?"

And I did, for the umpteenth time. After eating a steak with a salad for dinner, I'd read on my Kindle and taken an edible and dozed off. When I awoke, I'd gone for my nightly bath, or swim, whatever they preferred to call it, and I'd bumped into Crenshaw's body in the water. He was, without question, dead.

"And then?"

"As I told you, I ran up to the building to tell his bodyguard. Carl."

"And he's . . . " The skepticism in the chief's voice hadn't wavered during the grilling. "Setting you up. Making you a patsy."

"The proverbial frame up," the other cop said.

"That's right. I was there and they could do it."

"And tell us again what Carl has against you?"

"How the fuck should I know?" I said. "Nothing, maybe. It's Crenshaw's kids you should be looking at, 'cause they're the ones with a reason to kill him."

"Which Carl did for them?"

"What have I been saying? It's not complicated."

If I could get to my phone, I'd play the cops the video I'd taken of the Crenshaw family fight. The father voicing his concerns about the plotting his children might be doing, and lo and behold, that very night, he'd wound up dead. Proof? We'd find out, but the cops would have a hard time holding me after I showed them that. On the other hand, how could I trust these bastards? They had a perfect dupe in their custody, a Black guy from downstate, urban, an interloper, someone they could use to close a case they knew would rock their peaceful white town. The local powers would demand an arrest, and with me in their hands, and a person they thought loyal to Crenshaw against me, why should they bother to look anywhere else?

Even if I somehow got to my phone and handed it to them, they might erase the recording. I didn't think it was a stretch, or paranoia, to fear them doing that. Yet the phone, the more I thought about it, was the best chance I had to help myself.

Their questions over for the time being, the chief and his underling had walked me from the interrogation room back to the cell. I sat on a bench, exhausted. Tired but wound up, as far from sleep as it's possible to be. The cops hadn't got rough, but they seemed to have no intention of letting me go. Didn't they have to charge or release me? Should I ask for a lawyer? I didn't have one and didn't know any, and if I invoked my right to an attorney, who knew what local shark, likely a bar pal of these guys, would stroll in?

"Chief."

I called through the bars, my voice loud but composed.

"Chief! I have something I need to show you."

No one answered but I repeated myself, and eventually the chief opened a door and plodded down the hall to me.

"What is it?"

"At the bungalow I stayed in—"

He cut me off. "What do you have to show me?"

"My phone," I said, and told him I had something on it that would support what I'd been telling him.

"What's on it?"

"Take me over there so I can get it."

"We can get it for you," he said.

"You don't know where it is. "

"Tell us."

"I'm not even sure where I left it. Maybe in my car, which is locked."

His round face looked sardonic.

"I'm not bullshitting, chief. You need to see what's on my phone."

He turned sideways and tramped back down the hall, and I plopped myself on the bench. Pushing any harder, I thought, calling out again, would not work.

I may have fallen off to sleep, tense as I was, because the next thing I knew, the chief's assistant and another young cop were outside my cell and unlocking it.

"Get up," the assistant said. "We're going to get this phone of yours."

"That's all I ask."

"Uh-huh. This better be worth it."

The two of them cuffed me in front, not all that tightly, and led me past the chief at his desk.

"I'll be waiting," he said, as if to remind me he had control and the upper hand. "Can't wait to see what you've got."

As best I could, I settled myself on the squad car's back seat, and both the subordinates sat up front. The late morning sun hit me through the vehicle's windows, hot and blinding. I lowered my head, shut my eyes. I was already grimy from the long night but could feel sweat drops breaking out on my body.

"Don't pass out,'" the cop on the passenger side said. He must have been watching me in the mirror. "Turn on the AC."

The other cop did.

The drive took half an hour, give or take, and I felt revived by the time we reached Crenshaw's land. Yellow tape had gone up across the bungalow's entrance, proclaiming a crime scene, and around my car parked behind it. The cops let me out of the squad car and had me bend under the tape to open the door and go inside, and I indicated where I'd left the phone the night before.

"You can get it."

But when I plucked my pants up off the bedroll and fished through the pocket, both pockets, I felt nothing.

"Not there?"

The cop who had helped interrogate me at the station asked this.

"No," I answered. "It's not."

I assumed somebody from the police had sniffed through my things while I was in custody, but if they'd taken my phone, the chief would have known and wouldn't have allowed me to come for it. This trip did not seem like a charade of any kind, and why would they put on an act in the first place?

"He's wasting our time," the other cop said. "Jerking us around."

I'd been a bit high on the edible last night, but I was one hundred percent positive where I'd left the phone.

"Anywhere else it might be?" the first cop said. "Your car?"

"It's not there," I said. "No."

"Come on then."

Reluctant to leave, I strained to think whether I'd mis-remembered anything, but I knew I hadn't. And I could conjure up nothing, no tactic, to delay them driving me back to the station.

We went outside and got into the car. We were backing

up and away from the bungalow, when I saw Carl standing by the road, arms folded, a green baseball cap on his head. He was watching my departure, stone-faced. Had he been nearby when we came?

"Wait!" I shrieked.

"What?"

"He's got it."

"Who?"

"Carl. Crenshaw's bodyguard."

The cocky prick should have stayed out of sight and celebrated his theft in secret.

"You said it was in the bungalow."

"He came and took it. I'm certain."

Despite the cuffs, I banged on my door, which had no button for lowering the window.

"Search him, I'm telling you. Search him."

With me thrashing around in back, the car braked and stopped.

"At least say something to him."

The cop driving powered down his window.

"Mr. Wells. You do know that bungalow's a crime scene? Probably best to stay clear of here till we say."

"I understand, officer."

"Call it," I shouted. "Call my number."

Carl avoided looking at me. "What's this?"

He chuckled, eyeing the officers.

"Call my goddamned number!"

Carl turned and began to walk away, and I said my number out loud.

"Call it please. What's there to lose?"

"Jesus Christ."

It was the cop in the passenger seat, but he did slip his phone from its holder.

"One second, Mr. Wells."

I could only hope that the phone had power left to ring, that it hadn't died while I was at the station. I had charged it last night, though.

We heard it chiming.

"I told you! In his pocket."

Carl halted as though he'd collided with a wall, and both cops opened their doors.

"If you let me explain, officers . . . "

"You'll have a chance for that," came their answer.

And indeed, soon, he would. I loved that thought. He'd gone in and looked for my phone just in case I had something on it that could help me. The phone restored to me, heading back to the station and the waiting chief, I managed to tap in my code and light up the home screen.

My recording. It would direct the focus to Carl and Crenshaw's kids. How would they react to the pressure? With lawyers in the mix, they might betray each other. I'd talk to the media about these scum and their arrogance, how they had believed they could frame an innocent man, a Black man no less, and I saw attorneys knocking on my door to help me with a civil suit.

Social media. Like I said before, I seldom use it. But in the right circumstances, when you want to ensure a story's not erased by the powers that be, a blast to the world like the one I just did can be a beautiful source of ugly truth.

POST-GAME

IIII Alex Segura

New Jersey, 2012.

The call that his father had dropped dead in Miami came the night before.

Pete Fernandez still couldn't believe it, even two shots and three beers in. Didn't want to believe it. But there it was. Pedro Fernandez: Miami Homicide detective, father, the man who'd raised Pete—was gone. There'd been no long goodbye. No meaningful last conversation. No memory to speak of. The last chance had been missed earlier that week. Replaced by Pete, sitting in a shithole bar, talking to a gaggle of strangers, ignoring the vibrations coming from his pocket. Pete remembered checking his missed calls the following morning, as he watched his fiancée, Emily, sneak out of their bedroom door, sunlight creeping in through the blinds. It wasn't until that afternoon that he thought about calling his dad back. But the headache was too nasty. His mouth too dry. Too much to do. Then nothing.

Then he was gone.

Now here was Pete Fernandez, faded star sports reporter of *The Bergen Light*, a once-promising enterprise journalist relegated to serving as a backup to the main Rutgers beat writer. It was pure luck—if there was such a thing anymore, Pete thought—that he was even sitting here, watching a New Jersey Generals team struggle to chip at a twenty-point deficit in a basketball game no one gave a shit about. He knew he should be doing something else. Planning a trip home to Miami. Calling family and friends to tell them what happened. Figuring out funeral arrangements. Sitting alone and feeling something. But that wasn't Pete's style. No, he thought as he took another long pull from the plastic Amstel Light beer bottle. He didn't like "feelings" these days.

Maybe that was why he drank. The thought was fleeting, ushered out of Pete's mind by an army of well-trained mental bouncers, but it was still there. Pete shrugged. He was mourning, he thought. He was allowed to drink like this.

His phone buzzed, he checked the display and picked up, hoping his voice sounded steady.

"Yeah," Pete said.

"Just checking on you." It was Emily. She sounded tired. Her voice hoarse. She'd been crying.

"I'm fine," he lied. He could hear the slur in his voice. He wasn't drunk enough to not give a shit yet. "Honestly, I'm okay. We'll get our stuff together and head down next week. I just need to file this game story and—"

"I mean, is this even a good idea, Pete?" she asked. "Working? Tonight? Your dad is . . . he's gone, baby. We need to deal with this. Together. I don't want to think of you just sitting in that stadium, drinking—"

"I gotta go," Pete said. He didn't wait for her to respond. He flicked the flip phone shut and looked onto the court.

The Prudential Center was a giant red brick of a basketball arena in the business district of Newark. It, like many buildings in the area, was not pretty. Stark, brown and red, jagged. Again, he was lucky to be here. Liz Garrett, the *Light*'s regular pro basketball reporter, had gone into labor the night before. The paper's backup, Josh Pinter, had called in sick. Not many papers were three people deep anymore. Hell, they were lucky if they were two. So, Pete got the call. He could remember the voice of his editor, Hal Bradley, over the phone. Apologetic. Soft. Desperate. Pete hated it. Hal didn't understand. Pete wanted the assignment. Needed the distraction. Was desperate to feel anything that wasn't the sharp pain in his chest that hadn't faded since he realized his dad was dead.

"What are you doing to yourself, *mijo*?"

Pedro Fernandez's words echoed in Pete's mind, cutting through the haze of arena noise and cheap beer. Pete closed his eyes for a second and opened them again. He watched as the Generals' undersized point guard, Elgin Starks, took the ball down the court, sidestepping the Milwaukee defender and dishing the rock into the paint. New Jersey forward Danny Grier was there to receive it, and made a quick sidestep to avoid the Milwaukee center's slashing arm. Turning around, Grier slung the ball into the air. It was an ugly, workmanlike shot that despite flirting with the rim, went through the net.

Afterwards, Pete didn't remember much more about the game, which was problematic because he had to write up a game story. But it was all about the color, he told himself as he made his way down the arena's winding underbelly to the Generals' locker room. The stats—well, he could drop those in later. He knew the final score. He knew the Generals had squeaked out another win. He knew the narrative—New Jersey had a scrappy team that could piece together a half-decent playoff run if they got their shit together. This win was another example of that, blah blah blah. Pete felt his head start to spin—that last beer coming up for a second.

"Shit," he muttered, reaching out his arm to touch the cold, peach-painted concrete wall to keep his balance.

"Hey, man, you okay?"

He felt a hand on his shoulder. He looked up to see a lanky man in a rumpled suit, a shit-eating grin on his face. It took Pete a second for his vision to focus and realize who was hovering over him.

The man, closer to fifty than forty, white, and sporting a salt and pepper five o'clock shadow, was Mike Slattery, the Generals' head coach. That was as far as Pete's brain got before the man spoke again.

"Fernandez, right?" Slattery said as Pete straightened up to reach his eye-level. "Do you remember me? We hung out a while back when I was on the Rutgers staff. Had some wild times, huh? So, you're the guy subbing in for Pinter? Man, no offense but, well, you look like shit warmed over."

Pete shrugged.

"Just having a rough night."

"You journalists, huh? Sure have a way with understatement," the coach said. He motioned for Pete to follow. "You realize you're late, right? The players cleared out a few minutes ago. Were you hoping to get any time?"

Fuck.

The coach's comment felt like an anvil dropping on Pete's head. How had he missed the post-game? Had he fallen asleep in the stands? Pete shook his head. No, that wasn't possible.

Was it?

The hand on his shoulder again.

"Dude, you okay?"

Pete stepped back to get a better look at the coach, who had lost the smile—a concerned expression taking its place.

"I'm not," Pete said, ashamed by the sound of his own voice cracking. "I . . . I fucked this up."

Slattery's smile came back, but seemed a bit forced.

"Hey, don't sweat it. Look, uh," he said, his voice lowering, becoming conspiratorial. "Do you smoke? I've got some hydropo—"

Pete chuckled as he looked down at his ratty sneakers. He felt delirious. Was the coach of the New Jersey Generals . . . asking him to smoke a joint?

"Let's go," Pete said. The night couldn't get any worse. *Could it?*

THE BUZZ HAD GONE from fun to fuzzy to dirty in what felt like no time. Pete was sure the drag from that giant spliff Slattery busted out in the alley behind the arena didn't help. But there was little he could do about that now, as they both stood in this darkened corner, their backs resting on the same wall of grimy concrete. They had a view of a small street that would lead you around and toward the arena's parking lot—into civilization. Slattery started to chuckle.

"Needed that," Pete said, nodding to himself. He felt himself sliding down the dirty wall, felt the floor start to climb up toward him.

Slattery turned to look at Pete, the joyous look of the recently stoned gone, replaced by one of mild annoyance and even milder concern.

"You are fucked up," he said.

Pete mumbled something, about needing some quotes—about being on deadline.

Slattery shrugged. Pete heard a vibrating sound. He looked up to see Slattery pulling his phone out of his pants pocket. His eyes narrowed. Pete thought he heard him mutter a short string of profanities under his breath.

"Gotta run, Pete," Slattery said with a wave of his hand. "Just make some shit up, I trust you."

Pete felt his ass land on the alley floor. Hard. He didn't care. His head was bobbing forward. He'd been here before. He deserved to be here now, he thought. Fuck everything.

He felt a pat on the shoulder, some vague, forgettable words of concern, then footsteps as Slattery walked back toward the arena. The loud *thunk* as the door into the locker room shut. Then his heavy eyelids drooped down for the last time and the blackout embraced him.

PETE'S EYES FLUTTERED OPEN, the sound of tires screeching. Then a scream, followed by a loud thud, crunch, and the sound of something soft hitting something hard.

Pete's brain struggled to keep up with the images his blurred vision relayed. A red car—older, a Le Baron, he thought?—was racing down the alley, swerving left. It was an unnatural move, jerky, reactionary. Pete saw a woman at the wheel. Blonde hair. Sunglasses. But he saw something else—a form left behind in the car's wake. A body.

More screeching as the car careened down the cramped alley, its sides hitting a metal dumpster on the left, its right scraping against the alley wall on the other. But the body. A middle-aged white man, curled up on his side, hands near his face. Frightened for what was to come. Had he known the car was coming? Had his eyes widened in fear, only to remain that way forever?

But that wasn't what kept Pete's eyes on him. It was the growing pool of blood under his head—and the blank, empty expression in his dead eyes.

"Fuck," Pete said to himself. He didn't need to be a detective to figure out what had just happened. He looked up just in time to see the red car exit the alley. Too far away to read its license plate, but that was just as well, because there was no plate to see. *Why?*

Another screech of tires. The car was stopping—reversing for a second, then stopping again. Pete could hear the car's engine still running when he saw it, popping out of the passenger side.

A face. He locked eyes with them as they turned around from the red car's window, a look of fear, pure adrenaline coursing through their every vein.

He watched their mouth, in the split second before the red car turned onto traffic, spinning out slightly as it made it into the outermost lane.

He could see the words forming and re-forming in his mind, as Pete Fernandez stood up and tried to think of what the fuck to do.

"Oh no . . ."

"PETE, YOU BOMBED ON the story, so your next move is to ask for time off? Are you —"

"Look, Hal, I just need a day," Pete said. He was sitting in his battered Saturn SL2, parked outside a luxury apartment building on Hunterdon, off Clinton Avenue. It was around eight the next morning, and Pete could barely drive, much less think. But he was here for some reason.

His editor Hal Bradley sighed loudly on the other line.

"Did you even get anything on the body they found around the arena?"

"Body?" Pete lied.

"Did you even go to the game, Fernandez?" Bradley said, his voice rising. "Some poor sap was walking down the back alley and got mauled by a car. No surveillance picked it up. Died on the scene."

"Who was he?"

Bradley paused.

"Guy named Artie Massengil," Bradley said. "Worked construction. Lifetime Jersey guy. Why?"

"Just curious," Pete said.

"Enjoy your day off," Bradley said, his voice sharp. "Might be a lot more where this came from."

Pete got the subtext, which was anything but. He flipped his phone shut without saying goodbye. He reached into the glove and pulled out a plastic water bottle. He opened it carefully and brought it to his lips. The water that came with the bottle had been poured out that morning. The vodka hit hard and fast, spreading down his throat, burning on the way down. But Pete needed that. Wanted it.

He let out a long breath and opened his phone again, punching the number in quickly.

"*Bergen Light*, archives," the voice said, flat and robotic.

"Ward," Pete said. "It's me."

"Pete? Shit, man," Ward said with a dry laugh. He was a lifelong archives guy—the person you went to when you needed something fast and you didn't have time to fill out a form. He lived in the library and he also appreciated a good bottle of scotch. Both things were related, sometimes. "Heard you bombed the Generals game last night. You desperate to get fired, bro?"

Pete ignored the comment. Ward gave him shit every time they spoke. Only difference now was that it was legit.

"Need a solid," Pete said. He heard Ward clear his throat on the other end.

"Ah, man, I heard about your dad, too," Ward said, remorse seeping through his voice. "Sorry, totally forgot about it. Here I am busting your balls and—"

"Don't sweat it. Look, I need you to run a name for

me," Pete said. "Guy named Massengil. Artie Massengil. See if he popped up on any stories."

Ward cleared his throat.

"Huh. Evans asked about him this morning," Ward said. "Gimme five and I'll hit you back."

"Thanks," Pete said. The click of his phone closing synched up with the doors of the condo building opening—revealing the man he wanted to see.

Pete felt Slattery's eyes on him as he stepped out of his car and started toward him. The usually calm and collected basketball coach appeared suddenly ruffled.

"Oh, hey, Pete," Slattery said with a slight wave. "You feeling better?"

Pete ignored the comment and stepped closer. When he stopped, he was a few inches from the coach. He watched a drop of sweat slide down the side of the man's face. It was cold as fuck in New Jersey today.

"I feel great," Pete said. "How about you?"

Slattery's smile sagged, but the media-savvy coach seemed to will it back into place.

"Glad to hear it," he said. "You looked half-asleep when I left you."

"Not totally," Pete said, stepping a bit closer. "Look, coach—let's not do this dance, okay? I saw what I saw. I don't want to call the cops because they wouldn't believe some drunk asshole sports reporter. But you saw it, too. Except your angle was a lot better than mine."

Pete watched Slattery swallow hard.

"No idea what you're talking about," he said with a faux, playful shrug. "We smoked a joint, you passed out, I left, went home. Period."

Pete started to open his mouth, but Slattery continued.

"But I will tell you this," he said, his tone different

now—sharper. "You even try and fuck with me and all hell will come down. Whatever you saw, kid? It's gone. You're just another drunk passed out in an alley, and nothing you say is gonna mean shit against my word. You're just a lush who can't even do his job. I'm something else. I'm a success. So don't fucking try me, okay?"

Pete nodded and stepped back. He watched as Slattery made his way toward a black Escalade parked on the curb, a driver waiting for him. The coach waved at Pete as he entered the car.

Pete felt his phone vibrate. He picked up.

"Got what you were looking for," Ward said. "But it's pretty wild, dude."

KAREN MASSENGIL, *NÉE* PARSONS, didn't seem surprised when she opened her apartment door to find Pete on the other side. Her eyes were red and she looked defeated. It was also only half past noon and she reeked of weed and cheap wine. Or maybe Pete was just projecting.

"Yeah?"

She lived on the third floor of an apartment building off Springfield and Clifford that had certainly seen better days. The exterior paint had long since peeled. The buzzer hadn't worked in years, Pete guessed, too. Those were the surface things. But the building had an air of resignation and defeat he couldn't put his finger on. Not because he didn't want to, but because his brain was just not there. The vodka had faded, but the dirty, fuzzy remnants would linger until Pete could get another round of drinks in to smooth himself over.

"Karen Massengil? Pete Fernandez. I work for the *Bergen Light* newspaper," he said. "Can I come in?"

"No, you cannot," she said, tilting her head slightly to

get a better look at Pete. "You aren't a cop. I don't have to talk to you."

Pete nodded.

"That's true, ma'am, but I think I need to talk to you," Pete said. He felt hot and itchy, like he'd just worked out for hours. But he knew he hadn't. He knew what he wanted. The next pull from the water bottle would have to wait. "That your LeBaron parked outside?"

Karen's eyes narrowed.

"Come on," she said, turning and walking into her apartment.

"Sorry for your loss," Pete said as he sat on the dusty, gray couch.

The living room was cluttered and messy—plates of half-eaten food, unopened mail, an empty box of cheap wine. Despite it being the middle of the day, the blinds were drawn, giving the cramped space a claustrophobic, desperate air.

"My what?" Karen said, before stopping and realizing what Pete meant. "Oh, yeah, I mean—we were separated. Artie lived a hard life."

He wasn't alone, Pete thought. Then realized he could also be talking about himself. He flashed back to the call. His father's call. The one he ignored. The sounds of the bar and the game on the television hovering over Pete as he ordered round after round pounding through his hungover skull.

He shook his head gently, trying to shake the memory loose. To send it away.

"You finalize your divorce yet?" Pete asked.

"This for a story?" Karen said as she took a seat on the couch. "'Cause I don't see any notebook or tape recorder. Didn't get any business card. Something tells me you're not here on official business, either."

Pete smiled. A dry, empty smile. Karen's eyes widened.

"This isn't official anything," Pete said. "But I'll cut to it straight, so you don't feel like I'm wasting your precious time."

Pete pulled out a thin envelope from his back pocket and tossed it on the couch. Karen reached for it and pulled out a few photos. After he'd spoken to Ward, Pete had put in a call into his friend, Matt Wilhoite, a freelance photographer who worked the Generals beat. And who sold other pictures on the side.

"That you?" Pete asked. "With the coach?"

Karen tossed the photos on the couch between them. They were inoffensive on their own. Just two adults having dinner outside. Clearly a couple. Holding hands, laughing, kissing. More complicated when you knew who the people were. One a mildly famous basketball coach with a wife and two kids at home. The other was the woman now sitting across from Pete.

"So what?" she said, her defenses not making up for the surprise on her face. "Mike's a grown man. You think he's the first person in the world to cheat on his wife?"

She stopped, as if catching what she'd said.

"I mean, they're separated," she continued. "That marriage is over, okay?"

"Separated," Pete said, nodding to himself. "Like you and Artie, right?"

"Yeah, like that. We're not together."

"But not divorced yet?" Pete asked.

"Why do you ask?"

"It's funny, because your husband knows a lot of people—he's a lifer in this town," Pete said. "And these photos? They're not new. In fact, from what I hear, your husband got his very own set. Just yesterday around this time. Seems like the kind of thing that'd drive a man to confront the guy fucking his wife, huh?"

Pete watched Karen's face. Waiting for the tell. Nothing. Cold as ice.

"You ask a lot of questions for a do-nothing reporter," she said, her voice a low rumble now.

"I'm not a do-nothing anymore," Pete said, more to himself than to this woman he'd just met. But the words rang true in his mind. Like the voicemail his father had left him that night. The last time he could've heard his voice. But he'd chosen the drink over his own father. "And I'm not going to just let this one slide, Karen."

"You need to leave," Karen said. "I know who you are, Mike told me. This isn't your thing. You're some washed up loser. What's any of this got to do with you?"

"I'm curious, I guess. And hey, I'm just wondering about something else, because I asked around," Pete said, leaning back slightly on the uncomfortable couch. "And it seems like Artie was in line for some money. Looks like that insurance settlement was finally kicking in."

Karen didn't respond. Her eyes seemed to tighten on Pete, as if she were imagining what she could do with a belt around his neck.

"Guess he got hurt real bad working on the arena refit a few years back, couldn't get another job," Pete said. "It was neat while they were fixing the arena, they were still able to have games there, huh? Did you ever make it out to see him while he was working there?"

Silence.

"Heard you and the other spouses got to meet the players, too," Pete said, sounding impressed. "Must've met Coach, too, right?"

Karen stood up.

"You need to leave," she said. Pete watched her arm twitch, as if she were fighting off the urge to point Pete toward the door.

Pete got up. They were close now. He could smell her sharp perfume. Could hear the rumble of a distant train.

"Don't do this," she said, her voice a broken whisper. "Please. I didn't mean to—"

"It's already done, Karen," Pete said, nodding toward the photos on the couch. "I didn't want to call the police myself. Not my bag. But my paper's got a helluva crime reporter. Woman by the name of Nina Evans. Been there forever. Seen everything. Once I handed her a copy of those photos and the settlement, well—she put two and two together faster than the cops ever could."

"You son of a bitch," she spat. "Who died and made you judge and jury?"

My father, Pete thought. But he didn't utter the words.

Instead, he just turned around and exited the dingy apartment. As he made it out onto the street, he saw the forensics team huddled around Karen's faded and scratched red LeBaron. Saw the two detectives making their way toward the vestibule. He fought the urge to call the office and see if the story had been posted on the paper's rudimentary website. He knew it must've. He knew Evans was smart enough to alert the cops, too. He also knew she'd keep his name out of it.

He didn't want a byline. He didn't want credit. He just wanted a little slice of justice, if that was even possible these days.

His phone buzzed.

Emily.

"I'm coming home," Pete said. "See you soon."

SPIDERS AND FLY

IIIIIIIIIII Gary Phillips

Cresston felt trapped like that poor bastard in the old film he watched the other night when he couldn't get back to sleep. The movie was *The Fly*, the original, and the scientist's experiment had gone haywire. His head and an arm had been shrunk and swapped onto a fly's body. The bug's head and furry appendage were now affixed to his human body. The transformed insect man was stuck in a spider's web. The eight-legged messenger of his doom crept toward him, fangs poised. In his little buzzy bug voice he kept pleading, "Help, me, help me," until the spider devoured him, head first.

His lungs burning, Cresston ran with as much urgency as remained in his aching thighs. In the gloom of night he banged full force into a shopping cart filled with who knew what, cocked sideways along the sidewalk. It rolled away, banging into the wall of the overpass. At the end where he came out from under the freeway, past the assortment of pup tents and makeshift shelters in which the homeless were asleep along the sidewalk's edge, there was an opening he remembered where the cyclone fencing began. This area was along his daily route to work. Cresston felt the links as he went, his fingers seeking and finding the gap. He wiggled through the slit, tearing his pant leg. He tripped ascending the earthen rise leading to the freeway on-ramp. At this time past midnight, there wasn't much traffic. But this was L.A. and there were always cars on the roads at all hours. Behind him he heard the now-familiar drone of the big SUV's engine. The hunted man did his best to hug the ground cover of ivy and ice plants, trying to will himself invisible. The vehicle containing his pursuers went past. For the moment he was safe. Cresston knew that wouldn't last.

Huffing, regretting he wasn't in better shape, he made it to the top of the rise. Hands atop his head to expand his lungs as his basketball coach taught him in high school, he took several moments to catch his breath. He then walked along toward the side of the ramp, which at its end veered onto the freeway proper. Keeping straight, he jogged along the strip of dirt bordering the freeway, cars and freight-hauling trucks zipping by. It wasn't even a week ago when his life had been normal, boring, his worries like those of countless others: make the rent, what to get for lunch that wasn't the same goddamn thing like the day before, and maybe finally meet that special someone. His divorce was almost four years final and when was it since then he'd had a meaningful connection with a woman? Cresston had worked a lot of brain cells crafting his profile on the dating site and had dinner dates with a couple of women who'd sparked him—but it turned out he hadn't sparked them.

Crazy funny how it all changed when he met Natalia. God . . . damn.

"MIND IF I SHARE the table with you?"

"Oh, sure, please sit down." Cresston wiped his mouth with the paper napkin and did his best not to stare at her, nodding his head like a goof. There were other seats available.

She sat with her lunch order, a mélange of garlic shrimp, sautéed veggies and brown rice. The meal was topped off with a sprinkle of sliced pepperoncinis. The woman nodded back at him as she removed the paper wrapped around her assembly line chopsticks. She was Latina and he estimated she was in her late thirties, maybe even early forties like him. He understood this was a new day but that didn't mean he couldn't inwardly acknowledge she wasn't bad looking. And she didn't have on a wedding ring. Did he register to her at all, he wondered? Not much, probably, if he was being honest. He really should renew his gym membership. They ate in awkward silence, the din steady in the Thai-Mex fusion joint, a storefront sandwiched between a brew pub and a used bookstore.

"This is the first time I've tried this place."

Cresston looked up from biting into his curry chicken taco. He hastily chewed and swallowed. "I've come here a few times since they opened. A change of pace from the usual."

"Um-hmm." A shrimp and clump of rice were trapped between the ends of her chopsticks. She smiled at him as she continued to eat. A thin sheen of oil glistened on part of her lower lip, an enticing look as far as he was concerned. Slow down, son. Outwardly he grinned.

Again, silence descended, but this time Cresston found it comforting. He said, "You work around here? I'm over on Commerce Way."

She nodded. "I just recently transferred from downtown." There were numerous municipal offices in the vicinity. "You know, trying out a different place each time to get a feel for the area."

"I heard that, I've been trying new places too." He stopped from saying something about the weather. Was he that out of practice? He supposed he was, he sadly admitted silently. He did say, though, "Over on Telegraph there's a good place to check out, Italian, but not just heavy pasta dishes. Great salads and sandwiches. Barzini's."

"I'll do that. Thanks."

He nodded again. Was this an opening to suggest they meet there in a day or two and get lunch? No, he concluded, swallowing the last of his two savory tacos, he better be cool. More than likely he wasn't going to see her again, so why spoil a nice time by coming on like a creepy stalker? He drank his water, trying to stall leaving as she continued to eat. He'd been eating for ten minutes or so when she'd shown up. Like a lot of people in here, she was now scrolling though messages or what have you on her smartphone.

He sat the plastic cup down quietly and, wiping his mouth once more, rose from the table. "It was nice sharing lunch time with you."

She looked up from her screen, regarding him. "Same here."

"Have a good day."

"Natalia," she said as he started to walk away. She stuck out her hand. "Natalia Merazzo."

He shook her hand and told her his name. "Nice to meet you."

"Okay . . . bye now."

"Bye."

Of course he fantasized about her once he got back to his desk. The bureaucratic drone of his work was enlivened by his daydreaming, veering from the PG mindscape of the two of them holding hands, traipsing through a field of flowers, to pulse-racing X-rated adventures in bed. Usually as he sat here his big excitement was deciding what streaming series he was going to binge-watch that evening. Whoopie.

Two days later, walking out of his building after work, he was pleasantly surprised to encounter Natalia Merazzo out on the sidewalk.

"Hi, there," she said. "We meet again."

"Yes," he stammered.

"Can I buy you a drink?" she asked.

"Uh, sure, there's the brew pub."

"My thoughts exactly. Another place on my list to try. And this way I'm not drinking alone. Wouldn't want to give anybody ideas."

"Happy to be your shill."

She laughed at that as they made their way to the tavern. Inside he waved to a couple of others from work, both men. One of them winked at him while Merazzo had her head turned. He refrained from putting up a thumb. Carrying their beers, they got a small table off to one side. A muted basketball game played on two big screen TVs while on a third one of those bake-off competition shows was on. This one wasn't muted.

"Mom's had a couple of health scares and she lives over this way in Maywood," Merazzo told him as they made small talk. "I'd requested and finally received a transfer." She told him she worked for the Department of Sanitation.

"That's great you can look after your mother. I know it can be trying. I had an aunt, my dad's sister, I wound up taking care of. Well, not full time really, but getting her to her doctor's appointments, getting her damn toenails cut, all that."

She shook her head, reflecting on her duties.

"Damn sure it's a burden sometimes," she sighed.

"For sure. But what're you going to do, it's family."

She looked at him over the rim of her glass as she sipped her beer. Setting the glass down she said, "Life can be complicated at times, right?"

"Yep," he agreed.

"Be right back." She got up and headed for the bathroom.

As she went past him, her hand lingered on his shoulder. It was only for a moment but a jolt of electric excitement shot through Cresston. Whatever she saw in him, he hoped her blinders never came off.

Not an hour later they were making out in the backseat of her car. The late-model Honda hybrid was parked on the third floor of a parking structure. Her hand massaged his inner thigh. He was getting stiffer but wasn't going to ruin things by getting carried away, forcing himself on her lest he be reading these signals wrong. Could be this was as far as they'd go this time, but he sure hoped there'd be a second time. They were in a tight embrace when he felt the car's rear door open on his back. He stopped kissing Merazzo to look around. The muzzle of a gun filled his vision.

"You can have my wallet," he blurted, assuming this was a robbery.

"Sorry it had to be this way," Merazzo said.

He gaped at her as she uncoupled from him. There was a grim cast to her face. She wiped at her smeared lipstick with an index finger.

The owner of the gun flicked the muzzle against Cresston's ear. "Get out."

He looked around again to see a good-sized white guy at the other end of the weapon. He was at least three inches taller than Cresston and even though he wore an unbuttoned sport coat, it was quite evident he possessed a broad upper body no doubt due to incessant weight-lifting. He was certain this must be the man he'd seen in silhouette at the end of the passageway. There was a dark blue SUV parked in the aisle, the driver's door open.

"You were right, partner," the man said. "This was the best way to get this chump."

Something about the way he'd said the word "partner."

"Cops, you're cops." Then it all fell into place who they were. "Damn," Cresston muttered.

"Get out," the other man repeated, taking two steps back. "We just want to talk, that's all."

An elevator door pinged open on the other side of a support column opposite the car. From where they were, the elevator wasn't seen but heard. All of them looked in that direction. A plump man in a rumpled coat carrying an attaché case came into view.

Cresston leapt out of the car and yelled, "They're trying to kill me!"

"He's high," the one with the gun said, chuckling a little.

"Sheriff business, sir, you can move on," Merazzo said, exiting the other side of her sedan by the rear door. Where she stood put the car between her and the unseen elevator.

The overweight man remained motionless. "Let me see some identification."

"What'd you say?" Merazzo's partner asked.

"ID. How do I know you all aren't drug dealers or something?"

"Are you fuckin' kidding?" the man snarled.

"Here you go." Merazzo held her badge up for the man to see as she stepped closer to him. She spoke to him in a low tone and the man nodded his head. He then walked away toward his car, his fading footfalls diminishing along with Cresston's hope of survival. Cresston considered reaching for his phone, but didn't want to provide the excuse for the man to blast him.

Merazzo held up her hand, signaling her partner to wait. Cresston's idea of trying to use the phone was a no go anyway. He hadn't noticed, given that less than a minute ago he was in the throes of lust, but Merazzo had slipped his phone out of his sport coat pocket and now held it up for him to see. She smiled crookedly as she tossed it to the ground before stomping it into uselessness.

The white guy laughed. "You're royally fucked, buddy."

Fear making him desperate, Cresston put his shoulder into the gunman's body, knocking him over as he kept running.

"Motherfucker," he said.

Cresston headed for the unseen elevator, his only chance of escape. Two bullets echoed in the parking structure, sending plaster dust from the column into the air as Cresston dove around it. Only now were the elevator doors closing. Partly sliding across the floor and scrambling on all fours, he dove inside. He pressed the buttons for the second and first floor and the car started up. He scrambled out onto floor two and, taking some back stairs, was let out onto an alleyway where he began his most dangerous journey.

Running, Cresston couldn't shed the regret that what at first seemed to be a serious upgrade in his love life turned out to be a goddamn honey trap. He focused on what was important, staying alive. Out on the streets, rushing past people laughing and enjoying each other's company at tables outside of cafés, Cresston longed to jump in a time machine and go back three weeks to that day, which had begun comfortably normal like so many others in a life of hum-drum routine. He would stay indoors and eat corn chips and candy bars from the snack bar. His fate hadn't been upended in the gloom of evening with a thunderstorm booming like in a foreboding gothic setting, but on a typical clear and sunny Southern California day.

CRESSTON HAD TAKEN A late lunch and was walking back to the office after trying a new spot, an old-fashioned diner, hoping to spice up his usual lunch choices. The steak sandwich he'd had wasn't bad, yet somehow wasn't as satisfying as it should have been. Could be though, he'd reflected strolling back to his desk, food wasn't the answer to the excitement he lacked. Coming to a passageway between two highrises, he'd turned his head at a sound. Initially he stared at an indistinct blob at the other end of the passageway, but then like a giant mutant amoeba, the shape separated. Two forms loomed over a third, who seemed to be down on a knee. All were backlit, though he had the impression the two standing were in business attire. One of the standing forms brought an arm up, holding a length of plumbing pipe, as Cresston would find out later. The pipe came down hard, striking the lower form in the head, and over it went. As this happened, for a brief moment, the face of the one wielding the pipe was partially visible in a thin strip of light. He looked Cresston's way.

Shit. Cresston hurried away. The way the lighting was, he knew they could see him quite well. He began jogging, praying he got lost in the pedestrians out and about. Back at his desk in the satellite office of the Department of Building and Safety, he considered calling the Sheriff's Department, as they patrolled this part of the county. But what was he going to tell them? "I saw someone attacked and they could be lying badly injured right now." What did the attackers look like? "Hell if I know exactly. Men, women? One was a man for sure, white and good-sized." Where did it happen? That much he could tell them. But if he called the Sheriff's from either the office landline or his cellphone, the cops could pinpoint where he was calling from. He didn't want to get involved, but it wasn't right not to do something.

Fuck it. On his break he stepped back outside and called the Sheriff's station. He told the person who answered what he knew and hung up, not giving his name. Would they send a deputy to the location? Would they track him down? He didn't figure he was on the line long enough for them to get more than a general idea, the ping off whatever cell tower was nearby. His palms sweating, he rationalized he'd done his duty as a taxpayer and returned to his work.

THAT EVENING IN HIS apartment, he perused news sites on his laptop. He scanned through Nextdoor and other such sites searching for a mention of a dead body from that area of the county. Nothing. Over the next several days he bought hard copies of the *Los Angeles Times*. The third day he read a small article about the body of a man named Sean Alworth, found in a boarded-up house near the 110 Freeway and Trade Tech college. His head had been caved in with a blunt object that wasn't found. Was he the one? Had whoever killed him moved the body? The theory advanced in the article, quoting an unnamed source, was that the body had been moved to that location from somewhere else.

Alworth had a record of doing time for various crimes over the last twenty-five years, the report stated, including burglary and grand larceny. He was Black and in his forties like Cresston. Maybe it was Alworth he'd seen being murdered that day, but if so, given the man's past, it seemed like his bad deeds had caught up with him. A rueful smile crossed Cresston's face. See, that was why he wasn't all gung-ho about the protesting and goings on about the police.

Sure, he agreed, if the police or whomever stepped over the line, they should have to answer for it like anyone else who broke the law. But come on, you can't make martyrs of guys like Alworth who don't do right and take care of their kids and sometimes have problems with drugs. Thinking like that didn't make him a Tom, did it? He was critical of such people but that didn't mean he felt they or anybody else deserved to be mistreated. He wasn't a fool, he knew racism existed. It was just that he didn't call it as the reason for each and every bad interaction a white person and a person of color had. On the other hand, it wasn't like he was on an intravenous drip of Fox News like that asshole in accounts payable.

CRESSTON CHUCKLED GRIMLY AT the memory as he dashed across the freeway, horns honking and headlights flaring as drivers bumped on their high beams. Abstract notions of who had what coming to them for real or perceived misbehaviors now had deadly specificity. He reached the concrete raised median. He bent over, breathing hard, hands on his knees. He had no choice, he had to keep moving.

"Fuck," he muttered, gulping hard.

The only way off the freeway was to reach the other side. Standing on the raised median, he gauged the flow of oncoming traffic. Soon there was a break and Cresston started off again. He was about halfway across when a set of brakes squealed and he was almost run over by a car with its headlights off.

"Watch out, moron," the driver yelled. A powerful blast of marijuana assailed Cresston as the vehicle roared past.

Heart thudding in his chest, he had to chance walking along the side of the exit ramp as the simplest way to get off the freeway. He couldn't be sure that at the bottom of the rise there would be any break in the chain-link fencing this time. Headlights swept past him. Reaching a low point in the fencing, fear his incentive, he climbed over and was on the street. Cresston looked around. For the moment he'd lost his hunters. Who was he supposed to call? Where could he go? Social media? Cresston didn't even have a presence on Facebook or whatever it was calling itself these days. He could call one of his friends and ask to spend the night at their place, but he couldn't bring his trouble to their doorstep. Fuck and double fuck. He kept moving, trying to figure out a plan. If he could stay alive until daylight, more people out and about meant a better chance to live. But shit, plenty of unarmed Black men had been cut down by the cops in the middle of the day, so what was the advantage there? Hell, there was even that brother who got shot and killed in his own apartment by a cop who claimed she got confused, said she thought the apartment was hers.

Goddamn.

What about a bar, he wondered? It wasn't exactly armor plating, but if they found him, at least maybe somebody would record a video of his arrest on their phone. Once his dead body surfaced, could he get justice from the other side of the grave? Would the man and woman be believed that he'd resisted arrest, tried to flee and given them no choice but to shoot him in the back? But what would they manufacture as to why he was being arrested? Plant dope in his apartment, he supposed, his customers the middle-aged, mid-level bureaucrats in his department. He snorted bitterly.

Cresston neared a bar called the Comfort Zone, music and laughter spilling onto the sidewalk from within. Its windows were aglow with warm light. He started to go inside but an older woman stepped in front of him as he cleared the doorway. She was smiling and wore a cardboard top hat cocked to one side.

"Sorry, private function tonight."

"What?" He looked past her to see some folks dancing, others standing around and talking. Drinks were in hand and food was laid out on a long table. There was a banner tacked to a wall announcing the retirement of somebody named Terri. Five-pointed stars were scattered around her name.

"Sorry, huh?" she repeated, a slight frown now evident.

He could bull his way in, make everyone uncomfortable, questioning why this dude was bringing them down with his intrusion. A couple of guys would come over and politely ask him to leave and he'd refuse while he grubbed on the food he'd piled on his plate. The music would be cut off and the deputies would be called. But the notion of feeling safe in lock-up was iffy. How much easier would it be for a jailhouse snitch to stick a knife in his side? Maybe that was farfetched and maybe it wasn't. Shaken, he turned away.

Cresston jaywalked in front of the bar. An SUV rounded a corner at the far end of the block. From where he was, he couldn't tell if it was his tormentors. He jogged on across as the vehicle got closer. No sense running full-out, he concluded as he reached the other side of the street, there was nowhere to hide. He let out a breath as the big vehicle went past. Covering several more blocks and a turn down a side street brought him to a residential area. He walked along, lights on in some houses, with a dingbat apartment building along the street as well. Past the apartments there was a '90s era pickup truck parked in the driveway of a modest one-story Craftsman. Once there, he could make out an old-fashioned detached garage at the rear of the driveway. There was a dim yellow light on over its double doors, which were ajar. There were no lights on in the house. He walked slowly down the driveway, listening for human or animal sounds. He figured to shelter in place, as they say, for the night and risk being awakened by the home's owner in the morning.

At the doors he paused. Was that snoring? He was going to call out but decided to peep inside. He opened one of the doors wider and did so. Strung from the exposed rafters of the wooden garage were two work lights. They illuminated a car engine suspended by chains attached to a rollaway hoist. The cylinder heads had been removed from the engine block and were on a nearby table to be worked on. There were two rollaway tool cabinets in here as well as other assorted items.

A white-bearded man snoozed in a chair just outside of the cone of light. On the walls, Cresston saw several framed photographs of lowrider cars, from customized models dating back to the 1930s on to the '80s. Instrumental music played quietly on a transistor radio that must be at least forty years old. The music had to be on an oldies program, Cresston figured. A train engineer's billed cap was pulled low on the bearded man's head. Cresston entered and looked around, picking up a screwdriver. Like that would be an effective weapon against guns. Not to mention it would provide the excuse his pursuers needed to pump him full of bullets.

No sense waking the man, he thought, as there was no phone call he could make to save Cresston. He turned to leave and found his death standing there.

"Fuck me," he muttered.

"Yeah," Merazzo said, smiling at the sight of Cresston holding the screwdriver. He'd provided them with a degree of plausibility. She brought her gun up to fire.

"Wha, what's going on?" The shadetree mechanic awoke, blinking at his visitors. He wiped a hand over his face. He was Chicano.

"Shit," the woman swore. Apparently she hadn't noticed him until now.

"Caught this dangerous dude, old-timer," Merazzo's partner said, advancing into the garage. "You just go on and catch up on your beauty sleep." He looked at the woman, both understanding the old man was a complication but one they'd figure out how to explain away. The story would be that Cresston lunged at them, and they had no choice but to shoot.

The hunted man dropped to his knees and cried out, "Hands up, don't shoot!" He hadn't tried to throw the screwdriver away, not wanting to give them the excuse he'd made a threatening move.

"Shut up," Merazzo's partner said, trying to maintain control of the situation.

The older gent took his hand away from where he'd been pressing it to his breastbone. "What did you say he'd done, officers?"

"That's not your concern," Merazzo said in Spanish, producing a set of handcuffs.

"You taking him to the station?" the man said in English.

"What the fuck about 'shut up' don't you get?" Merazzo's partner said.

"This is Security Alert," a soothing voice crackled. "What's the nature of your assistance?"

"Yes, send an ambulance," the bearded man declared.

"One has already been dispatched."

Glowering at him, Merazzo's partner grabbed the older man out of the chair. Popping out from underneath his shirt on a lanyard was the two-way emergency pendant he'd activated. Angered, the cop ripped it off the old man's neck and stomped it to pieces.

"A little late for that," the other man said. A siren could be heard in the near distance.

"Time to blow this clusterfuck," Merazzo's partner said. He was holstering his weapon when the woman shot him.

The shocked look on the faces of the old man and Cresston were only surpassed by the one on the wounded man's face. He'd fallen back against the wall, sliding down to a sitting position on the grease-stained floor. Blood seeped out of a corner of his mouth and his lips puckered and unpuckered like a fish lying on a dock. He was still alive and Merazzo stepped over to the man, her gun steady on him. His gun was still in his hand, resting on his lap, but he couldn't seem to lift his arm. The beam of a flashlight shined inside the garage and the voices and footsteps of the arriving EMTs caused Merazzo to look toward the door as they entered.

THE STORY SHERIFF'S DETECTIVE Natalia Merazzo spun was one of fearing for her safety from her partner, Brian Scofield. The dead man, Sean Alworth, had been one of Scofield's confidential informants, she said. He'd given them bad intel on a dope bust and Scofield was certain Alworth was lying to them, that he'd known the truth but double-crossed them to profit by warning the drug dealers. Things got heated that afternoon and the next thing she knew, Scofield had bashed in Alworth's head with a lenth of pipe. Totally catching her off-guard, she insisted.

He'd told her unless she helped him move the body, he'd do the same to her. Scofield was a known tattooed member of a Sheriff's gang, one of several cliques—such as the Spartans and the Reapers—within the Department. More than a handful of its members had come under fire in recent years for questionable use of force and deaths in the field.

Merazzo said she feared going to her bosses with this predicament as she couldn't be certain she'd be backed up. As had been reported in the *L.A. Times* and other sources over the years, no one knew how deep this gang was entrenched. Yes, she admitted, she helped Scofield set Cresston up, as he'd seen Alworth's alleged murder happen. Merazzo maintained she had no intention of harming Cresston, and was waiting for the opportunity to get the better of Scofield and turn him in.

Cresston's account, of course, differed greatly from hers. He was even contacted by a writer-producer who wanted to turn his story into a film. He told him it would take time to set matters up but he'd be back in touch. For the time being, Cresston kept going to work, a mid-level bureaucrat in a mid-level anonymous job.

A FAMILY MATTER

Sarah M. Chen ||||||||||||

After jabbing herself with her dad's dull knife for the tenth time, Vanessa Chu was ready to chuck it across the kitchen. The thing was useless for slicing scallions and ginger. She made a mental note to buy her dad a new one. If she was going to be stuck here in Taichung for the next twelve weeks to help him with his recovery, she needed a knife that worked.

The Runner was now on lap three.

Every morning before sunrise, she'd stand at the kitchen window which overlooked the building next door and watch the same man run the roof's perimeter ten times. Afterwards, he'd face the rising sun and do tai chi.

Sometimes she did tai chi along with him. Her heartbeat would slow. Her breath would even out. The one time of the day she could lose herself and not be reminded of her failing marriage back home in Los Angeles and lack of job prospects. Unless you counted caring for the most stubborn man in all of Taiwan as a job.

A couple days ago, her dad had surprised her by waking up early and joining in. She'd seen him reflected in the window behind her. When she turned around, he dropped his arms like he'd been caught making funny faces behind her back.

"Let's do tai chi together at the park," she'd suggested.

"Bah." He'd waved his hand. "Too slow for me."

This despite the fact he was recovering from a stroke and could barely do the leg lifts and knee extensions the doctor had instructed him to do.

This morning, however, she was too frazzled to do tai chi. Michael, her husband, had sent her a lovely message last night.

I want a divorce.

It wasn't totally unexpected. When she'd left for Taiwan five days ago, their conversation had been cold and stilted.

"Typical," he'd said when she told him she'd be gone for a while.

"My baba has no one else," she'd said. "Let's talk when I get back. Maybe look into counseling."

"It's too late for that."

"You don't even want to try."

"I've been trying for years. I'm done trying."

The rice porridge boiled, and she turned the heat down. The Runner had moved onto his stretching exercises. The black sky was now softening into a midnight blue, the usually bustling city blanketed in the quiet of the pre-dawn glow.

Movement at the other end of the roof caught her attention. Another man—heavyset, with broad shoulders—emerged from the stairwell. She'd never seen anyone else this early on the roof before.

He strode purposefully toward the Runner. Maybe he was a building worker telling him he had to vacate for maintenance. She continued chopping scallions when the Runner turned around. It looked like the two men were talking.

The Runner turned his back to continue stretching. The heavyset man lingered. Then he wrapped his arms around the Runner from behind. The Runner instantly squirmed and struggled.

Vanessa froze. The two men staggered around like drunken dancers, moving toward the roof's edge. There was no guardrail. Just a one-foot-high ledge. The large man lifted the Runner like he weighed nothing. The Runner's legs peddled uselessly in the air.

The man dangled him over the ledge, and then the Runner was gone.

The killer ran back to the stairwell, vanishing into the darkness.

It happened so fast, but Vanessa was absolutely sure of what she saw. Her knife clattered to the counter.

"Baba," she called out, rushing to her room for her phone. She had to dial nine one one but didn't know the equivalent in Taiwan. "Call the police."

"YOU DID NOT SEE his face," the female police officer said. "This other man."

Vanessa sighed in frustration. "No, like I said, it happened so fast. It was still pretty dark. The sun hadn't risen yet."

The two police officers from the North District had been questioning her for what seemed like hours but was probably only twenty minutes. Her father had called one one zero, the emergency line in Taiwan, about an hour ago. Vanessa waited on the balcony until an ambulance arrived a few minutes later. All she could see was a body covered with a sheet being loaded onto a stretcher. That was enough.

The female officer sat across from Vanessa while her male partner stared out the kitchen window, the exact spot where Vanessa had watched the Runner being dropped from the roof like a water balloon.

"I didn't see the man's face, but I remember his body," she continued. She flexed her arms, mimicking a weight-lifter. "Big muscles and large. Heavyset."

Her dad sat beside her. Every now and then he and the officers would babble in Mandarin. Then the female officer would write something in her notebook.

Vanessa couldn't help noticing the woman never wrote anything during their conversation.

When they left, Vanessa turned to her dad. His cup of jasmine tea sat in front of him, barely touched. The porridge now congealed on the stove.

"What did they say to you?" she asked.

He frowned. "Nothing."

"C'mon. You guys were a bunch of chatty Cathys."

Her dad hesitated. "Maybe you didn't see what you thought you saw," he said. "Maybe you were confused about two men."

She stared at him. "I hope you told them I wasn't confused."

He flinched and she knew he told them no such thing.

"I know what I saw, Dad."

"Let the police figure it out." He stood up and headed back to his room, his left leg dragging slightly behind him. "Focus on your own problems and your marriage instead of distracting yourself with this."

She scowled at his retreating figure. Wondered what he'd think if she told him the marriage was over. He knew they were having issues, but had no idea Michael had moved out six months ago, leaving her alone in the house they'd bought together. A house she'd never even liked and planned to sell as soon as she returned.

She added it to her endless list of regrets when it came to Michael. The number one being selling her bookstore for him. Her "little hobby" had been draining their savings. When she finally broke down and sold it, he didn't even seem to care.

Now she had no marriage, no job, and no home.

She threw the porridge in the trash and began cleaning up. Her appetite was gone.

VANESSA LEARNED THE RUNNER'S name the next day at the nearby Starbucks.

"Lam Tsung-fan was sixty-eight," Susan Tseng read, her long black hair falling forward onto the table. "No children. Never married. No next of kin. Retired engineer."

"What else? Anything about the other man?" Vanessa gripped her black sesame matcha tea latte in both hands as her friend from grad school scanned the newspaper. She was exhausted, having slept very little last night. Every time she closed her eyes, she saw the Runner with his legs in the air.

When she'd listened to the daily ICRT news report—the one English radio station in Taiwan—with her dad earlier, there had been a brief mention.

"On October second at five forty-nine a.m., a man at the Funja Building in the North District of Taichung fell from the building's roof and died instantly."

She had hoped the *Taichung Daily News* would have more information so she snuck her dad's copy from Wang, their building security guard, and called Susan, hoping she'd read it for her.

"The North District police are investigating but not ruling out suicide," Susan continued reading. "He suffered from a terminal illness." She took a sip of her coffee and looked at Vanessa. "The police probably don't want to appear incompetent, since they have no clue about the killer. So they tell the media it's suicide."

Exactly what Vanessa was thinking. She stood up. "I have to go."

"Seriously? I finally get to see you after five years and you drop 'I witnessed a murder' in my lap and now you have to bail?" She folded her arms. "This is crazy. At least buy me lunch or something while we talk about this more."

Vanessa hesitated, not wanting to admit she was eager to get to the police station. "I bought you a latte."

Susan stared at her.

"I know, I know. I suck," Vanessa said. "My dad will be looking for his paper." Not a total lie. "Why don't we go walking Saturday? I'll fill you in on everything then."

Susan sighed. "Fine. Meet me in front of the Star Hotel at nine A.M. You know that swanky one by the Calligraphy Greenway?"

Vanessa nodded.

Susan waved her off. "Go. I'm sure the police will love having you hassle them on why they're doing a shitty job."

VANESSA STARED UP AT Lam's building, unsure what she was looking for but not knowing what else to do after hitting a dead end with the police. The same female officer had told her nobody else had seen the large man. A check of the security cameras showed nothing either. All signs seemed to point to suicide.

"Why would he run every morning if he planned to kill himself?" Vanessa had asked.

The officer had no answer to that.

Vanessa scanned the street. There was no crime scene tape anywhere. Just a faint discoloration on the sidewalk in front of her where they must've cleaned him up. She shuddered and went inside.

A desk sat in the rear of the lobby with a security guard who looked no older than twenty-five behind it, reading a book.

"Excuse me, did you know Lam Tsung-fan?" Vanessa asked.

He looked up from his book with no indication of whether he understood her or not.

"Were you working the day he died?" Vanessa tried again. Nothing.

She sighed. "Okay, thank you." She was about to turn to go when he said something in Mandarin and slid the book toward her.

Curious, she looked at it. A stark red cover with a Chinese title.

"Oh, um, I can't read Chinese," she said, embarrassed.

He said something that sounded like *"dong xi."* Vanessa shook her head.

"I'm sorry, I don't understand."

He pointed to the book and said it again.

She picked it up and noted the author looked like an American woman. When Vanessa tried to hand it back, he held up his hands, gesturing for her to keep it.

"Xie xie." She thanked him, wondering if it had something to do with Lam or he just wanted to get rid of the book.

As soon as she got home, she skimmed it, but it was all in Chinese. After Googling the author, she determined the book was called *Shut It Down* and was about activism. But what that had to do with Lam, she had no idea.

Vanessa thought of something and pulled up her Google Translate app.

"*Dong xi*," she said into her phone.

The word "thing" popped up. She snorted. That was helpful.

Frustrated, she tossed the book aside on the table. A small bookmark slid out. She picked it up.

Something Bookstore.

The address was in Taipei.

She wondered if this was what the security guard was saying to her. Maybe Lam worked there. It was the only lead she had. Plus it wasn't like she needed an excuse to visit a new bookstore. She'd already been to all the local ones.

She scribbled a note to her dad that she'd be back before dinner. No point telling him she was going all the way to Taipei. It was two hours by car or an hour by high speed rail, but he'd wonder why the sudden desire to go there. He was at the gym, which she knew meant gossiping in the sauna for two hours with Teddy and Mimi, an elderly couple she'd met briefly. At least he had a social life. More than she could say.

Vanessa had been to Taipei only once before—many years ago—and recalled how cosmopolitan it was compared to Taichung. Now it seemed even more so with its posh boutique stores and high rises.

Amidst the sound of scooters whirring by, Vanessa dug around in her pants pocket for her map. She'd asked Wang to show her where the bookstore was. He'd drawn an arrow from the high speed rail station to the Zhongzheng District.

The Something Bookstore was on the fifth floor of a nondescript building. When she got out of the elevator, she found herself in a narrow hallway paved with mustard-colored tiles. She passed an acupuncture clinic and a dumpling shop, and finally reached the bookstore. She breathed in the familiar scent of paper and books, feeling at home for the first time since arriving in Taiwan.

An elderly man—close to her dad's age—sat at the register talking in Chinese on his cell phone. She noted that it sounded different than the Mandarin she was used to hearing. He nodded at her.

She found the English-language section off to the side. There were books on the 228 Massacre and the White Terror era. Copies of *Formosa Betrayed*, *Brave New World*, and *Fahrenheit 451*. There was even a small children's section in the corner dominated by Winnie the Pooh books.

"Can I help you?" the man asked in perfect English.

It amazed her that everyone automatically assumed she didn't speak Chinese. Even though she was only half Chinese, she thought she looked Chinese, but apparently not. She was an outsider and always would be.

"Hi, yes, I came from Taichung to visit your store," she said. "I used to own a bookstore back home in America."

He smiled. "Welcome," he said. "Is there something in particular you're looking for?"

Vanessa walked over to the register and pulled the book out from her tote bag. She slid it across the desk toward him.

"This was purchased from here, I believe."

He leaned over, his glasses sliding down his nose. "Ah, yes. A guide to the resistance movement." He looked up at her. "We take action when there is something—or some-one—important we want to protect."

"What did Lam Tsung-fan want to protect?"

The bookseller stiffened. "How do you know Lam?" Suspicion clouded his face. "Who are you?"

"My name is Vanessa Chu. I'm taking care of my dad

and his building is next to Mr. Lam's." She paused, not sure how much he knew. "We never met, but I felt like I knew him."

He said nothing, his eyes sharp. She plowed ahead. "I saw him get killed," she said in a low voice despite no one else being in the store. "I can't stop thinking about it. The police are suspecting suicide because he was terminally ill, but it was murder." The image of Lam dangling over the ledge flashed in her mind.

The bookseller blinked at her but said nothing. She noted he didn't seem surprised Lam was murdered.

"Do you know who would kill him?"

He pushed the book back. "I'm sorry. I can't help you."

Vanessa wanted to protest, but another customer walked in. The bookseller seemed eager to end their conversation and hurried over to greet him.

She browsed while she waited. Post-its with handwritten messages covered a nearby wall. Mostly in Chinese characters but a few were in English.

Free Hong Kong

Love is Love

I Stand for Taiwan Independence

She had watched the news with dismay when pro-democracy protestors flooded the Hong Kong streets to protest a possible extradition bill with China. The bill was scrapped, but Beijing passed the controversial national security law that essentially cracked down on any form of dissent, including books.

Vanessa feared Taiwan could suffer a similar fate.

When the customer left, Vanessa pointed to the Post-its. "I think you would be someone who cared about justice."

He crossed his arms across his chest. "You know nothing about me."

"So tell me." She waited. "Look, I know you must think I'm a pushy American, but I have to do something. Like you said, we take action for things that are important to us."

"Why is he important to you?"

"Because he didn't deserve to die like that," she said. "Because if I do nothing, they win."

Whoever *they* were.

He sucked his teeth as he stared at her from behind his desk.

"I came all this way," she pleaded. "Just tell me how you know Lam."

He hesitated, then softened. "You are a bookseller so you may understand. The importance of knowledge and exchanging ideas." He spread his hands on the desk and leaned forward. "I don't know if you know what's been happening in Hong Kong, but my home has become unrecognizable."

At the mention of Hong Kong, she realized he must have been speaking Cantonese earlier.

"The CCP didn't like the books I was selling. Books about the history of China, social activism, that kind of thing. So I left Hong Kong and opened my store here."

"CCP?"

"Chinese Communist Party." Off her nod, he continued. "Lam was one of my best customers. We became friends and eventually business partners. He convinced me to open a second location in Taichung. We were scheduled to open next month."

"Oh?" Vanessa would love to have such a bookstore near her. "Whereabouts?"

"In the West District. On Yingcai Road. Right next door to the Star Hotel."

The hotel where she and Susan were meeting Saturday.

He shook his head. "But without Lam, I can't sustain two stores."

Vanessa was genuinely sorry to hear that. "So what are you saying?" she asked, steering him back. "It's the CCP? They killed Lam?"

"I'm not saying that." He frowned. "But maybe some people don't want me in Taichung. They want to silence our voices."

"If you know who did this, come to the police station with me," she said. If the both of them went together, the police would surely investigate Lam's death as a homicide.

His face tightened. "Go home, Ms. Chu. You don't know what you're getting into." He sat down and picked up his phone. Turned away from her as he babbled in Cantonese.

Frustrated, Vanessa wrote down her contact information on a piece of paper and left.

WHEN VANESSA RETURNED TO her dad's condo, she found him at the kitchen table with a copy of the *Taichung Daily News*. Beside that was her note.

"Where did you go?" he asked.

"The museums." She smiled. "What do you want for dinner, Baba?"

"Don't lie to me." He scowled. "I know you went to a bookstore in Taipei."

Vanessa winced. "How did you know?"

He shook his newspaper at her. "I didn't get my copy this morning. Stupid security people downstairs keep forgetting to deliver it."

She swallowed, feeling a twinge of guilt for stealing his paper.

"Wang mentioned you asked about directions to a bookstore in Taipei." He waited. "So why didn't you tell me you were going all the way there?"

Thanks a lot, Wang.

She sat down across from him. "Someone gave me a book that belonged to Lam. The bookmark was inside and it was the only clue I had."

"Clue to what?" His scowl deepened. "You're still wasting time with this dead man?" He pointed to the paper. "It says here he was sick and probably killed himself."

"No, he didn't. I have proof now that it wasn't suicide."

Alarm crossed his face. "What proof?"

"The bookstore owner came to Taiwan from Hong Kong. He's like a social activist. Lam was helping him open a second location here and now he's dead."

Her dad frowned.

"Do you think it's the CCP? Beijing sent someone to quiet him?" she asked.

He snorted. "You watch too much TV."

"Aren't you concerned, Dad?"

"About what?"

"About China doing to Taiwan what they did in Hong Kong?"

He waved his hand. "Bah. It won't happen."

"But what would you do if it does?"

He pursed his mouth. "We are all Chinese. We come from the same family."

That surprised her. She thought he considered himself Taiwanese since he'd grown up here. "So you would be fine if China took over? A country that censors what they don't like and violates people's civil liberties?"

"It's not so simple as that." He gave her a sharp look. "Let it go, Vanessa. This isn't your home."

"But it's *your* home, Dad. Don't you care that this is happening?"

Her dad took a long time to answer. "I'm proud to be Chinese," he said finally. "Whatever will happen will happen. There's nothing I can do but live my life." He suddenly looked old and tired.

Vanessa impulsively reached out and grabbed his hand. His papery thin skin felt rough. When did he get so many age spots on his arms?

"You need to stop with this Nancy Drew stuff," he said. "I'm too old for this."

She wanted to reassure him that she would drop it. "Don't worry, Baba," she said. That was the best she could do for now.

They sat quietly together at the kitchen table, the uncertainty of their future weighing on them both.

"THAT'S CRAZY," SUSAN SAID.

"Which part?" Vanessa asked. They powerwalked along the Calligraphy Greenway, a wide stretch of parkway dotted with sculptures. The gray Saturday morning was thick with the threat of rain. "The revolutionary bookseller who fled Hong Kong to open a store here? Or that the CCP may have killed Lam?"

"The part about such a cool bookstore opening here in sleepy Taichung. I don't believe it."

"*That's* what you think is crazy?"

Susan snorted. "I'm kidding."

"Ha ha."

"No, but seriously, all of the above," Susan said. "I mean, it's like right out of a spy novel."

"Yeah, my dad isn't too happy about it."

"I'll bet. His only child playing Mission Impossible."

They walked in silence, their heavy breathing in sync, until they arrived back in front of the Star Hotel. They stretched their legs and Vanessa glanced up at the building next door.

"I wonder where the bookstore is going to be." She frowned. "*Was* going to be."

Susan raised her eyebrows. "It's not opening now?"

Vanessa shook her head. "He said without Lam, he doesn't have the funds to run two stores."

"Too bad."

"Do you ever think about it?" Vanessa asked suddenly. She knew Susan identified as Taiwanese.

"About what?"

"The One China policy."

Susan seemed surprised. "What's the point? I mean there's always the possibility of an attack, but too much is at stake for China to actually go through with it. But what do I know?" She shrugged. "We can only do our best. Keep moving forward and fighting when we need to." Then she brightened. "Hey, there's an idea."

"What?"

"We can raise money for the bookstore."

"Like a GoFundMe?"

"Yeah, why not? My students organize fundraisers all the time for causes they believe in. I'd be happy to set one up, and they'd spread the word, I'm sure of it."

Susan taught international affairs at a local university. Vanessa smiled, grateful. "That'd be awesome, thanks."

After saying goodbye, Vanessa hurried back to her dad's. It was half past twelve. She was late for lunch and the ICRT news hour. It had become part of their daily routine. She and her dad would sit down and eat while listening to the news. He said it helped him brush up on his English while it gave Vanessa a sense of being back home.

Although home was a vague concept these days.

She found him at the kitchen table, the radio in the center blaring loud. A bowl of rice in front of him. Platters of leftover beef stir fry and scallion pancakes on the counter. "I waited for you."

"Sorry, I lost track of time." She scurried around the kitchen and heated up the food. Placed it in front of him and he immediately started eating. She chopped up fresh ginger while vaguely listening to the news report.

"And out of the Zhongzheng District in Taipei, the Something Bookstore owner, Cheng Wen-je, was found badly beaten late last night in an apparent burglary gone wrong."

Vanessa whirled around. Her dad looked just as startled, his chopsticks frozen in mid-air.

". . . the store had recently opened to much fanfare, including a visit from the president, and hosted several book events featuring social activists and local authors. A second location is scheduled to open in Taichung. Cheng remains in critical condition but is expected to survive. And now onto the weather. A cold front . . ."

Her dad turned down the volume. "This is the bookstore you went to yesterday?"

She nodded, feeling sick.

Worry lines creased his forehead. "Were you followed?"

Her stomach flip-flopped. "You're scaring me, Dad." She swallowed. "I don't know. It wasn't like I was looking behind me all the time." Her chest tightened from the mounting panic. "Do you think this was my fault?"

He shook his head. "Don't blame yourself. You don't know if it would have happened anyway." He set his chopsticks down. "Someone doesn't like the books they sell."

Exactly what the bookstore owner said.

"Will you admit now that Lam was murdered?"

He pursed his mouth, narrowing his eyes.

Stubborn old man.

"I have to contact the police," she said. "I'm sure it's connected."

"No." Her dad pounded the table with his fist, making Vanessa jump. "What's wrong with you?" He scooted his chair back and stood up, wobbling before he steadied himself against the table. "You must stop this. Before you get hurt."

She'd never seen him so upset. "Just a call to the police in Taipei. Then I'll stop."

He looked like he was ready to throw his rice bowl at her. "Vanessa. Why are you so stubborn? Just like when you were a kid." He glared at her. "You never change."

"Look who's talking."

They faced off across the table, both of their arms folded in defiance.

Vanessa thought of her late mother, who had died of cancer ten years ago. Her parents divorced when she was thirteen because her mom got tired of her dad acting like his way was the only way. Their shouting matches had Vanessa running to her room and slamming the door. Blasting her music so she wouldn't have to listen.

Too stubborn to forgive and too proud to apologize.

He was the first to break the silence. "You need to go back to L.A."

Heat flushed to her face. "Are you kicking me out, Dad?"

"No." He sighed. "Yes."

"What about your recovery?"

He waved his hand. "Bah. That doesn't matter. You aren't safe here." He turned to go like it was settled. "I'll arrange your flight."

"I'm not ready to go."

"Too bad. I'm your father. You do as I say."

She felt like she was thirteen again. "This is ridiculous."

He shuffled toward the door. "I'm going down to the gym," he said. "I'll arrange your flight when I get back. You stay here. And no more bookstores." The slam of the door echoed throughout the condo.

At least he has no problem with his arm strength.

She dumped their lunch in the trash, her stomach too knotted up with guilt and anxiety to eat.

VANESSA LOOKED UP FROM her laptop and fund-raising research to glance at the clock. Almost two and a half hours had gone by since her dad stormed out. He was probably complaining to everyone in the steam room about his troublesome American daughter whom he was packing up and sending home.

She could still contact the police about her suspicions. Her dad would never know. But she decided it wouldn't do much good. They hadn't been very helpful so far.

When over three hours had passed, Vanessa knew something was wrong. He'd never been gone this long.

She called him and immediately heard ringing down the hall. His phone lay on the coffee table in the living room. In his haste to end their argument, he'd left it behind.

"Crap." Vanessa hung up.

A hollowness formed in her chest. She grabbed her key card and ran out, darting into the elevator. Just as the doors were about to slide shut, someone from the hallway yelled, "Hold the elevator."

Vanessa reflexively hit the "door open" button and a large stocky man wearing a baseball cap pulled down low slithered in.

He stood close behind her.

Too close.

Something picked at the back of her brain as the doors slid shut. Like an itch she couldn't quite reach.

Why didn't he yell "hold the elevator" in Chinese?

When strangers spoke in English to her it was because she looked like a foreigner. But this guy had no way of seeing her from the hallway.

She tensed. The oxygen seemed to suck right out of the elevator.

The man's fist hit the emergency stop with lightning speed. The elevator jolted to a standstill and she stumbled into him. He yanked both of her arms behind her and twisted them up while shoving her face into the wall. She yelped in pain as her right temple smashed against the cold steel, momentarily stunning her.

"You nosy American. We will hurt your baba," he said into her ear. His breath was sour and hot.

"Where is he?" she croaked.

"You stay away from police. You forget this. Or he will die."

She struggled to break free, but the hold on her wrists and the back of her neck tightened. White-hot pain shot through her, reverberating down her spine.

They had her father and it was all her fault.

"Let him go." She choked back a sob. "Please. He has nothing to do with this."

She tried to turn around to get a glimpse of the man,

but he banged her head against the elevator wall with such force black spots danced in her vision.

This was it. She would die right here.

"We are watching you, Vanessa."

Suddenly, she went flying to the other side of the elevator. Her left shoulder slammed into the wall and she crumpled to the floor. The elevator dinged and the doors slid open. When she looked up, the man was gone.

She awkwardly got to her feet and scanned the hallway. He had vanished. It had happened so quickly. If it wasn't for the pain she felt all over, she'd wonder if she hadn't imagined the entire thing.

With shaking hands, she hit the "gym" button. She'd take stock of her injuries later. Time couldn't be wasted. If she wasn't sure something had happened to her dad before, she was convinced now.

The second the elevator doors slid open, she bolted out, wincing at her throbbing head and shoulder. She burst through the gym's double doors and headed straight to the back for the pool area.

If something happened to her dad, she'd never forgive herself.

One lone swimmer sliced through the water with a methodical breast stroke. Chlorine stung Vanessa's nostrils as she walked past the pool to the sauna. When she opened the door, the humidity practically suffocated her.

"Baba! It's me, Vanessa." She peered inside, waiting for her eyes to adjust to the dim light. She recognized Teddy and Mimi. They sat in their robes, chattering in Mandarin but stopped when they noticed her. "Hi, was my dad here?"

Mimi shook her head. "He did not come today."

Vanessa mumbled a *"xie xie"* as she staggered out of the sauna. Her head throbbed.

We are watching you, Vanessa.

She dashed back to the elevator and hit the "lobby" button. As soon as the doors slid open, she made a beeline for the security guard desk. A woman sat there. No sign of Wang.

"Have you seen my baba? Sam Lai?"

The woman's eyes widened. She said something in Mandarin and pointed to the right side of her face. Vanessa realized she must look banged up.

"My dad? Have you seen him?" she repeated, ignoring the guard's stare.

The guard shook her head.

"*Xie xie.*" When she turned to leave, she spotted her dad strolling in from outside, heading for the elevator.

"Baba!" She almost collapsed with relief before rushing over to him. "Where have you been? I looked everywhere."

"I went to the park to do tai chi."

She gaped at him. "I've been trying to get you to do that since I got here and you choose *now* to go?" She didn't know whether to hug him or slap him upside the head.

He peered at her. "What happened here?" He touched his right temple and frowned.

She felt her head and winced. A lump had already formed. She wasn't going to tell her dad about the attack. No use making him worry even more. "I slipped at the pool looking for you."

"You have to be careful, Vanessa. Don't be so clumsy."

"I know, Dad." She guided him to the elevator. Fortunately, he seemed to believe her.

VANESSA SAT UP IN bed, waiting for her eyes to adjust to the darkness. She glanced at the clock, feeling uneasy. Maybe a bad dream. It was three thirty in the morning.

Slowly, she got out of bed and went to her window. The roof of the building next door loomed in the darkness like a vast concrete sea.

A rustling from down the hall. She froze. That was what had woken her up. She'd heard something, like someone trying to quietly move about the kitchen.

Did the man who threatened her break in? It had been three days since the attack in the elevator. Three days of going to the gym with her dad, afraid to let him go on his own. She'd even joined him in the steam room with Teddy and Mimi. Listened to them chattering in Mandarin and laughing. She'd been concerned her dad would pick up on her edginess, but to her relief, he seemed oblivious.

Although he stayed true to his word and booked her a flight back to L.A. next week. There was no way she was going to leave him alone now, but she couldn't tell him why. She'd pretend to miss her flight.

We are watching you, Vanessa.

She crept down the hall and glanced back at her dad's bedroom. His door was shut. Hopefully he was sleeping through this. He never got up before seven.

When she checked the kitchen, it was empty and dark. The only sound the ticking clock above the sink. Something was off, but she couldn't put her finger on it.

The click of the front door closing. Was somebody coming or going? She tiptoed down the hall, her breathing shallow, but nobody was there.

Ding!

The elevator. She hurried to the front door and cracked it open, scanning the hallway. Empty.

She grabbed her key card from the tray by the door and ran to the elevator. Her dad's unit was on the tenth floor. The indicators above glowed with each passing floor. Nine, eight, seven, six. She pounded the "down" button.

Where are you going, Dad?

She knew it was him. His key card had been missing when she'd grabbed hers. Why was he sneaking out in the middle of the night?

Impatient, she watched the indicators light up one by one. Finally, it stopped. P for parking. Which was weird since neither of them had a car.

She banged on the elevator button, but P remained lit up. "Dammit."

She ran to the stairwell and hustled down, her footsteps clanging on the metal steps. The fluorescent lights buzzed above her. Despite the chilly night and wearing nothing but boxers and a T-shirt, she was sweating.

When she got to the lowest level, she hit the push bar and stumbled into the garage, blinking at the harsh lighting.

Where was he?

She waited, listening. An electrical buzzing somewhere, probably a generator. A murmur of voices to her left at the far end of the garage. Hunching down between cars, she hurried toward them.

As she darted out from behind a large SUV, the roar of an engine came from behind. She whirled around to see a sedan barreling down the aisle, heading straight for her. Panicked, she dove out of the way just in time as the car hit the brakes. It squealed past her before coming to rest a few feet away.

Vanessa wobbled to her feet, stunned by the close call of almost becoming roadkill. She ducked behind the SUV, shielded by a tire. Her heart seemed to pound in her ears, and she strained to hear footsteps.

The rev of the engine. Were they leaving?

She crawled out just as taillights flashed, momentarily blinding her. She froze. The car suddenly reversed, tires squealing, and zoomed toward her. She scrambled to safety at the last second.

Whoever was at the wheel of the car was definitely trying to run her over.

Her breath was quick and shallow as she scuttled away. Where was her dad? Was he being held hostage somewhere? Was he in the car?

She crouched down, darting in between cars and losing all sense of direction. Unsure if she was heading back to the elevator or away from it. Frustrated, she stopped and listened. The distinct sound of a car engine. It purred quietly, maybe three aisles away.

They were hunting her down, looking for her.

Gulping down her terror, she continued scurrying in between cars, moving from aisle to aisle. If they had her dad, how would she be able to save him? She didn't have her phone to call the police, but even if she did, she had little faith they would be able to help her in time.

No, she had to handle this on her own.

The voices again, this time closer. Talking in Mandarin. If they were in the same location as when she first entered the garage, they were near the freight elevator. She hurried in that direction and hunkered down behind a car to sneak a peek.

Two people huddled in the shadows near the elevator. She couldn't make out their faces. Couldn't tell if her dad was one of them.

"Vanessa?"

She turned to see him standing behind her a couple car lengths away. Startled and relieved at the same time, she got to her feet.

"Dad?"

"What are you doing here?" He shuffled toward her. "Why aren't you in bed?"

"I was looking for you." She scanned the parking garage and spotted the car heading toward them. She clutched his arm. "That guy tried to kill me." Panic gripped her and she pulled him toward her to get him out of the car's path. "C'mon."

Her dad turned and waved at the car. Confused, Vanessa watched as it screeched to a stop in front of them. The driver climbed out and said something in Mandarin, gesturing at her. Vanessa recognized him as Teddy from the steam room.

What the hell?

"You tried to run me over," she said.

Her dad and Teddy went back and forth in rapid-fire Mandarin. Her dad nodded and turned to Vanessa.

"He's sorry. Said you came out of nowhere and he didn't recognize you. Thought maybe you were another building resident. He was afraid you saw something."

Vanessa frowned. "Saw what?"

More talking behind her in Mandarin. She turned to see the two people by the freight elevator waving at them. It was Mimi and Wang, the security guard.

"What's going on?" she asked again.

Her dad said something in Mandarin, and Teddy got back into the car and popped the trunk.

"Vanessa, go back to bed," her dad said. "You shouldn't be here."

Ignoring her dad, she walked over to Mimi and Wang. They loomed over a heavyset man on the ground with tape over his mouth and his hands bound behind his back. His feet were zip tied together at the ankles. He squirmed and struggled until Mimi gave him a good kick in the ribs.

"Omigod." It was the man from the elevator.

He glared back at her with hate-filled eyes from his prone position on the ground. Angry muffled shouts in Mandarin.

She looked at her dad in disbelief, but he was too busy talking to Teddy.

Teddy waved to Wang, who hurried over. The two men bent down and picked up the bound man. They struggled and strained. Finally, they hoisted him up, awkwardly duck-walked him over to the opened trunk, and, with Mimi's help, heaved him inside. The man took up the entire trunk. Her dad slammed the lid down. It popped back up. Teddy moved her dad out of the way and slammed the lid down. It popped back up again.

"I told you we need SUV for him," Mimi said.

Her dad waved his hand. "Bah. He'll fit." He tried again. The lid refused to close. Mimi shoved Vanessa's dad aside and slammed the lid, pressing down with all her strength. She couldn't have weighed more than ninety pounds. Muffled cries from the trunk. The lid latched closed. Teddy patted his wife on the back.

Wang climbed into the back seat and Mimi rode shotgun. Teddy and her dad jabbered back and forth in Mandarin. Her dad nodded and Teddy ran over to the driver's side. The car revved to life. Her dad yanked the back door open and was about to scoot in beside Wang.

"Hang on a second," Vanessa said, frustration surging through her. "Dad, you've got to tell me what's going on. Right now."

He looked at her. "He told me he would kill you if you didn't stop. Wang here saw him lurking around the building, so . . ." He shrugged. "I had no choice. You're so stubborn. You would find a way to miss your flight home."

He knew her better than she thought. "So wait, how did you—?"

Her dad stuck his arm out and said, "Zzzzzz." He gestured to Wang in the car. "Wang here tased him."

Vanessa was stunned.

"Don't worry," her dad said. "We'll take him far away."

She lowered her voice. "Are you going to kill him?"

He waved his hand. "Bah. We'll just scare him."

Teddy stuck his head out the window and barked something in Mandarin. Her dad nodded and said "*hao, hao*," while he eased himself into the car. He rolled his window down and stuck his head out.

"Go back to bed," he told her. "I'll be back in time for congee."

He slammed the door and Vanessa stared in disbelief as the car sped down the aisle, its taillights winking at her as it braked and skidded around the corner.

When she got back upstairs, she boiled water for tea, knowing she'd never be able to get back to sleep, and that was when she realized what had been bothering her earlier. Several kitchen drawers were left ajar. Annoyed, she closed each one wondering what her dad had been looking for until she spotted the space where the chef's knife she'd recently purchased should be. She stared at the empty slot before easing the drawer shut.

IT WAS FIVE DAYS later when her dad turned on the radio for their daily ICRT news report that Vanessa learned not only the murderer's identity but his motivation.

"Taichung police have arrested Hsu Chi-lung, the outspoken billionaire hotel mogul, in connection with a conspiracy to murder Lam Tsung-fan, a

*retired engineer thought to have committed suicide
fifteen days ago. During the police's investigation
into the disappearance of Star Hotel security guard
Tsai Feng-kee, they discovered numerous communi-
cations between the two men regarding a plot to stop
the Something Bookstore from opening its second
location in the building next to the Star Hotel, one of
Hsu's luxury properties. Hsu, a staunch pro-China
sympathizer and vocal critic of the president and
her party, is known for his extremist op-eds blaming
'dangerous propaganda machines like the Something
Bookstore for poisoning the minds of today's youth
with progressive thinking.'*

*"The Something Bookstore is owned by Cheng
Wen-je, a social justice advocate from Hong Kong,
who was badly beaten two weeks ago. The investigation points to Tsai Feng-kee as the assailant hired by
Hsu. The new bookstore location is still on track to
open in one week, thanks to fundraising efforts that
went viral."*

Vanessa stole a peek at her dad, who sat motionless
in his chair, avoiding her gaze. Neither of them had mentioned that night. Every time she wanted to ask him, the
words stuck in her throat. She'd noticed the knife had
been returned the next day but couldn't bring herself to
use it.

Her dad leaned over and turned off the radio. "Maybe
we can go to the bookstore opening together." He stared
down at the table. The remnants of their lunch in front of
them.

Vanessa blinked at him. "Really?"

He shrugged. "I could use a book."

She'd never seen him read a single book. Only newspapers. "I'm supposed to fly home tomorrow."

He waved his hand. "Bah. We can move it." He paused. "You stay here as long as you need."

She wanted to hug him. But the question burning inside her rendered her immobile.

Did he kill Tsai?

Did she really want to know?

He cleared his throat. "I will do whatever it takes to protect you, Vanessa. You're the most important thing in my life."

We take action when there is someone important we want to protect.

Vanessa felt the stinging behind her eyes. The burning of her nose as she blinked the tears back. She reached across the table and touched his arm. Now was not the time to ask. It wouldn't change things. Or how she felt about him.

He put his hand on top of hers and held it there.

She didn't trust herself to speak but knew without a doubt that he could feel what was in her heart. The same way she could feel what was in his.

That no matter what happened with her marriage or where she ended up, she'd always have a home here with him.

HAVANA CALIENTE

||||||| Teresa Dovalpage

Like most people my generation, I grew up in a pixelated world that often felt more vivid and trustworthy than real life. My mother, *Dios la bendiga*, put a cheap digital camera in my hands when I was eight years old and taught me to take pictures to keep me entertained. It worked, and I was hooked. See, eyes can deceive you, words can be misinterpreted or drowned by noise, but images captured by a camera are faithful witnesses of reality.

This early fascination with photography led to my love of movies. Soon I discovered that telling a story was more fun than documenting it. All through my teenage years, I longed to become a screenwriter. I bought Final Draft, took a number of online courses, and finally enrolled in film school at Southwestern College.

By the end of the first semester I teamed up with a girl named Ashley to produce a short film, *Havana Caliente*. It was a Cuban love story with a sassy heroine used to pulling herself up by her bootstraps—or rather stiletto straps. Truth is, neither of us knew much about Cuba. I grew up between Tijuana and San Diego and Ashley in Pasadena, but we both felt the allure of an island of which so many things, good and bad, have been said.

The project as such was quite simple. We planned to

feature two students from the college acting program and use archival images of the Malecón, the Havana seawall. Then Zurdo joined us and everything changed.

Juan Pérez, a Cuban guy who owed his nickname to being left-handed, was in his late twenties. His long slick hair tied up in a ponytail, he looked casual and easygoing. He had worked, he claimed, with Tomás Gutiérrez Alea, of *Guantanamera* and *Memorias del Subdesarrollo* fame, and other well-known Cuban directors. Zurdo was, in fact, an aspiring director himself. Invited to an L.A. film festival in 2014, he had stayed to try his luck in the business. In 2015 he moved to San Diego and, two years later, at the time we met, was part of the Southwestern College janitorial crew. When he found out that our short was about his country, he offered to help us.

I was supposed to be the director, producer, and screenwriter while Ashley multitasked as the director of photography, editor, and everything else. Suddenly we found ourselves displaced by the frantic energy of a guy able to raise ten thousand dollars in two weeks through a Kickstarter campaign, though he barely knew enough English to get by at work. I helped him write the description, but still, he did most of the work, contacting people who were interested in Cuban movies and spreading the word. Our original idea morphed into a Spanish-language short with English subtitles; we would shoot it in Havana. Zurdo was listed as the production assistant, though he called himself *el director*.

At first, I felt uneasy. There were times when Zurdo felt more like competition than an ally. He was the one handling the money, since he had raised most of it. He made me change the script more than I wanted to, even if it was for the better. Basically, he took over, but Ashley and I were too intimidated by his credentials and know-how to confront him. I also feared that our professor wouldn't like the idea of an outsider "helping" us. But Zurdo insisted, and what a smooth talker he was!

"See, Lupita, I know everyone who's anyone in the Havana movie scene," he boasted. "With all my contacts there, you girls will be in good hands."

He emailed the script to two Cuban actors and they agreed to work with us. A couple in real life, Ramón and Yuli were pros, Zurdo assured us—established theater people who wanted to break into movies. Ashley said it would be a shame to miss the chance. Our professor okayed the collaboration, and I finally put my doubts aside.

Getting a legal permit to fly from the United States to Cuba is a mass of red tape. Zurdo suggested we avoid it by simply leaving from Tijuana. He purchased the tickets from an airline he knew and traveled first to have everything ready for us.

WHEN ASHLEY AND I arrived at the José Martí International Airport, Zurdo was waiting for us in an *almendrón*, a very vintage bright blue '57 Ford Fairlane. The actors were there too. Ramón was in his thirties, tall and handsome, with well-defined muscles and a black penciled mustache. His wife, Yuli, was ten years his junior, slender and graceful, a dead ringer for a young Halle Berry.

"Thank you so much for giving us this opportunity," she gushed. "It means a lot to us!"

As we all squeezed inside the *almendrón*, I wondered if they knew that ours was a student film with expenses financed by Kickstarter patrons. But it didn't feel right to bring it up.

Ramón and Yuli lived on the third floor of a former

tobacco factory now turned into an apartment building. It had two entrances—each with their own cracked marble staircases—and long, dimly lit halls. We helped them carry upstairs the props and costumes Ashley and I had bought in San Diego—clothes, wigs, and makeup. Yuli was delighted with the wigs. She had just cut her hair for a play, but our protagonist's look called for long, flowing tresses.

Their apartment was one single room. A cast iron double burner on a cement counter constituted the kitchen. The refrigerator was a capsule Frigidaire contemporary of the *almendrón*. The only modern touch was a 32-inch plasma TV.

Zurdo had made reservations in a *casa particular*—an Airbnb for foreigners—that was on the same block. The *casa* had seen better days. Ashley and I shared a room furnished with two creaky beds, a basin-and-towel contraption that acted as a sink, and a claw-foot loveseat. There was a window to the street that didn't close properly. No five-star situation, but, after seeing the actors' residence, I didn't dare to complain.

I spent our first day in Havana taking pictures with my cellphone. There were too many photo ops everywhere—the multicolored *almendrónes* that drove up and down the street, the mahogany dining room set polished by time and use, and a gilded mirror that Margarita, the *casa* proprietress, said was over a hundred years old.

That night we all met at a private restaurant called El Paladar de Carmela. The food was scrumptious, and the aromas of fried chicken and plantains wafted in from the kitchen as we ate.

Yuli and Ramón appeared to be very much in love. They called each other *mamita* and *papito* and were often canoodling or holding hands. Their public displays of affection were a little over the top, but I assumed it was a Cuban thing. Anyway, I took dozens of pics of them.

Listening to Zurdo, you would have thought that we were on the verge of something momentous.

"I'll send the movie to the Sundance Film Festival. And to Venice, of course. Then, you know, the sky's the limit!"

Ramón and Yuli nodded, smiling and starry-eyed. I kept clicking away. If the movie turned out as expected, the crew would be grateful that someone had documented our humble beginnings.

THE NEXT DAY WE all read the screenplay together and decided on locations. Zurdo had already picked them out, but most were changed at Ramón's requests. Filming began. In the opening scene Yuli was wearing the wig, a tight red blouse, hot pants, and high heels—a *jinetera* outfit, Ashley remarked, having learned a few Cubanisms. Yuli *did* seem quite whorish, but the look was perfect for the plotline.

"Let the camera caress Yuli's body," Ramón told Ashley. "You are the audience's eyes. People will see what you want them to see. There's an *almendrón* speeding down El Malecón Avenue, but unless you focus on it, they'll just notice a blur of red."

Ashley captured the sensual cadence of Yuli's walk, a rhythmic sway of the hips that I tried in vain to imitate. But my friend's hands shook a little, and she kept stealing looks at Ramón.

AS FILMING PROGRESSED, IT BECAME clear that *el hombre* there, the real director, was Ramón. He not only had better knowledge of the trade, but, Havana-born and raised, he was more familiar with the city than Zurdo, who got us lost more than once. Ramón also made changes to the script and noticed details Zurdo had overlooked.

"Nobody here would say *No me chingues*. The right way, the Cuban way, is *No me jodas*. We don't send people to *la chingada* either; we send them to *el carajo*."

I realized he was treating Zurdo just like Zurdo had treated Ashley and me in San Diego. Karma's a bitch, *que no?* Not to be outdone, Zurdo regaled him and Yuli with stories about his time in Hollywood. Time that, for all I knew, had been less than a year in length.

"So I told Guillermo, 'You need to put something in Spanish here, man.' That's how *Babalú* came to be in *The Shape of Water* soundtrack!"

He made it look like he was on a first-name basis with Brad Pitt and had breakfast on Tuesdays with Leonardo DiCaprio. Ashley kept quiet because she didn't always understand what Zurdo said in his rapid-fire Cuban Spanish, but I rolled my eyes so often that they seriously began to hurt.

HAVANA REMINDED ME OF Tijuana in some ways—the murals, the colorful façades, the performers around Cathedral Square, *la gente* speaking *español*. But places to eat were few and far between. (El Paladar de Carmela turned out to be the exception, not the rule.) A *tortilla* was a one-egg omelet. There were no *taquerías*. My inquiries about *burritos* made people laugh as they thought I wanted to buy small donkeys. On the other hand, there were no beggars or street kids, though we were often approached by adult hustlers. But they weren't aggressive. It felt safe to walk anywhere, even after dark.

Our little team got along well. We had chemistry or, like

Zurdo put it, *sandunga*. While Yuli and Ramón worked on our short, they also rehearsed for a play—the opening night was scheduled for three months later at the prestigious Sala Teatro El Sótano. They were, no doubt, real actors, and we were lucky to be working with them.

WE RAN INTO THE first stumbling block when attempting to shoot a scene at the National Library, where the protagonist met her lover—a bookish literature professor masterfully played by Ramón. At the sight of Ashley's camera and tripod, a library employee blocked our way.

"Do you have permission to film inside?" she demanded.

Ramón and Yuli argued that the library was a public place. The employee didn't budge. Ramón got pissed and sent her to *el carajo*. She kicked us out, unceremoniously, and threatened to call security if we went back.

I was crestfallen because the library location was central to the plot, but Zurdo promised that his "contacts" would take care of the issue.

Days passed. Zurdo said he was in talks with the Cuban Institute of Radio and Television higher-ups. He also reached out to his former colleagues. The permit never materialized.

"Why don't we shoot the scene in Coppelia, like a homage to *Fresa y Chocolate*?" he proposed with fake enthusiasm.

Ramón wasn't pleased with the change.

"*Coño, chico!*" he snapped. "I thought you knew some people. But it seems like no one even knows you!"

In the meantime, Ashley found excuses to get close to Ramón, asking him about low angles and bird's eye views, but obviously more interested in his square shoulders and bulging muscles than camera shots. These exchanges created some friction as Zurdo was still, technically, the director. They also gave Zurdo a chance to be alone with Yuli. I started to feel like the fifth wheel.

THE MALECÓN SEAWALL WAS the perfect setting for a romantic scene. "Passionate but tasteful," my parentheticals read.

"Guys, keep it mild," Zurdo said.

But Ramón and Yuli went wild. Zurdo yelled "cut" with more force than necessary. His mouth twisted, he looked jealous and annoyed. It suddenly dawned on me that he had a crush on our leading lady, like Ashley did on our leading man.

The next day, Yuli and Ramón behaved differently. Less than actors, more like a couple that had had an argument the night before. When not on camera, Ramón addressed his wife in a curt, bossy manner. It was awkward for all of us, but nobody dared to intervene.

Tensions rose. Ramón got rude, bordering on abusive. Ashley amped up her attempts to win his attention. Yuli, as if to spite her husband, started flirting with Zurdo. The team chemistry changed. My plot took a backseat to real-life drama.

Not long afterwards, on a break, I caught Zurdo and Yuli kissing behind a baroque column at Cathedral Square.

At lunchtime, the actors walked together to a peso cafeteria. Ashley and I opted for the dollar-only establishment La Bodeguita del Medio, which had a better and more varied menu. Zurdo went somewhere else on his own. We should have invited them all, but Ashley and I needed to be alone. Let's face it—an affair happening right under your nose is always worth discussing.

La Bodeguita is known for Hemingway's words: "My

mojito in La Bodeguita, my daiquirí in El Floridita." The walls were covered by the signatures of famous and not-so-famous patrons. A huge black-and-white photo of Hemingway presided over the room.

Sipping our drinks, Ashley and I assessed the circumstances.

"Yuli's way out of Zurdo's league," she said. "He doesn't have a chance."

"*Pues*, he does," I countered. "Not because Yuli's so much into him, but she probably sees him as her ticket to Hollywood."

"Come on, Lupita! Do you think they believe he's friends with Guillermo del Toro?" Ashley laughed so hard that she spat her mojito, then got serious again. "Though it wouldn't be a bad idea if Yuli ends up with Zurdo as that would free Ramón for me."

I wasn't about to tell her that Ramón was way out of *her* league.

ONE AFTERNOON, RAMÓN HAD another commitment and left the set early. Then Zurdo brought Yuli to the *casa particular*. He asked Margarita for permission to use her phone—a prehistoric device with a rotary dial—because our cellphones didn't work in Havana. As Yuli stood nearby, Zurdo called the American embassy.

"How can I get a visa for a Cuban citizen? Uh, I am . . . well not an American citizen, but a permanent resident. Yes, a business visa, a work visa, whatever . . ."

There was no way to know what response he got, but Yuli seemed impressed. She blew a kiss at Zurdo when he hung up the phone. Margarita glowered.

"*La* Yulita and that guy with the ponytail are up to no good," she said when the pair left.

Ashley chuckled, but the incident left a bad taste in my mouth.

ZURDO AND YULI'S AFFAIR heated up quickly, but Ramón failed to notice Ashley's puppy love. It wasn't like he rejected her. He just didn't *see* her, at least the way she wanted to be seen. Her hopes shattered, she stopped finding the situation funny and turned into Miss Morals.

"Those two have no shame!" she fumed. "Someone should tell Ramón!"

"He knows, *pendeja*. Don't you hear how he talks to Yuli? The guy's mad, but what can he do?"

"Then someone ought to tell *her*. Zurdo is not taking her anywhere! I can't believe she fell for that 'work visa' sham."

"Stay out of it."

At that point, a fight could mean the end of the movie. Wait until we finish shooting, I thought, then let hell break loose.

Unexpectedly, Zurdo moved out of the *casa*. He said he was going to stay with a friend who had a nicer home and a better bed. I suspected it wasn't the accommodations he cared about. He wanted privacy—a "love nest" away from prying eyes.

TOWARDS THE END WE were shooting in Parque Central, an iconic square surrounded by palm trees. Ashley kept asking Yuli to get close to the statue of José Martí, which made for a great background against the clear blue sky, but she insisted on standing under a tree because it was "too hot."

"I'm so tired of you playing diva!" Ashley yelled.

She kicked a tripod. It hit Yuli in the chest. Then things

got out of hand. Yuli went for Ashley's hair. Ashley shoved our leading lady. Ramón pulled his wife aside and slapped her hard. Think Steve McQueen and Ali MacGraw in *The Getaway*.

The crew disbanded.

Chinga.

That evening Zurdo took Ashley out to "have a talk" with her. I stayed in the *casa*, feeling dejected about the collapse of what had started as a great partnership. Even if we got the movie finished, it wouldn't be the same. No matter what happened with Zurdo and Yuli (and I expected it would be *nada*, and he would forget her as soon as we left), the experience had been soured for all.

ZURDO MANAGED TO UNRUFFLE feathers and convinced Ashley and Yuli to shoot the last scenes. The spell, though, had been broken, at least for our leading man. Ramón recited his lines without much feeling or expression, his passion gone. Yuli, on the contrary, did some of her best acting, either to please Zurdo or to show her husband *she* was truly a professional.

After the closing scene was over (Ramón and Yuli staring into each other's eyes near the Malecón wall), Zurdo yelled "Cut, it's a wrap!" A deep sense of relief filled me. Good or bad, the movie was finished. Ashley and I high-fived each other, but nobody else seemed to be in a celebratory mood.

Zurdo excused himself, exchanged a knowing glance with Yuli, and left.

Ramón approached Yuli. "*Mi amor . . .*"

She turned her face away.

"Ah, *chica, vete pal carajo!*" he yelled.

He raised his hand as if to hit her, but then backed off and left. To my surprise, Ashley handed me the camera and trotted after him.

Now that our project was over, I finally allowed myself to feel sorry for Yuli. It was time to have a heart-to-heart conversation with her and show some sisterhood.

"Are you and Zurdo . . . ?" I asked softly.

She sat on the Malecón wall. "You figured it out, eh?"

"Everyone has. But your husband . . ."

"He suspects," she shrugged. "Anyway, I'm telling him tonight."

"*What* are you telling him?"

The sun hung low, casting her in a light that Ashley would have loved. The breeze ruffled her short hair. She had gotten rid of the wig as soon as the last shot was over.

"That I'm leaving."

Long strands of seaweed had washed up on the rocks. A pungent, almost putrid smell filled the air.

"Yuli, do you know who Zurdo is?"

She lifted a perfect eyebrow but said nothing.

"He's no Hollywood insider," I told her gravely. "All the stories he told you? Lies. *Pura mierda.*"

"You mean he didn't give music advice to Guillermo del Toro?"

"In his dreams! He works at the community college Ashley and I attend. The short's a class project."

Yuli's response was long, hearty laughter. Her eyes twinkled. She obviously thought I was kidding her.

"Zurdo's a fake," I added, curtly. Her naiveté was getting on my nerves. "He can't get you an American visa any more than he can cast you with Brad Pitt!"

She stared me down for a long time. When she spoke at

last, only three words came out of her pretty mouth. "*No me jodas.*"

With that, she stood up and walked away. So much for sisterhood and heart-to-heart conversations!

Carrying the camera as if it were a baby—indeed, it had *my* baby inside—I returned to the *casa* and spent the afternoon looking at the videos stored in the memory cards. Ashley hadn't come back. I wondered if she had hooked up with Ramón after all. Which made little sense, as we would be flying back to Tijuana in three days. But maybe she had to scratch that itch. Whatever, I concluded. To each their own.

Around 8 P.M., Ashley was nowhere to be found.

"She must have found a Cuban boyfriend," Margarita joked.

"I'm starting to worry."

"Don't, *mija*. Havana is very safe."

I didn't feel like eating out alone. Margarita made supper for me—fried chicken, rice, and a small salad. Though still concerned about Ashley, I got in bed and fell asleep as soon as my head touched the pillow.

A thud against the outside wall woke me up. It sounded as if a rock or some heavy object had hit it. The light switch was in the other end of the room. I grabbed my cellphone, turned on the flashlight and looked around. Ashley's bed was still empty.

I ran to the window and opened it. A woman was lying on the curb, under a lamppost. A man was leaning over her, hitting her on the head with his fist. They weren't fighting, though, as she didn't attempt to defend herself and her body looked strangely limp. The guy had his back to the building, which made it impossible to see his face, but I did see his ponytail swinging behind. I cried out and, almost instinctively, took a picture. The flash must have alerted the man, who ran away while Margarita's cries came from the second floor.

"*Ataja al criminal!*"

BY THE TIME I threw on a dress and left the room, Margarita and a neighbor had carried the woman inside and put her on the couch. I glanced at her and recoiled in horror. It was Yuli, her dress torn and her face covered in blood. She didn't seem to be breathing. She looked, in fact, dead.

"It was Zurdo!" Margarita yelled. "I saw him run away!"

Other neighbors rushed in. Someone went to fetch Ramón, who came over wearing only a pair of shorts.

"*Mi amor!*" He began to clean the blood off Yuli's face.

An ambulance arrived. The paramedics pushed Ramón aside. Someone said that the police were on their way.

In the middle of this chaos Ashley showed up, disheveled and smelling of beer and sweat.

"What—what's going on?" she stammered.

She tripped over the leg of a rocking chair. Ramón took her by her arm and steadied her, leading her away from the scene. When he came back alone, the paramedics had taken Yuli to the ambulance. Ramón left with them.

A police car, blue lights flashing, parked in front of the *casa*. I hurried to our room. Ashley was slumped over the loveseat.

"Where were you?" I asked.

"With Ramón."

"You mean in their apartment? All this time?"

She looked down, avoiding my eyes.

"Yes. We were in bed when the racket began downstairs."

It took me a while to process *that*.

"We were drinking together." Her voice quavered. "I'm so scared, girl."

She began sobbing. Margarita came over.

"The *policía* wants to talk to all of us," she said.

IN MY STATEMENT, I was as specific as possible without mentioning Zurdo's name because I wasn't totally sure that he had been the assailant. Margarita, however, had no such qualms.

"I always knew that the guy was up to no good!" she declared.

I kept mum about the photo, afraid that the cop, a young and wiry lieutenant, would confiscate my phone and keep it after I left. (And at that time, I was hoping to leave as soon as possible.) The picture I had taken was probably too dark to serve any purpose. But mostly, I didn't want to get entangled in that mess. Getting involved in a crime, in a foreign country where I didn't even know the laws and my rights? No, thanks. Besides, it didn't seem necessary. The first neighbor who showed up had gotten a glimpse of the attacker and described him as well.

Slurring her words, Ashley repeated that she and Ramón had been together for most of the evening.

"Weren't you afraid that his wife would catch you?" the lieutenant asked tersely.

"Eh . . . no," Ashley mumbled. "Ramón said they had already broken up for good."

The cop took notes. He left an hour later, after handing out cards with his phone number.

"Make sure to call me if you remember any other detail."

THE NEXT DAY WE learned through the grapevine that Yuli was already dead by the time they took her to the hospital, which didn't surprise me. Zurdo was the main suspect because he matched the description of the attacker. But he claimed he had been waiting for Yuli at his friend's house. Alone. That night, his friend had left "to give them some privacy." And after all, why would he kill Yuli, people wondered, when she was willing to leave her husband for him?

The day of our return flight came, but Ashley and I weren't allowed to leave the island because the investigation was still underway. We weren't suspects, the *policía* told us, only "persons of interest," whatever that meant.

After talking it over with Ashley, who wasn't much help ("I don't care what you do, I just want to go home," was all she said), I called the lieutenant and related my last conversation with Yuli. Not an easy decision, as she hadn't said anything of substance in response. But I figured that, afterwards, she had confronted Zurdo and they had had a fight. She must have been on her way home when he attacked her. Or maybe they had started to argue right there, in the street.

By then I didn't care about our film anymore. *Havana Caliente*, which had meant so much to me, had only caused trouble. Yuli was dead. Zurdo, guilty or not (okay, probably guilty, but still), had been thrown in jail. (Since he wasn't an American citizen and we hadn't traveled to Cuba legally, he couldn't ask for help at the embassy.) And Ashley spent hours holed up in bed, barely acknowledging my presence or Margarita's.

"Do you know," she asked me once, after I tried to comfort her, "that I was a suspect too?"

"How come?"

"The fight I had with Yuli . . ."

She hung her head. I thought she was exaggerating but didn't argue. Though I hadn't been a suspect, I felt guilt-ridden as well. Ah, if I hadn't told Yuli anything about Zurdo! Then their affair would have fizzled out, and she and Ramón would have reconciled after we all left. But I had opened my big mouth. Yuli's death, hard as it was to admit it, had been my fault.

A WEEK LATER, WE were informed that Zurdo had been formally charged with Yuli's murder. The investigation over, Ashley and I were free to go home. I can't even start to tell you how relieved we were to leave behind that Cuban nightmare. We got new return tickets for the earliest flight.

Back to the *casa*, Ashley was in the kitchen settling the bill with Margarita. I had finished packing but stayed in our room. Neither of us went outside much. Last thing we wanted was meeting Ramón again. It would have been awkward and painful. What could anyone say to him, poor guy?

Alone in the room, I took out my cellphone and noticed that the storage space was full. Of course, all those pics I had been taking. Why keep them? I didn't need reminders of that fateful trip. As it was, all its excruciating details were forever etched in my mind. All I wanted to do at that point was get out of Cuba, go on with my life and forget *Havana Caliente* and its protagonists.

Our table at El Paladar de Carmela. Delete. The *picadillo*. Delete. Ramón and Zurdo standing by an *almendrón*. Delete, delete. Parque Central, minutes before the fight. The strain on Ashley's face was clear. Not Yuli. She didn't wear her feelings on her sleeve. Well, she was an actor.

Pretty girl, *pobrecita*. Delete, delete. And there, *Dios mío*, was Zurdo beating her. The picture was dark but you could see his ponytail clearly. No room for mistakes.

I took one last look.

"Zurdo, *cabrón*," I whispered.

But a second before I pressed delete, a realization hit me.

The man in the picture was striking the woman with his right hand.

Numb, I stared at the screen for a long time. My mind went back to Yuli sitting on the Malecón wall. Her twinkling eyes, her laughter. *You mean he didn't give music advice to Guillermo del Toro?* And then another realization made my cheeks sting. She had been laughing at *me*.

Yuli knew from the start that Zurdo was a liar. But she still wanted to take her chances with him, either because she had fallen in love or because he looked like an opportunity, no matter how small, for her to start a new life. That day, she had gone home and told her husband that she was leaving him.

And then Ramón . . .

People will see what you want them to see.

I enlarged the image, focusing on Yuli's limp body and suddenly understood that, by the time the picture was taken, she had already been dead.

ASHLEY CAME BACK FROM the kitchen, nibbling a guava pastry.

"Did you actually spend that evening with Ramón?" I asked point-blank.

She turned pale.

"Why . . . why are you asking me now?"

"Because I think you lied."

"I didn't."

But her voice quavered. She plopped down on the loveseat.

"*Ay*, Lupita . . ."

I sat next to her.

"You can tell me the truth, girl," I whispered. "We are friends, *que no?*"

She nodded dolefully. I squeezed her hand.

"Come on, *chiquita*. Did you meet with Ramón at all?"

"Not really." Her cheeks flushed. "When I caught up with him, he blew me off. I went to La Bodeguita and ordered like a couple of mojitos. Afterwards, I careened in El Floridita for daiquiris. That's all I did that evening—get drunk."

"Yes, you were pretty wasted when you got here."

"Then Ramón took me aside and said that, if Yuli was dead, as it seemed, we both would be suspects. He, because he was next of kin and she was cheating on him. Me, because of the fight we had had."

"But that wasn't enough reason to . . ."

"I know, but I was drunk. And he made me *feel* like a suspect. I didn't have an alibi. He convinced me to say that we had been together, to protect each other. It all happened so fast that I didn't have time to think it over. After you guys recognized Zurdo, I saw no point in changing my story, but it has been eating at me ever since . . ."

I exhaled heavily and reached for my phone.

"Because, no matter what you guys saw, and even if Yuli had broken up with Zurdo," she concluded, "I don't believe he'd have killed her."

"You're right," I said. "But Ramón had more at stake. His pride was wounded, for one thing. He had a temper, too. He slapped her once, remember? And he had that awful argument with the library employee."

"But how come you all saw Zurdo?"

I showed her the last, and by now the only picture on my cellphone. Her eyes grew big and terrified.

"When did you take that pic?"

"Look at it."

"I *am* looking. That's Zurdo!"

"Are you sure?"

She squinted. "He looks a little thinner. But see the ponytail? That's him!"

"That's Ramón wearing a wig tied up in a ponytail. After killing Yuli, he left the apartment with her body. He threw a rock at our window and maybe others so people looked out, saw them, and 'recognized' Zurdo. He hit Yuli again before running away and going back home, likely through the building's other entrance."

Ashley stared at me in horror and recognition.

"I always suspected . . . But why did he get me involved then?"

"To add an extra layer of security, I guess. In any case, it doesn't matter anymore," I stood up. "We are going back to the *policía* right now. You're going to tell the truth, and I'll show them this picture."

"Will they believe us?" she asked in a shaky, hopeful voice.

"There's no reason why they won't."

"But we'll have to buy new tickets. And we don't have much money left!"

"So what? We may end up begging our families to rescue us and selling *burritos* in TJ to repay them, but it doesn't matter. Zurdo is only a self-aggrandizing asshole, not a killer. And this photo may be the only way to exonerate him."

So that was that. And here we are, still stranded on an island of which so many things, good and bad, have been said.

FATAL ASSUMPTIONS

||||||| Pamela Samuels Young

"But why two weeks?" Mia asks. "Laura never stays longer than a weekend."

I don't normally make a habit of eavesdropping, but my brother's cracked bedroom door beckons to me like that second piece of cheesecake I couldn't resist last night.

"We haven't seen each other since this whole COVID nightmare started," Larry tells his wife. "Laura and I have a lot of brother-sister bonding to make up for."

I've always viewed Mia as the sister I never had. And I thought she felt the same way about me. Apparently not. Knowing that Mia doesn't want me here—at least not for two weeks—stings a bit. Actually, it stings quite a bit. But my brother's right. We desperately needed to connect. Two years is a long time to be unable to reach out and touch the one person in the world you love the most. The fact that I flew all the way from New York to Los Angeles in the midst of a COVID spike is a testament to just how important this trip was to me.

It's hard for most people to understand the connection between twins, especially ones like me and Larry. Our parents never encouraged our individuality. We came as a pair and have happily stayed that way for the past forty-one years. And since losing both of our parents, we've clung even tighter to each other. I always joke that Larry is my phantom limb. Even when he isn't near me, I can still feel his presence.

I hear Mia walking toward the door so I continue down the hallway, maintaining my same carefree stride, resisting the urge to pick up my pace. That's the mistake guilty people make. When they're caught in the act, they *act* like they're guilty. Stuttering when asked a simple question or nervously looking around instead of making eye contact. And, of course, the true sign of guilt: making a run for it.

I know a lot about guilt and guilty people. As a prosecutor, I've spent the last ten years putting away bad guys. And a fair share of wayward women too.

"Good morning, Mia," I call back over my shoulder as I'm about to enter the guest bedroom.

"Hey, Laura," Mia says flatly as she continues past me and heads downstairs.

My one and only sister-in-law has been in an unusually funky mood since my arrival two days ago. Perhaps it's my desire not to be the interloper, but my gut tells me her errant disposition is about more than my unexpected invasion of her personal space.

My first inkling of trouble in paradise was the vibe, or lack thereof, between Larry and Mia. It's solidly off-kilter. This is the first visit where I haven't witnessed a single kiss on the cheek "just because." The glaringly easy laughter they used to share is hidden behind a wall of pretense. I haven't seen them touch each other even once. Their giddy, adolescent-like love connection that I'd envied for years seems to no longer exist.

Larry lumbers into the guest bedroom dressed in jeans and a T-shirt, work attire that aptly fits his personality. My brother greets me with a much warmer welcome.

"What's up with the best sister in the whole wide world?" he says, squeezing my shoulder.

This handsome six-foot, gregarious marketing executive epitomizes the phrase "people person." When his company instituted a work-from-home policy over a year ago, Larry was one of a handful of employees who eagerly volunteered to continue coming into the office. Unlike his buttoned-up wife, my brother prefers face-to-face consultations over aloof Zoom meetings.

"Thanks for getting Kelli to school this morning. She's absolutely thrilled to have her favorite aunt around."

"Ditto for me. But what's going on with Mia? She's not her normal cheery self."

I don't mention the noticeable disconnect between them. I know Larry had been planning a surprise trip for the two of them, which he'd recently put on the backburner. I assumed COVID was the reason it was on hold. Perhaps there's more to that story.

"She's ticked off that her company ordered all the managers back to the office while everyone else still gets to work from home."

I'm not buying my brother's cover story. Something much bigger than where Mia plugs in her laptop is at the core of her bad attitude.

"You sure?" I prod. "She just doesn't seem like herself."

Larry shrugs. "It's probably just a hormonal thing. But if you figure out what's going on with her, please do share."

WHEN MIA ARRIVES HOME from work, I'm determined to lift her spirits and get things back on track between us. I ignore the disinterested look on her face and focus on her beige designer pantsuit. The bronze satin blouse perfectly highlights the dark undertones in her skin.

"I love that power suit," I say, gazing up at her from the couch in the great room. "If I stepped into a courtroom wearing an outfit that snazzy, the judge would have to declare a mistrial because I'd literally have the jury eating out of my hands."

Mia works as a senior manager for a major pharmaceutical company. If I got stock options every year, I'd be able to dress like a *Vogue* model too. She smiles, kicks off her heels, then wearily plops down on the couch next to me and Kelli. Since picking her up from school, I've kept my 10-year-old niece busy munching on popcorn and binge-watching cartoons on Disney+.

"Aunt Laura ordered pizza for dinner," says Kelli, who looks more like me than her mother. "It'll be here in thirty minutes."

Mia yawns and gets to her feet. "Thanks for doing that. Let me change clothes and I'll be right back."

Nearly an hour later, Mia still hasn't rejoined us. So I tiptoe down the hallway to find out what's up. She's sitting on her bed, still dressed, staring down at her iPad.

"Hey, Mia, the—"

She slams her iPad case closed, but not before I see the red Wells Fargo logo in the upper left-hand corner of the tablet's screen.

Only the guilty act guilty.

"The pizza's here," I tell her. "And Larry's just pulling up."

Protectively tucking the iPad under her arm, Mia stands. "Sorry. I had a work thing I needed to deal with. I'll be there in a minute."

When Mia finally joins us in the great room fifteen minutes later, Kelli, Larry, and I are enjoying a good, loud laugh.

"What's so funny?" she asks, an amused look on her face.

For the last five minutes Larry's been ribbing me about his best friend Jack, a blowhard who would flirt with a floor plant just because it was there.

"Mom, tell Aunt Laura she should've gone on a date with Uncle Jack before he got married again," Kelli says. "He's really nice and rich too. Even richer than Daddy."

Larry chuckles. "Not with two ex-wives he isn't."

Mia makes a show of rolling her eyes. "Aunt Laura definitely made the right decision by taking a pass on Uncle Jack."

She walks into the kitchen and starts dishing slices of pizza onto four paper plates.

"Make sure you add lots of parmesan cheese to mine," Larry tells her.

"Yuck," Kelli says, screwing up her face. "Daddy always puts a ton of parmesan on his pizza."

"It's a family tradition," I say. "Load mine up too."

I step into the kitchen and see Mia grating swirls of fresh parmesan cheese over one of the plates.

"Can I help?"

"Nope. I have this under control." She sends me back to the couch. "You already did the hard part. You ordered the pizza."

Minutes later, she hands Larry a plate of pizza piled high with parmesan, just the way he likes it.

"Oh, that's a little sexist," I protest. "Why does he get served first?"

"Yeah," Kelli chimes in.

Larry grins. "Because I'm the man of the house."

"Hold your horses," Mia says, stalking back over to the kitchen counter. "Your plates are on the way."

She hurries back to us and hands Kelli a plate with no added cheese. My pizza is covered with parmesan, but it's not freshly grated like Larry's. I glance toward the kitchen and see the plastic container of parmesan cheese sitting on the counter.

How petty, I want to say, but don't. This is obviously Mia's passive-aggressive way of letting me know I'm not wanted here. *Too bad. I'm staying.*

Larry takes a big bite of his parmesan-smothered pizza, then tries to get Kelli to taste it. "You have no idea what you're missing. Just try it."

"No, way." Mia stuffs herself into the small space on the couch between father and daughter. "That much cheese would have her constipated for days."

Kelli grimaces. "Don't worry, Mom. You and me are gonna eat our pizza like normal people."

"Bro," I say with a smile, "we gotta get to work on making a cheese head out of my niece."

I WAKE UP TO the sound of animated voices. My eyes gravitate to the digital clock on the nightstand. It's just after three in the morning. I hop out of bed and hustle downstairs toward the sound of the commotion.

My brother is leaning over the kitchen island, cupping his forehead. I rush up to him as Mia flanks him on the opposite side, her face etched with worry.

"I feel like crap," he mumbles in a thick, raspy voice that sounds nothing like his own. He's gasping for air, his breath coming out in short, fast gasps. If I didn't know his medical history as well as I know my own, I'd think he was having an asthma attack.

Mia presses an ice pack to Larry's sweaty face. His T-shirt is soaked with perspiration and matted to his chest.

I reach down to feel my brother's forehead. "My God. You're burning up!"

"I don't know what's wrong," Larry says, barely able to speak. "I can't breathe."

COVID is my first thought, but I can't bring myself to say the words out loud.

Instead, I snatch the house phone and dial 911.

FEAR.

That's the only emotion I can muster as Mia and I sit on the bed staring at Larry's image on the screen of her iPad. Seeing my brother hooked up to a breathing machine, barely conscious, is wreaking havoc on my heart.

"I love you," Mia says softly.

The maze of tubes stuffed down Larry's nose makes it difficult for him to respond, audibly or otherwise. Acknowledging us with a quick wave or even a faint smile would require a level of energy Larry no longer possesses.

"You're going to be okay," I whisper. "You have to be."

Mia's eyes are wet with tears. "We love you so much."

The steady humming and beeping of the machines surrounding Larry's bed are like a sad lullaby. The whole scene reeks of gloom.

"We should probably sign off now," the nurse says gently. "He needs to get some rest."

The screen of the iPad fades to black but Mia and I continue to stare at it like an anxious audience waiting for an encore.

"I don't understand why the virus hit him so hard," I say.

"Larry didn't take COVID seriously enough." Mia sniffs and wipes her eyes with a tissue. "He never thought it could happen to him."

Mia often complained to me about my brother's bad habit of walking into a store without a mask on and having to run back to the car to retrieve one. When he didn't forget to put one on, he often carelessly let it slip below his nose. Larry genuinely believed his upbeat attitude about life would place a wall of protection around him, keeping the virus at bay.

Mia pulls me into a tight embrace. "I'm so glad you're here. There's no way I could get through this without you."

"I just can't believe it's really happening," I mumble.

Earlier in the day, an unfocused, obviously overworked doctor advised us that Larry might not make it through the night.

"You have to be kidding," I said, horrified that he was making such a grim prediction so soon. "It's only been two days. And he's vaccinated."

"There's no way to predict with any certainty how quickly the virus will attack someone's immune system," the doctor explained. "And being vaccinated doesn't provide one hundred percent protection. Your brother is obviously a breakthrough case."

"Is Daddy going to die of COVID?" Kelli opens the closed bedroom door and steps inside. Her face is even sadder than ours.

Mia and I instantly straighten up and try to pretend we haven't just been crying our eyes out. Kelli's question catches us off guard. We'd been careful not to discuss Larry's condition in her presence, hoping to shield her from the pain we were all experiencing. An impossible task.

"Come here, sweetheart." Mia spreads her arms wide as Kelli rushes to her.

I wait in silence, leaving it to Mia to respond to her daughter's agonizing question.

"Daddy is very, very sick," she finally says. "And we're praying really hard that he's going to be okay."

As I close my eyes to do just that, I'm thankful that Kelli didn't enter the room a few seconds earlier. Otherwise she would've seen the image of her listless father on that iPad screen. If Larry doesn't make it, that should not be the last image a daughter should have of her father.

Or a sister of her brother.

EARLY THE NEXT MORNING, we receive the call we had hoped would never come. Larry died at 4:47 A.M.

Death by COVID intensifies the magnitude of our loss. We could not be at Larry's bedside during his final moments. And even after death, the virus steals our chance to say a final goodbye.

The following few days are a blur, whizzing past us like a fast-moving snowstorm. Mia and I lean on each other, just as Larry and I would have done. When Mia refuses to get out of bed, I busy myself making sure Kelli has breakfast, lunch and dinner. I make the calls to family and friends. I proudly wear a mask of strength during the day, only surrendering to my own grief in the solitude of darkness.

As I numbly carry on, I cannot shake the ominous feeling that something isn't right. I refuse to accept that COVID could've taken my brother so quickly. The prosecutor in me wants answers beyond the ones provided by the doctors and nurses.

After confirming that both Mia and Kelli are asleep, I search for Larry's cell phone. I have no idea what I'm looking for, but this seems like a good place to start. If Mia happens to catch me snooping, I'll just say I'm searching for more of Larry's friends to contact.

I find his phone on the desk in his home office. After locking the door and plugging the phone into the charger, I hold it up to my face, wondering if the facial recognition might mistake my face for Larry's since we're twins. That, of course, fails. Luckily, since college, my very predictable brother has used a variation of the same passcode: our mother's maiden name plus the street address of our first home. I'd watched him type it in once, and told him it wasn't secure enough. He ignored me. When an account forced him to change it, he simply rearranged the order of the numbers.

It takes me only three tries before I'm successfully scrolling through Larry's emails. Other than the occasional spam, his emails are nearly all work-related. Not a single clue jumps out at me. His internet browsing history, phone call log and voicemails offer no answers either.

I'm about to reach the same conclusion regarding his text messages when a string of texts jumps off the screen at me.

> *I love you.*
> *I love you more.*
> *When can you get away?*
> *Maybe Thursday night.*
> *I don't know if I can wait that long.*
> *Don't worry. I'll make it worth the wait.*
> *I know you will.*

My first reaction is disbelief. *How could I not know my brother was having an affair?* Larry wasn't the type of guy who cheated on his wife. Or was he?

Without warning, my shock is replaced by a sensation of outrage so potent I can feel it oozing down my throat.

For our entire lives, we shared everything. The good and the bad. He knew my most embarrassing moments. My disappointments. My failures. And I thought I knew his.

As I struggle to come to terms with my brother's disgusting betrayal, I think of Mia. How could Larry deceive her like this? I'm not sure how long I sat there, motionless, my fury escalating. In that moment, some of the clues to this shocking puzzle start falling into place.

Mia knew.

That would certainly explain why she had been so aloof lately. The image of Mia slamming her iPad case closed so I wouldn't see what was on the screen came back to me. Why would she need to hide the fact that she was looking at her bank account? Was she searching for proof that Larry was spending *their* money on his mistress?

I return to Larry's cell phone and try to open the Wells Fargo app. Multiple attempts at guessing his password fail. I give up when the app warns me that I'm about to be locked out of the account and will have to contact customer service to reset it.

Then another memory hits me.

The day after I arrived, I was relaxing in the great room when Larry left for a run. A couple minutes later, a soft chime caught my attention and my eyes gravitated to his cell phone sitting on the coffee table in front of me.

I leaned forward to take a look at the screen. Before my eyes could register what was on it, Larry's big hand appeared from nowhere, snatching it away.

"Forgot my phone," he said breathlessly, as he tucked it into the pocket of his sweats.

A spark of panic flashed across his face, quickly replaced by a smile.

"I see you're still just as nosy as you were at twelve."

Only the guilty act guilty.

Now, I'm even more motivated to keep digging. I dial the number attached to the text messages and a woman picks up. I speak before she does.

"This is Laura, Larry's sister. I need you to tell me everything."

IT'S BEEN MORE THAN a month since my brother's death, and I'm still barely functioning. I returned to New York the week after Larry's memorial service and spent the first few days walking around in a fog of grief. After a co-worker found me locked in a ladies' room stall bawling when I was supposed to be arguing a motion, my boss suggested I take some more time off. So I flew back to Los Angeles to be with the only family I have left: Mia and Kelli.

I haven't told Mia about the texts I found on Larry's phone or what I learned from the woman who sent them. I've been patiently waiting for the right moment. For weeks, I've fretted over what I know. After all, I still love Mia like a sister. But it's finally time.

The next day, after we have lunch, I make sure Kelli is safely upstairs, occupied with a video game. I can't risk the possibility of her overhearing what I have to share with Mia. Since Larry's death, we've all found our individual ways to deal with our unbearable grief. Kelli copes by gluing herself to a computer screen.

Mia is sitting on the patio sipping a glass of white wine when I step outside.

I'm happy to see progress in Mia's emotional resolve. She no longer spends all day in bed and is at least showering and getting dressed in the morning. But she still sits on the patio for hours at a time, staring at nothing.

"We need to talk," I say, taking a chair directly across from her.

Mia quickly waves a hand in front of her face. "I'm still not ready to discuss the finances. Larry made you his trustee. Whatever you want to do is fine with me. I trust you."

"That's not what I wanted to talk to you about." I pause to take a breath as I fight to control my own emotions.

"Right after Larry died, I went through his phone. And I came across some text messages. Some very disturbing text messages."

For several seconds, Mia's face displays no reaction. Then she exhales. "You and Larry were so close. I always wondered whether you knew he had a mistress." Her tone is thick with accusation.

"No, I didn't know," I say. "And for the record. Larry didn't have a mistress."

A cynical smile curls Mia's lips before she takes a sip from her wineglass. "You just told me you saw those text messages. How can you say that?"

"How did *you* see them?" I ask.

"I logged into his Apple account. So don't tell me he wasn't having an affair. I'm not stupid."

I was about to ask how she got into Larry's account, but if I could guess my brother's password, of course his wife could easily do the same.

"I called the telephone number those texts came from," I say. "The woman who answered admitted sending them, but said she wasn't having an affair with Larry."

"Of course she'd say that. She's lying."

"No, she's telling the truth. Actually, she was having an affair with Jack, not Larry. Larry was simply covering for his best friend."

"What?" Mia glares at me, her gaze so intense I can almost feel it graze my cheek.

"It was Jack she was sleeping with, not Larry. Whenever they were in the office together, Larry let Jack use his phone to text her because his wife was constantly checking his."

An expression I'm having trouble deciphering distorts Mia's pretty face.

"He . . . Larry wasn't having an affair?"

"No," I say again. "And I've confirmed all of this with Jack. What in the world made you check Larry's phone in the first place?"

A snarl stretches across her face. "I guess I could ask you the same thing."

Before I can respond, Mia's anger evaporates and she hangs her head.

"I checked his phone because he started being really secretive. Always keeping it close to him. Turning it face down whenever I came into the room. He never acted like that before. So I decided to check his Apple account. That's when I saw those texts."

Mia closes her eyes and traces the rim of the wineglass with her index finger.

I take another long breath before disclosing my next earth-shattering revelation. "And my brother didn't die from COVID."

Mia flinches and her eyes spring open. "But the doctor said—"

"Before I went back to New York, I called the hospital and demanded written proof that Larry had COVID. And you know what? He'd never been tested."

Her mouth gapes open.

"When they checked Larry's records," I continue, "they

discovered that no one gave him a COVID test when he first got to the hospital. Things were so chaotic and the hospital was so understaffed, it was just overlooked. The nurse who was supposed to do it became ill during her shift and went home early. No one noticed that the test hadn't been done. Since his symptoms looked like COVID, everyone assumed he had it, so they concentrated on getting his fever under control and helping him breathe."

"But what made you suspect that he didn't die from COVID in the first place?" Mia asks.

"Larry was so strong and athletic. I know it kills healthy people too, but I just couldn't accept that it could happen to him. And after we took those at-home tests and found out we were all negative, I was even more suspicious. You would think that at least one of us would've come down with it."

Mia's expression is unreadable now.

I quietly inhale, then proceed. "Isn't there something you want to ask me?" My tone is almost taunting.

Her eyes refuse to meet mine. "What? I . . . I don't know. I think I'm in shock."

"You haven't asked me how Larry *really* died."

Mia swallows hard. "Well, how *did* he die? Was it pneumonia?"

"No, it wasn't pneumonia," I snap at her. "You already know how he died."

"What are you talking about?"

"Admit that you killed my brother!"

The wineglass slips from Mia's trembling hand and shatters against the cement patio.

"The stress of Larry's death is obviously making you crazy," she says. "You were here when that ambulance took Larry to the hospital. He was alive. What are you saying? That I snuck into the hospital and killed him?"

I can no longer hold back my rage. "You put all of this in motion. Anybody who walked into that hospital with a breathing problem would probably be treated like a COVID patient. And that's exactly what you were banking on."

Mia presses a palm to her forehead. "Laura, please stop talking nonsense."

"After they told me Larry didn't have COVID, I demanded that he be tested for poisoning. The results just came back two days ago and it turns out my brother *was* poisoned. By you!"

A single tear begins to trickle down Mia's cheek. "That's . . . that's not true. I—"

"You poisoned him with thallium."

"Thallium? I don't even know what that is."

"I doubt that. Your company is one of the biggest manufacturers of thallium in the country. One of the researchers or even a sales rep could've told you everything you needed to know about its symptoms and then some. Or maybe you just Googled it."

"This is nuts. You're just grieving. I can't believe you're actually accusing me of killing my husband. I loved him."

I ignore her weak professions of innocence. I've heard similar pleas from the guilty far too many times.

"I didn't actually put all the pieces together until I remembered a murder case I had two years ago where the defendant killed his wife with thallium. The symptoms of thallium poisoning are very similar to COVID. Shortness of breath, fever, chills. It's tasteless and very easy to hide in food. You almost got away with it. Almost."

"I told you, I didn't—"

"I was racking my brain trying to figure out when you could've poisoned him," I go on. "Then I realized it had to be the pizza Larry had the night before he was rushed to the hospital. You gave him freshly grated parmesan cheese, but gave me cheese from the jar. At the time, I thought you were just being mean because you weren't happy about me staying for so long."

Mia begins to weep.

"I also remembered how you inserted yourself between Larry and Kelli on the couch when he tried to coax her to take a bite of his pizza. I didn't realize it then, but later on, it hit me. You weren't about to let Kelli taste that pizza. You wanted your husband dead, but not your daughter. I guess I should be grateful you didn't poison me too."

"I thought he was cheating on me," Mia says, sobbing now. "I had planned to confront him, but you came to visit, so I decided to wait until you left. But then I discovered the money he took out of our account. Twenty thousand dollars. When I went through the search history on his computer, it was clear he was planning a trip to Paris with his mistress. If he'd be bold enough to do that, I knew he was eventually going to leave me."

"Larry wasn't leaving you. And he wasn't taking anyone to Paris." I intentionally pause for dramatic effect. "Except you."

Mia's cries screech to a stop. "What?"

"Larry was going to surprise you with a trip to Paris. He even asked me to look at some of the hotels he was considering."

"But what about the money he took from our account? A trip to Paris doesn't cost twenty grand."

"That was a loan to Jack. He was twenty grand short on the down payment on the condo he was buying for his mistress. Larry didn't tell you about it because he knew you wouldn't go along with it."

Mia's whole body starts to spasm.

"According to Jack, Larry intended to put the money back into the account before you ever found out. Jack knows I'm handling Larry's affairs. Two weeks after Larry died, he sent me a check for the entire amount, plus interest, and asked me not to mention it to you."

"Oh my God! What did I do?"

The sound of the doorbell, which I'm expecting, interrupts us. As I head back inside, my footsteps grow increasingly heavy with regret.

After grabbing a mask from the table near the door, I welcome inside a middle-aged man wearing a sports jacket. A mask covers most of his face, but not the resolve in his eyes.

I didn't realize Mia was standing a few feet behind me.

"Who is it?" she asks.

"It's Detective Miller," I say, feeling both mentally and emotionally drained. "From the LAPD. He's here to arrest you."

ON GOSSAMER WINGS

||||||||| Gar Anthony Haywood

Melinda Cortez fell down. All the way down. From the balcony of her eighth-floor apartment in Carson to the concrete walk below. It happened somewhere in the neighborhood of 6 P.M. on a Thursday afternoon. If the young woman had made any sound at all, it had come upon her landing, and no one reported hearing even that. The calls to 9-1-1 only started dribbling in after neighbors discovered her lifeless body, broken and spilling blood like a slaughtered calf in front of the complex.

The uniforms who canvassed the building and those nearby with a clear view of Cortez's balcony couldn't find a single witness to her death, nor anyone who saw or heard anything they would describe as suspicious beforehand. So the two Los Angeles County Sheriff's detectives who caught the call had their work cut out for them, figuring out whether Cortez had jumped to the ground of her own accord or received some kind of help.

Just another average day for Detective Jimmy Lattimore.

M.E. ARCHIE FUKUYAMA'S PRELIMINARY examination revealed little that wasn't already obvious to the naked eye. Death had been caused by blunt force trauma to various parts of the body, most significantly Cortez's head.

Archie saw no signs of injury that would not have been a result of her impact with the ground, he said, but he wouldn't know for sure until he got her body to the lab for a full autopsy.

"She landed head-first?" Jimmy asked, giving Cortez's body the once-over. A small group of onlookers was still murmuring nearby behind a fence line of yellow tape.

"Most definitely," Archie said.

"Isn't that a little unusual for a jumper?" In Jimmy's experience, people who committed suicide by leaping from great heights did so feet first, so their legs and spine almost always took the brunt of their fall.

"A little," Archie said. "Depends on how committed they are. When they really want to make sure, they come down like a member of the Olympic diving team. I've seen head-first cases where their faces left an imprint in the cement where they landed. You know, like the handprints of movie stars at Grauman's Chinese?"

"Nice visual, Archie," Lattimore's partner, Leila Downs, said. "Thanks for that."

"You're very welcome, detective."

WHEN THEY QUESTIONED THE building manager up in the dead woman's apartment, the cops found Kathy Anderson to be a chain-smoking white woman with watery eyes and less meat on her bones than an SPCA rescue animal. Between expressions of shock and disbelief that such a terrible thing could happen under her charge, she gave the detectives a snapshot image of the deceased. Melinda Ann Cortez, age twenty-eight. Single, no children, employed as a dental technician at an office in Sherman Oaks. No pets, but she shared apartment 803 with her boyfriend Jeffrey Smart, age thirty-three, a transmission specialist at a Toyota dealership in Torrance who wasn't in when Anderson led the first responders up here to his and Cortez's apartment to see if anyone was inside.

"Was the door locked or unlocked?" Lattimore asked.

"Unlocked."

"Have you seen Mr. Smart today at all? Either before or after Ms. Cortez's body was discovered?"

Anderson said she hadn't.

"Any security cameras in the building? Either inside or out?"

"One outside the front door and another out in the parking lot. The only one inside the building is in the gym on the second floor."

"Anyone else live here besides Mr. Smart and Ms. Cortez? Any members of his or her family, for instance?"

"Not that I'm aware of. It was just her and Jeff."

"What about frequent visitors?"

"I don't know about frequent. But they had visitors, sure. At least Jeff did."

"How do you know they were Jeff's visitors and not hers?" Downs asked.

"Because he was usually with them when they came and went. I never saw anyone come in with her."

"Would you happen to have names for these people?" Lattimore asked. He and Downs liked to ping-pong like this, so an interview subject never knew what the next question was going to be or which of the two detectives was going to pose it. It made lying to them just that much more difficult.

The building manager shook her head. "But why would you want their names? The poor thing just jumped, didn't she?"

"Is that what you think?" Jimmy asked. "That she jumped?" The uniforms who'd checked the apartment said they hadn't come across anything resembling a note from Cortez, so suicide was just a theory at this point.

"Well, what else could have happened?" Anderson asked. Off the detectives' silence, she said, "Oh, my God. You don't think—"

"Us? We don't think anything yet," Jimmy said. "We don't start thinking until we're at least two, three hours into an investigation, and this one's just getting started." He turned to Leila. "Wouldn't you say that's about right, detective? Two or three hours in?"

Downs nodded, straight-faced as a mugshot. "Yeah, give or take."

Lattimore turned back to Anderson. "How would you describe Ms. Cortez's general attitude of late? Would you say she'd been in a good mood or a bad one?"

"Her mood?" The building manager tossed the butt of her cigarette into the kitchen sink, then lit up another one. "Well, I wouldn't say she was particularly happy. She wasn't that kind of person, right? She rarely smiled on her best day."

"You're saying she seemed depressed?" Downs asked.

"Yes."

"More so than usual?"

"Yes. Though, like I said, I never knew her to be a sunflower."

"Any idea why she was so down?" Lattimore asked.

"No. But I don't think it had anything to do with money. Their rent was always paid on time."

"How about her relationship with Mr. Smart? Would you say they were getting along?"

Anderson shrugged. "As far as I know. I never saw or

heard them argue myself, and we got no complaints about arguments from any other tenant. But who can really say if two people are getting along or not? Not me."

"And everyone else in the building? She have any issues with any of them?"

"No. Never. Although . . ." She paused to think something over. "She got into it with Mr. Givens, once. Everybody does, eventually."

It was now Downs's turn. "Mr. Givens?"

"Barry Givens. Apartment nine-oh-three. He's something of a character."

"What does that mean?"

"It means he always has something or somebody to complain about. The plumbing. Missing mail. Noise in one unit or another."

"Nine-oh-three. Would that be the apartment directly above this one?" Jimmy asked.

"Yessir."

"And would this be one of the units he thought was making too much noise?"

"Yes, but that's not what he and Melinda got into it about. It was his car. He accused her of hitting it in the parking lot."

"When was this?"

"About a week ago, I think."

"And did she?"

"Hit his car? Somebody did. But Melinda denied it and I believed her."

"You said there was a camera out there," Downs reminded her.

"Yes, but it only catches half the lot. Barry's space and Melinda's are out of its view." Anderson put a hand over her eyes and lowered her head, a crack finally showing in her hard-ass exterior. "Jesus, I still can't get over it. The poor child's dead. It's horrible."

Lattimore gave his partner a look. It was time to talk to the boyfriend.

THEY HAD TO LEAVE two voicemail messages for him before Jeff Smart called them back. He took the news of his girlfriend's death exactly as they would have expected, had he been learning about it for the first time and had deep feelings for the woman. But they withheld exactly how she had died, wanting to see if he'd ask the question. He did.

Jimmy told him he'd better just come home and see for himself.

Smart showed up less than thirty minutes later. Cortez's body had already been removed to the morgue but strips of crime scene tape remained out front for him to see, along with the bloodstained sidewalk his girlfriend had left behind. A tall, brown-haired white man with the soft, spongy exterior of a plush toy rabbit, Smart looked every bit like the shocked and heartbroken lover, from his red-rimmed eyes right down to his unsteady hands and legs. Downs offered him a seat in his own apartment, afraid he might collapse under the weight of either his genuine grief or the effort of his performance, but he declined.

"She finally did it. She kept saying she would, but I never really thought she'd go through with it," he said, once the detectives told him the circumstances of his girlfriend's death. "Goddamn her!"

"You're saying she jumped?" Jimmy asked.

"Of course she jumped. What, do you think she just *fell*?" He almost laughed at the thought.

"Stranger things have happened. There's a wine glass

out on the patio along with an empty bottle of white Zin-
fandel. If she'd been drinking, it might have just been an
accident."

"No." Smart shook his head frantically. "It was no
accident. She's been working up to this for a long time."

"Any particular reason?" Downs asked.

"Her weight. Her childhood. The inability to have kids.
Mel was just a mess." His eyes misted over. "I tried to keep
her off the ledge—God, what a terrible choice of words!—
but it was hopeless. Like trying to put smoke back into a
jar."

"So why take her life today?" Jimmy asked. "I mean,
in the absence of a note—at least, we haven't been able to
find one, yet—what could have happened to finally make
her go through with it?"

Smart didn't answer right away. The way it looked to
Jimmy, given a choice, he would have never answered at all.

"We were talking about breaking up. That is, *I* was
talking about it, as usual, and she wasn't hearing it."

"When was this?"

"This morning, before I left for work. She'd stopped
taking her meds again and refused to go back on them, so
I told her I was done." He saw the look on the detectives'
faces, said, "You have no idea what it was like. Every day,
the same thing, trying to convince her how much I loved
her, how much we had to look forward to if she could just
. . . just . . ."

"Get her act together?" Downs suggested.

"No. Just find some peace. That's all I wanted her to
do. Find some peace."

He let the tears go now, and Jimmy had a hard time
imagining they were strictly for show. The guy seemed
legitimately broken.

"You said you went to work today?" Jimmy asked.

"Yes." Smart wiped his eyes with the back of one hand and nodded.

"From what time to what time?"

"What? Oh. I got in around nine and left a little after five-thirty. Why?"

"Mind if we ask where you've been for the last hour and a half?"

Cortez had died around 6 P.M. and it was almost 8 now. That meant Smart had over ninety minutes to drive home from the Torrance dealership where he was employed, kill his girlfriend, and then leave again.

"It's Thursday. I do yoga in the park twice a week after work, Tuesdays and Thursdays. Anything wrong with that?"

"Which park would that be?"

"Oh, I get it." Smart bristled. "You're thinking I killed her. Picked her up and threw her off the balcony. Well, you can forget it. Mel didn't need my help killing herself, and I wasn't here to give it to her, in any case."

"The name of the park, Mr. Smart. Please," Downs said.

"Hickory Park, on Two-thirty-second. And before you ask, I doubt anybody saw me because nobody ever sees me. I practice way on the north end of the park, as far away from other people as possible. There wouldn't be much point, otherwise."

Lattimore thought that was pretty damn convenient, as alibis went, but that didn't mean it couldn't be true. Smart did strike him as the kind of gentle soul who would find yoga a fine way to connect with the spirit gods after a long day of manual labor.

"Your landlady, Ms. Anderson, says the door to your

apartment was unlocked when she let the patrol officers in here earlier," Jimmy said, changing the subject.

"Yeah, so?"

"Well, it just seems a little strange. You'd think she'd lock it to keep from being interrupted. Considering what you think she was planning to do, that is."

Smart shrugged and said, "I don't know what to tell you. Sometimes we lock the door when we're home and sometimes we don't. Why is that important?"

"If the door was unlocked, somebody could have come in and surprised her while she was out on the balcony," Downs said.

"Somebody besides me, you mean."

"Yes." She didn't bother to add that this scenario seemed doubtful, in that there'd been no sign of a struggle, either on the balcony or anywhere else in the apartment. If somebody tossed Cortez off the balcony, it probably wasn't a stranger.

"Can you think of anybody who might have wanted to harm Ms. Cortez?" Jimmy asked.

"No. No way."

"No one?"

"No one. Who would want to hurt her? People felt sorry for Mel, they didn't dislike her."

"What about Mr. Givens?"

"Who?"

"Your neighbor upstairs in nine-oh-three. Barry Givens. Ms. Anderson tells us he and Ms. Cortez had an argument over his car not long ago."

"Oh." Smart nodded. "That idiot. He's harmless."

"Why do you say that?"

"Because he's all talk. He's got anger issues, to be sure, but that's it. He got it in his head Mel had backed into his car in the parking lot and was threatening to put her lights out. Those were the exact words he used, 'put her lights out.' I asked him if he'd like to try that with me and he did a full retreat. That was the last we heard of him."

He started tearing up again. "Look, I want to see her. Where can I go to see her?"

JIMMY AND DOWNS WENT up to 903 to talk to Barry Givens. In the elevator, Jimmy asked, "So what do you think?"

"I think he's had it rough," Down said. "My brother Reggie's been clinically depressed for years, and it's made his wife more suicidal than he is."

"Still—"

"Do I think he killed her? I don't know. Sounds like he had opportunity, if nothing else. 'I was doing yoga alone in the park.' Yeah, right."

"What we need," Lattimore said, "is a witness."

"Yeah. You'd think somebody somewhere would have seen her taking the plunge, right?"

"Except we're on a cul-de-sac here, so pedestrian traffic would have been limited and the closest buildings are all facing the wrong way."

"True. Our luck."

"And if it all happened real fast, there may not have been time for anybody to see anything. She makes up her mind, climbs up on the railing, and . . ." He made a diving motion with both hands pressed together.

Downs nodded and the elevator doors opened.

"SORRY, WOULD YOU MIND repeating that?" Downs asked.

"I said I wish I could say I gave a shit, but I don't. Or would you rather I lied and said I do?"

Smart and his landlord had both neglected to mention it, but the word for Barry Givens was "obese." Not "fat" or "overweight," but "obese." A middle-aged Black man with jowls like a buddha and more folds in his neck than a geisha's fan, he was heavier than anybody Jimmy had ever seen who was capable of standing on their own two feet.

"The simple truth will do," Downs told him.

"And that's what you got. Next question?"

"We understand you had issues with Ms. Cortez on at least one occasion. Would you like to tell us about that?"

"If by 'issues,' you mean I wanted to break her neck for plowing into my car, I confess. We had issues."

"That's a little extreme, don't you think?" Jimmy asked. "Lady puts a dent in your fender, you take it out on her insurance company, you don't threaten her with violence."

"It was more than a dent. And it's not just any fender. My car is a '69 Pontiac Bonneville coupe, detective." Givens's voice was rising, his face getting flushed. "It was my mother's car before she passed and there wasn't a scratch on it until that halfwit damn near tore off the right rear quarter panel!"

"You saw her do it?" Downs asked. This was a sensitive subject for her, men who liked to accuse women of being lousy drivers without cause. Her own driving drew comments from Jimmy all the time.

"I didn't have to see it. I heard it!" Spittle was starting to fly. "She was just getting out of her car when I got down there, trying to pretend like nothing happened, but she wasn't fooling anybody!"

Jimmy and his partner traded a look. This guy was a loose cannon.

"So you threatened to put her lights out," Downs said.

"Damn right I did. You know what my car's gonna cost to get fixed?"

"Were you home when Ms. Cortez died, Mr. Givens?" Jimmy asked, cutting to the chase. "That would have been somewhere around six P.M. or so."

"Sure, I was here. But if you're gonna ask me if I saw her jump, the answer's no. I would have been in the bath around six."

Seeing Givens naked in the tub was not a fate he would have wished on anybody, but Lattimore had to ask: "Were you alone?"

"Of course I was alone."

"You said she jumped. If you didn't see it happen, how do you know she didn't just fall?"

"Jump, fall, whatever she did, it was bound to happen. Like I said, the girl was a halfwit. You sit on a balcony railing once too many times, eventually you're gonna go over the side of it, whether you were planning to or not."

The two detectives traded another glance. "Excuse me?" Downs said.

"You heard me. She liked to sit on the railing. I'd seen her do it once before, from my own balcony."

"You could see her?" Jimmy went out to Givens's balcony to see for himself, Downs and Givens trailing behind him. He looked out over the railing and, sure enough, the staggered arrangement of the building's balconies gave him a decent view of the one for apartment 803, directly below.

"I couldn't see her face," Givens said, "but I could see almost everything else. Her body, her legs, the works. I thought she was gonna jump then, but she didn't. If she had, my poor mother's car would still be spotless."

"When was this?"

"A month ago, maybe. Maybe longer."

"Did you see anybody else down there with her? Mr. Smart, perhaps?"

"Her boyfriend? The great protector? No. It was just her."

"Okay, Mr. Givens. Thank you very much for your time. If you can think of anything else you think might be helpful to our investigation, please let us know."

"Investigation?" Givens took the business card Lattimore was handing him like it was something foul-smelling. "What's there to investigate? A crazy woman killed herself. Shit happens."

IT TOOK LATTIMORE AND Downs another two hours to canvas the rest of the building. Nobody had seen Melinda Cortez die and few tenants even knew who she was. The detectives asked if anyone had ever witnessed her behaving dangerously on her balcony and no one could remember doing so. "No" was also the answer they gave when asked if they'd ever seen Cortez and her boyfriend engaged in an argument.

The only interview Jimmy and Downs conducted that night that stood out from all the others was with a lady named Angela Breen in apartment 1105, and it wasn't because Breen had anything useful to tell them about the death of Melinda Cortez.

Breen was the neighbor Jimmy had desperately wanted when he was fourteen years old and developing an abiding appreciation for the female form. Which was to say, she was built like a Playboy centerfold and happy to give anyone interested an unobscured view of all that God had given her. Closing in on forty, by Jimmy's estimation, with copper red hair and light brown eyes, she answered the detectives' knock wearing an emerald-green kimono barely cinched at the waist. That was it. Jimmy could see more skin above and below the kimono's sash than he'd seen in the shower that morning.

"It's a shame. That poor kid," Breen said. "Why would someone want to do such a thing?"

"Such a thing as what?" Downs asked.

"Are you serious? She was murdered, wasn't she?"

"Well, we don't know what happened to her, yet. That's what we're trying to find out."

"You want my opinion? She was murdered. This world. I swear to God, there's no end to the insanity."

She liked to wave her arms when she talked and the robe kept flowing open, giving Lattimore flashes of things his eyes couldn't avoid latching onto. She caught him looking once and gave him a smile; Downs pretended not to notice the exchange.

"If she was murdered, who do you think might have killed her?" Downs asked, trying to keep her partner focused.

"How would I know? This building is full of cretins. Take your pick."

"Cretins?"

"You want a for instance? The sexual deviant with the drone. Find him and you'll probably have your killer."

"What drone is this?" Jimmy asked, his mind snapped back around to police work.

"The one flies outside my window two or three times a month. Sometimes more. It was out there earlier today. Recording me on video, no doubt. Sick fuck."

"A drone. With a camera. You're sure?"

"I know what a drone is, don't I? Looks like a toy helicopter and sounds like a giant bumblebee. And I don't *know* it has a camera, but why else would it hover out there when I just happen to be half-naked? To catch flies?"

Jimmy looked over at Downs and Downs looked right back. Could God possibly be so kind?

JIMMY HAD NOTICED THE photos on the walls when they'd been inside apartment 202 earlier. Large black and white city- and streetscapes of Los Angeles in all its disparate glory: tents on Skid Row, an upshot of new office buildings downtown, skateboards stacked like Ritz crackers against a tagged brick wall in Venice. And two aerial shots, one taken high above the checkered rooftops of East L.A. and the other a bird's eye view of Wilshire Boulevard and Vermont Avenue, choked with gridlock at the height of rush hour.

"Great stuff," Jimmy had said then, just making a casual observation.

The guy who'd taken the photos was a thirty-something white man named Stephen Sutton whom Jimmy could have mistaken for a Mormon missionary had his white shirt been closed at the neck and *Grand Theft Auto* not been cued up on his living room Xbox. He was mild-mannered and cordial, but anxious to have the cops leave because he'd just returned from a business trip in the Bay Area, he said, and was dead on his feet.

Having them come back to question him a second time did nothing to improve his mood.

"I've already told you everything I know," he said. "What more can I tell you?"

Jimmy stepped over to the aerial shot of East L.A. and pointed. "This was shot with a drone, yes?"

"Yes. Is that why you came back? To talk about photography?"

"In a way," Downs said. "But more specifically, your drone photography."

"I don't understand." The indistinct sounds of a stereo or television playing in another room seemed to be creating a greater distraction for him than for the detectives.

"We're wondering if you ever use it here at home. The drone, that is."

"My drone? No. Why would I?"

"To take pictures or record video," Jimmy said. "Why else?"

"If I thought there was something worth shooting here, I probably would. But I don't."

"Is there anyone else here who might have been using it?"

"Not a chance."

"You live here alone?"

"With my son, who was at school all day today. Why are you asking me about this?"

"Frankly? Because one of your neighbors reports seeing a drone flying outside her window earlier today and we were hoping it might have been yours. We don't really care why you were using it if it was, but if you happened to catch what happened to Ms. Cortez on video . . ."

"It's a long shot, obviously," Downs said, "but—"

"I'm sorry. Pardon me a moment, will you?" Sutton said. He went to the back of the apartment, out of their view, and the music that had been murmuring in the background came to a halt. When he returned, he said, "As I told you detectives earlier, I only arrived from the airport a little over an hour ago, so whoever's drone my neighbor saw, assuming it really was a drone, it wasn't mine. I'm sorry."

"Sure, sure," Lattimore said. "But again, just to be clear: You wouldn't just say that to protect your integrity, right? Because, like I said, Mr. Sutton, if it was your drone and you were using it today for, shall we say, less than professional purposes, that really isn't something we would give a damn about. All we're interested in here is whether or not the video you captured can tell us how Ms. Cortez came to fall off her balcony. Period."

"I didn't capture any video. It wasn't my drone because it's under lock and key and I wasn't here to fly it. I told you two earlier, at six o'clock tonight, when you say Ms. Cortez died, I was sitting in an airport shuttle stuck in traffic on the four-oh-five, and I can prove it. Jesus, if I had video of the lady falling, why wouldn't I just tell you?"

Because you wouldn't want to lose your apartment for being a goddamn perv, Jimmy thought but did not say. Primarily, because he believed the man. Sutton came off as something of a humorless stiff, but he didn't have the vibe of—to use Angela Breen's term—a sexual deviant. Nor a murderer, for that matter. And if he could prove he wasn't around when Melinda Cortez died, well, that was the end of that, in any case.

"Sorry to have bothered you again, Mr. Sutton," Jimmy said, and he gave Downs his time-to-leave nod.

"YOU WANNA DO ME a favor and slow down?"

The two detectives were heading back to the station and Downs was behind the wheel of the car, as usual putting the fear of God in her partner with maneuvers Richard Petty in his prime wouldn't have tried at Daytona.

"You want to talk about my driving or Melinda Cortez?"

"Just take it down a notch, please. And try staying in the same lane for ten seconds, for chrissakes."

"I think she jumped. The boyfriend says she'd been working up to it for a long time, and if that wasn't a test run Givens says he saw her do a month ago, I don't know what else you would call it."

"Can't say I disagree," Jimmy said. "Givens is a loud-mouthed hothead, no doubt, but he doesn't seem crazy enough to kill somebody over an affront to his mother's car. Plus, big as he is, I'm not sure he could get back up to his apartment from our deceased's without somebody seeing him. Just getting from the elevator to his front door would probably take him fifteen minutes."

"And I can't see Smart killing her because he's too bro-ken up. The way everybody describes her, Cortez was a real downer, and you don't stick around somebody like that for long unless you love the living shit out of 'em. Take it from me."

"Still. Why didn't she leave a note? Why leave Smart to guess what made her finally go through with it today of all days?"

"What's to guess, Jimmy? He said he told her they were done. He might have said it before, but maybe she believed him this time, even if he didn't mean it."

Lattimore nodded his head, Downs's thinking right in line with his own. Homicide cops were predisposed to see murder behind every death they came across, and Jimmy and Downs were no different. That was their job, after all. But sometimes, a slip-and-fall was just a slip-and-fall and the person who put the gun in the dead guy's mouth was nobody but the dead guy himself, and all the detective work in the world wasn't going to make a homicide out of it.

"Too bad that wasn't Sutton's drone Breen saw outside her window," Jimmy said.

"Yeah. But you heard the man. 'Not a chance,' he said."

"When a simple 'no' would have sufficed. What an asshole."

"Could take us days to find that drone owner now. And even if we do, what are the chances the video will tell us anything?"

"Slim and none. I know. But we get lucky every now and then, don't we? Like that time we"—Jimmy bolted upright in his seat—"*what the hell are you doing?!*"

Downs had tried another one of her signature moves, running a yellow with a car turning left right in front of her, and they'd missed a head-on by just something short of a foot.

Jimmy put a hand to his chest, checking for a heartbeat. "Seriously, Lee, who the hell taught you to drive, a blind man?"

Downs just grinned, as unfazed by this near-death experience as all the others she was responsible for. "Nobody taught me. I taught myself."

"That figures."

"No, really. I had to teach myself. My mother refused to teach me and my father never had the time. So when I was sixteen, I started taking our car out at night when everyone was asleep. Drove out to Glenville Mall and practiced in the parking lot for an hour, sometimes two. Nine weeks later, I passed my driver's test with flying colors."

"And your folks never found out?"

Downs laughed. "Never. Every night, I put it right back in the driveway where I found it, without a scratch on it. I even put gas in it sometimes. How would they know?"

She laughed again and Jimmy joined in. He thought about his own teenage years, and all the wild shit he'd pulled on his parents without their knowledge.

"Hey, wait a minute," he said, no longer laughing.

"What?" When he didn't answer, Downs looked over and saw he was suddenly deep in concentration over something. "What?"

"He's not just an asshole. He's a specific *kind* of asshole. The 'nothing happens under my fucking roof I don't know about' kind."

"Excuse me?"

"Turn the car around," Lattimore said. "We gotta go back."

THERE WAS A REASON the Xbox and *Grand Theft Auto* didn't mesh with Stephen Sutton and the reason turned out to be Mike Sutton, Stephen's thirteen-year-old son.

Stephen Sutton wasn't happy to see the detectives back at his door for the third time in as many hours but he became downright surly when he learned they hadn't returned to talk to him.

"What's my son got to do with this?" he asked.

"We'd just like to talk to him, Mr. Sutton," Downs said. "Anything wrong with that?"

Unable to say why there should be, the elder Sutton led them back to his son's bedroom, where more of the muffled music they'd heard here before—Jimmy recognized this as a Wu-Tang Clan song his own daughter Marcie liked to play incessantly—was again beating its way through the closed door.

Stephen Sutton knocked and entered, skipping the step of waiting for an answer entirely. Jimmy and Downs came right in behind him to find Mike Sutton sprawled upon his bed, fully dressed, shoes still on his feet. His shoulder-length brown hair was emblazoned with a streak of orange running front-to-back and he had black plugs in both earlobes. Jimmy figured he had to tower over his father when he stood on his feet.

"Mike, these are detectives with the Sheriff's Department investigating the death of that woman who fell from her apartment today," Stephen Sutton said, turning off his son's Bluetooth speaker to silence the Wu-Tang Clan. "They'd like to ask you some questions."

"Me?"

Lattimore couldn't tell if he found the idea frightening or simply ridiculous.

"Your father tells us you were at school when it happened," Jimmy said, moving in closer to the bed. "That would have been around six, six-thirty. Is that right?"

"Me?" the kid asked again, sitting up to address them all directly now.

"Or were you here to see her fall? And 'see' might not be the best word for it, would it? 'Recorded' would be more accurate."

Jimmy watched to see if the boy would flinch, and he did. It wasn't much, but it was there.

"Hold on a minute," the elder Sutton said. "Are you suggesting—"

"No, of course not," Jimmy said. "Take it easy." He turned back to Mike Sutton and came right out with it. "You like to skip school and fly your father's drone when he's away. And we think you were flying it today, before he got back from his trip. Have you looked at the video yet?"

The boy was like a block of ice, his expression flat and body motionless. Only his eyes, flitting from Jimmy to his father and back again, told the tale of his fear.

"I know what I'm asking you to do is hard," Jimmy said, leaning in, "but I promise you, we aren't interested in what you were recording or why. We just need to see if the video you shot shows how Ms. Cortez died."

"This is ridiculous," Stephen Sutton said angrily. "You're trying to say it was *my* drone somebody saw flying around here today and that Mike was the one flying it?"

"It *was* me, Dad," Mike Sutton said, meeting his father's gaze straight on. Jimmy thought it might have been as great a show of underage courage as anything he'd ever seen.

A brief silence fell. Then the boy looked back at Jimmy and said, "He pushed her."

IT WASN'T MUCH. JUST a little push. A love tap. But the one-handed nudge Jeffrey Smart gave Melinda Cortez had been just enough to send her toppling off the balcony railing where she sat. The camera on Stephen Sutton's quad-engine drone had caught it all from two floors above and in striking, 4K/HD detail. The video footage that had been shot before, featuring Angela Breen prancing about her apartment in panties and bra and nothing else, was equally impressive, though Lattimore and Downs refrained from watching all of it.

Smart took one look at the video and collapsed like a stack of Jenga blocks. Jimmy could have left the interview room for lunch and it would have all come pouring out of their suspect just as easily. Downs had been right—he *did* love Cortez desperately—but every man had his limits and Melinda Cortez had finally, after years of stretching the envelope of his emotions, pushed Smart beyond his.

He'd come home after work to find her up on the balcony railing again, a new favorite spot for one of her regular pity parties, and she was almost too drunk to put three words together. Their usual routine called for him to talk her down, to beg and plead and profess his love for her until he was in greater hysterics than she was, but for some reason, he couldn't find the will this time to follow the script. Instead, he just let her mumble softly from her perilous perch, filled with more pity for her than affection, until putting them both out of their mutual misery was the only thought he could keep in his head.

A little push. That's all it was. And when it was done, he raced from the apartment and drove out to Hickory Park, having never even bothered to look down over the balcony railing to see if his beloved girlfriend had survived her tragic fall.

From what Jimmy could tell, the man was truly sorry for what he'd done, and was likely to feel sorry about it for the rest of his life. Stephen Sutton's son Mike, on the other hand, was also sorry, but for reasons completely different from those of Jeffrey Smart. The boy's remorse was all about his hesitancy to come forward on his own when he'd witnessed Cortez's murder; he knew he should have contacted the police the minute he saw the crime occur over the live video feed from his father's drone. But then, of course, the game he liked to play when Stephen Sutton was not around—freeing the big black bird from its cage with a key he had made months ago—would have been over, and there'd be no more home movies of their neighbor Angela Breen to ignite the fires of his burgeoning adolescent lust.

"Still. The kid did the right thing," Downs said, after she and Lattimore had formally booked Jeffrey Smart.

"Yeah. He didn't have to come clean at all. And considering what it's going to cost him . . ." Jimmy figured, when his father got through with him, it would probably be months before Mike Sutton could touch that Xbox again. And yet, little "cretin" that he was (to use Angela Breen's word for him), the odds were good that, somewhere in that room of his, he had an SD memory card hidden where Stephen Sutton was never going to find it.

THIS NIGHT IN QUESTION |

Tod Goldberg |||||||||||||||||||||||||||||| |

The night is when the visitors come. When the past and the present seem to converge. Fifty-three and already lost to time?

Did it happen like this at all?

Here it is. 6 P.M. Sundown.

There's two cops at the door, so I know it's bad news. I recognize one of them through the peephole. Blake Dilley. Went to high school together. Thirty-five years ago now. He was one of those guys who always wanted to be a cop, his career path set for him from second grade on: Boy Scouts. Eagle Scouts. Search and Rescue volunteer. ROTC. Two years junior college. Academy. Cop. He's been on the job three decades, still wearing a uniform, but now he's Watch Commander. What he's doing here I can't imagine. Last time we spoke was in the parking lot outside my nightclub, Cecil's on Sunrise. There'd been a shooting. I drove over to see what was what. Ex-boyfriend of one of my bar girls showed up with a gun, killed himself in the parking lot. One of those fucking things where you think, well, it could have been worse, and man, maybe that's true, but what a way to think.

Other guy is in a suit.

So. A detective.

Blake must be here to make sure I don't kill anyone.
Or vice versa.

"Cecil," Blake says, "can you open up? We need to talk."

"I've got a gun on my person," I say. "So I need to know what the situation is with the guy in the suit before I open the door."

The detective shares a look with Blake, who just shrugs.

"We're not here to arrest anyone, Cecil," Blake says. "We just need to ask you some questions. You can trust us."

Shit. It is bad news.

Show them in, Caroline says.

THE DETECTIVE, HIS NAME is Nitch, goes to find me a garbage can from my own bathroom in case I get sick again, but I don't see that happening. Because I'm not looking at the videos on his phone again. Blake says, "I should have warned you."

"No way to warn a person about that," I say.

Detective Nitch had shown me a video of my daughter, Diane, getting the shit kicked out of her by a man. He mashed her face into the flat screen TV I'd bought her for Christmas, then picked up Diane's baby, Little Luke, and boned out the front door. All of it caught on Diane's nanny camera. My wife, Caroline, paced in the kitchen. I couldn't make her look.

But then the guy, two minutes later, he came back in without the baby, dragged Diane out by her hair, my daughter limp the whole way. That's when I lost it, threw up in the plant next to my sofa. Caroline sobbing.

Blake says, "You know him?"

"It's her ex-boyfriend," I say. "Kirby Colton. Last I heard, he was up in Corcoran."

"You sure?"

"Yes," I say.

Blake says, real quietly, "Look, before Detective Nitch comes back, between us, I need to know if you're still . . . active."

"What do you think?"

"I mean," Blake says, "do I need to worry about a bunch of mobsters killing this Kirby guy's family?"

"No," I say, "you don't need to worry about that."

Blake says, "Understand, I don't care what you do for a living. You and me, we played AYSO together, so, whatever happens at night in your private life, hey, great. My job is to find your daughter and your grandkid, number one."

Detective Nitch comes back, sets a wicker garbage can down in front of me. "You only got wicker," he says.

"Caroline puts a liner in it, usually," I say. She's not in the kitchen. She's not in the house. She's drifting above the pool out back.

"Usually?" Nitch says, like it matters to the case.

"Diane's mom, she was in charge of that."

"Where's she now? Caroline?" Nitch asks and I see Blake wince.

"She's in heaven," I say, "with Elvis and Jesus Christ."

"Shit, I'm sorry," Nitch says. "I've done this all backwards."

"Cecil has an ID on the guy," Blake says, gives Nitch the name.

"Who called this in?" I ask.

"Neighbor heard the ruckus," Blake says. "She went by this morning to check on things, found the place empty, saw the blood on the TV and everywhere else, made the phone call. Now here we are."

"Diane," I say, "she looked dead to me."

Nitch says, "We didn't find any brain matter on the TV. A lot of blood, I'm not gonna lie. A ton of hair and skin. But no brain matter. My feeling is she was concussed, but alive when this Kirby dragged her out."

"I've seen plenty of dead people who didn't even leave blood somewhere," I say. "She was dead."

"This isn't like in the movies," Nitch says.

"I look like I'm talking about the movies?"

I get up, walk into the kitchen, pour myself a glass of mineral water to help settle my stomach. On the fridge, under a magnet, is a photo of Diane and Little Luke.

"That baby isn't even his," I say. "Not sure if he knows."

"Whose is it?" Nitch says.

"Guy Diane was dating off and on," I say. "Bartender at Hunters in Rancho Mirage named Greg."

"Thought that place was gay?" Nitch says.

"It is," I say.

Another look between Nitch and Blake.

"How long you been in town, detective?" I ask.

"This will be my first summer," he says. "That's why I've got Lieutenant Dilley with me. Introduce me to key players. Fill in some gaps."

You're never going to find my grandson and my daughter, I think, and then I say it out loud, because fuck it, it's the truth.

"Hey, hey," Blake says, "let's take it easy. We're here to help. But we need your help first. Can you do that for me, Cecil?"

"You keep my name out of the paper?"

"Don't see any reason for it to show up," Nitch says.

I finish off my mineral water. "All right."

"Is there any reason to believe," Nitch asks, "that someone would get this Kirby to hurt your daughter, anything like that? Like to get to you?" He's got a notebook out now, taking notes.

Blake looks at his feet.

"Yes," I say.

"Yes?"

"Blake," I say, "keep me from incriminating myself."

Blake says, "Detective? Cecil has been a good friend to our department. If he thought this was about him, we'd know already."

"A CI?" Nitch says.

"Hey," I say.

Blake says, "Hey, hey, let's not put a name on anything. Let's just say all the way up the line, Cecil has been a friend to the department and the city. Okay? So we know his known associates and people we think might have grudges. None fit this guy's profile."

Nitch taps a pen against his lips. "This Kirby run with anyone?"

"Inland Empire Peckerwoods," I say. "White supremacists living in basically occupied Mexico. Stupid shit. I don't approve of that race-war shit. Part of the reason Diane was trying to get him out of her life."

"How long he been in Corcoran?" Nitch asks.

"Two years," I say. "Jacked a car."

"Two years up there," Nitch says, "he's probably come out worse than he went in."

"The kid," Blake says. "Was he here for the birth?"

"A week before he got pinched," I say.

"So he's not a primary caregiver," Blake says. "Fair to say?"

"Fair to say. He's got a sister. Manages the Hot Dog on

a Stick in the mall. I remember them being close. Darlene. Marlene. Something like that."

Blake says, "She have kids?"

"I dunno," I say. "I'd bet yes. She had the 'knocked up in high school' vibe. Responsible, but only to a point."

Blake looks at his watch. "Mall's open for another hour. Let me put in a call."

He steps outside, leaving me and Nitch alone, which I don't like, so I say, "I need to hit the head. Help yourself to whatever in the kitchen." Once I'm in there, I text Mad Tony, tell him what's up, tell him to burn down where the fucking Inland Empire Peckerwoods hang, a bar in Cathedral City called the Capri. Mad Tony says, "Don't you own part of that?" I tell him it's fine, fucking torch it, I'll explain later, and then flush, wash my hands, stare in the mirror. Wait. Caroline sits down on the edge of the tub. *She's gone*, she says. *Go back out there.*

Blake's still outside, on the phone, when I step back into the living room. Nitch is staring out a picture window into the darkness.

"There's a fairway out there," I say, "if you've got night vision."

Nitch says, "Nice house."

"I've lived here thirty years," I say. "It was my Pop's before that."

"I like the Modernist style," he says.

"That's how it came."

"Why are you so calm now?" he says. "Fifteen minutes ago, you were throwing up."

"I was calm then, too," I say. "It just made me sick to see Diane like that."

Nitch looks at photos on the wall. A mix of family photos and my old man with local celebrities. Frank Sinatra.

Sonny Bono. Bob Hope. "I never found Bob Hope funny," Nitch says.

"Different era," I say.

"Your father," Nitch says, tapping a photo on the wall, "was Bobby D'Amico?"

"That's right."

"Learned about him in that Netflix documentary series," Nitch says. "I forget the name. Watched it for like eight nights. Crazy shit. All those New York families capping each other in broad daylight. No one gets out alive for doing some stupid shit. Everyone always gets theirs. That's how it should be. How your father got out alive, I do not know. What was it called? Do you remember?" I tell him I don't remember. "So, you're a capo? Got your own crew? That the story?"

"Just a businessman."

He leans in, looks at a photo of Caroline and me in Hawaii. "Your wife?"

"Yeah."

"Beautiful." He looks closer. "Kauai?"

"Maui."

"I honeymooned there twice myself," Nitch says.

Blake comes back in then, saves the conversation, says, "We're going to run an Amber Alert in about two minutes. We'll get everyone home safe and sound, Cecil."

"I'll let Greg know," I say. He's a good kid. Diane told him the baby was his, he immediately offered to pay his share, but Diane said no. Still, he comes and visits, is in the child's life, does whatever he can, whatever Diane will allow. Part of that, I think, has to do with Kirby. Keep Greg out of his bullshit.

Greg's relationship to Diane, that's more complex, not my business. But he should know about this. Cops go tell him, he might seem suspect to them, because he's a suspect guy. Fought Golden Gloves, does a little work for me now and again. He doesn't love Diane but he loves Luke and that's been fine.

"Okay, okay good," Blake says. "Anybody pops in your head that wants to hurt you, call Detective Nitch, okay? Same with Greg. We've got a cruiser at the mall sitting on the sister. We're gonna go talk to her. Maybe she's got the boy. Otherwise, stay frosty, Cecil, okay?"

I tell him I will. I wait twenty minutes, call Mad Tony, he says it's happening now, it's basically done, the Capri about to be ashes, and in fact, an hour later, I can already hear the sirens in the distance when I get into the car and drive over to Hunters, Caroline beside me, telling me to breath, to keep real calm.

IT'S A TUESDAY NIGHT, so it's a little light in Hunters. There's a group of ten guys on the dance floor, shirtless, dancing lazily to some disco song. At the bar, there's another half-dozen men sitting around nursing drinks and watching the baseball game on the TV. Greg's shaking a martini when I step up to the bar. It's my first time in the place in years, even though I've been a silent partner since the '90s. You run a bar in the Coachella Valley, you either cut me in or maybe you drown while fishing in the Salton Sea.

"What's wrong?" Greg says immediately.

"Easy," I say. I wave over the manager, a lady named Rose Pollard whose brother is doing ten at Pelican Bay for me, tell her I need Greg to go on break and meet me out front.

"Is it Luke?" Greg says when he finds me smoking beside my Cadillac.

I tell him what's happened, and Greg has almost the

same response as me. He leans over. Tries to catch his breath. Gags. Swears. Then says, "Where do we find this fucking guy?"

"Was hoping you might know. Diane mention him at all recently?"

"Only that he was out," he says. "You really think she's dead?"

"She was a ragdoll," I say. "If she was alive, she'd fucking kill that guy on her own. He's not a tough guy."

"Jesus," Greg says. "I'm sick." He paces. "He's some Nazi fucker, right?"

"Yeah," I say.

Greg cracks his knuckles. "What are we waiting for?" he says. "Let's go to the Capri. That's where they hang."

"I heard it burned down," I say.

"When?"

"Tonight."

Greg flinches, then says, "Cecil, if he hurts my kid I will go insane."

"I got a kid in this, too," I say.

"I didn't mean it like that. Shit. I'm all fucked up."

"I know," I say. My cell rings. It's Mad Tony.

"They scattered out of there like roaches," Mad Tony says. "No sign of Kirby."

"Stuberville there?" Nick Stuberville is the de facto boss of the Peckerwoods. Only OG not in prison. Like everyone else in this fucking town, we went to school together.

"Yeah, yeah," Mad Tony says. "Saw him hop his bike and get out. Not waiting around for cops, I guess."

I tell Mad Tony to hold tight, maybe I'll need him later, tell Greg to go back to work, that I'll check in with him soon, that he might hear from the police and to just be cool.

"How am I supposed to be cool?" Greg says. He stares up in the night sky. "There's supposed to be a meteor shower tonight. One of those 'first time in ten thousand years' things. I was gonna go by and see Diane tonight. Wake up Luke. Look at history. And now here we are. Jesus fuck, Cecil."

"He'll see it," I say.

NICK STUBERVILLE LIVES IN a gated trailer-park golf community in La Quinta called Rancho Park Estates, which seems like pretty good living for a fucking Nazi, but everyone out here lives behind a gate and estates is a word that has lost all meaning. These estates don't even have a security guard at the gate, so I sit and wait for five minutes and then get behind a couple in a Honda Accord and get into the place. I wind around for a few minutes and then find Stuberville's trailer. Same place he's been living for ten years. He was a couple years ahead of me in school. My pops and his pops did some work together back in the day. Stuberville's father was in the cement business. This Stuberville fronts in the motorcycle repair business.

I knock on the brushed-steel door. Stuberville's living in a souped-up trailer, all right. Looks to be two stories. Hardwood floors on the enclosed patio. View of the lake. A car port for his bike. I knock again. I could kick a window in, but I need information. I come in hard, I might catch one in the chest. Best to go slow. I hear some shuffling around and then hear Stuberville say, "That you, Cecil?"

"Yeah."

"What's the occasion?"

"I'm looking for one of your soldiers."

"He ain't here," Stuberville says.

"You gonna let me in?" I say.

"I don't like you just showing up at my house like this," he says, "on the same night someone throws a Molotov into the Capri."

"That was me, too."

"The fuck?" He opens the door. He's 6'5, skinhead, covered in tattoos, old school Aryan Nation motherfucker, not one of these new breeds who wear a suit and tie, tries to fake being a civilian.

"My daughter," I say, "Diane. And her kid, Luke. One of your fucking guys ran off with them both. I needed to see what was what. Insurance will rebuild the Capri. Better than ever."

"Who?"

"Kirby Colton," I say. "Cops got it on video."

"Shit. Come in, come in," he says, so I do. Stuberville goes into his kitchen, comes out with a bottle of something brown, two glasses, pours me a shot. I take it down.

"I need to find Kirby," I say.

"Last I heard he was up in Corcoran," Stuberville says. "If he's out, he's not come by."

"Come on," I say. "I know you watch your fucking guys."

"I'm on my way out," Stuberville says.

"Bullshit," I say. "You were at the Capri."

"Only so many places a guy like me can go get a beer and catch a ballgame."

"This is my grandkid we're talking about. And my daughter."

"Ain't she your step?"

"Raised her like my own," I say. "Does it fucking matter?" The walls of the trailer are covered in shitty paintings of sunrises and wolves, but not outright Nazi shit, so that's a relief. The community is on a golf course, so Stuberville does have a bunch of golf shit sitting around. Clubs. Balls. A little putting machine.

He puts his hands up. "Heard about your wife. I would have sent a card. Or something. If I was a different person. Hell."

"It's fine."

"Co-workers," he says, "should be able to console each other outside the game."

"Is that what we are? Co-workers?"

"Our dads knew each other, come on." He pours himself some more whiskey. "Cancer?"

"Ten different kinds." I look out the window. Half expect Caroline will be out by my car, smoking, but she's nowhere.

"You say Kirby took his boy?" Stuberville says.

"Yeah," I say. "It's not his boy, though."

"He know that?"

"Intellectually, maybe."

"That's not a thing with Kirby."

"Diane told him, but he didn't believe it. Not that he ever asked for a test or anything."

"Must have been thinking on this the entire time he was in," Stuberville says. "What a crazy thing to do. Not like he's the changing diapers type. Kirby's a dumb fucker but he's not . . . mean, you know?"

"He put Diane's head through a flat screen TV."

"Shit," Stuberville says. "You don't touch a woman. That's code."

"Just Jews and Blacks and Asians and Muslims and the rest of the non-white fucking world?"

"Look," Stuberville says, "my belief system has changed. Okay? I live in California, too." He points to his right arm, a sleeve of iron crosses. "I'm getting this shit lasered off. I'm fifty-six years old, walking around like this? It's stupid. This January sixth shit, that turned me around."

"Are you fucking serious?"

"I served in Desert Storm," he says. "I love this country, even if I count that time in the service as responsible for half the dumb shit I've done. I'm trying to retire. Aren't you tired of this yet?"

"Are you hearing me?" I say. "One of your guys maybe killed my daughter and for sure took my grandson. I don't give a fuck about your retirement."

"It's all related," he says. He takes down his drink. "I find Kirby for you, maybe you help me out of some trouble I've got. Boss to boss?"

"What kind of trouble?"

"Cop shit," he says. "I know you got sway in this town. I got a drug charge hanging over me. They want me to snitch, make it go away."

"Then make it go away." I stand up. The whole idea of this fucking guy is nauseating me now. I start to leave. "You bring Kirby," I say, "or maybe everyone in your club of fascists is getting one between the eyes. That's my code. And then we can talk."

I'm already starting my ignition when Stuberville comes out and stands in front of my car, cell phone in his hand. I roll down my window.

"You crazy fuck," he says to me, "I'm trying to help you." He hands me the phone.

"Who is this?" I say.

"I've got the baby," a woman says. "Luke. He doesn't look anything like Kirby. Jesus. What a terrible mistake."

"Who is this?" I say again.

"Lisbeth," she says. "Kirby's mother. I'm sorry. This is all my fault."

GREG IS WAITING FOR me in the parking lot of the Stater Brothers on Washington. It's close to midnight. "She's going to show?" he asks. He's chain-smoking. I've never seen him smoke before.

"Yes," I say.

"You believe her story?"

"I believe it's a story," I say. Lisbeth told me that Kirby dropped Luke off this morning at her place in Joshua Tree, told her that he and Diane needed some time alone, see if they could work out their problems, and then they'd be by to pick the boy up tomorrow. But then the cops rousted her daughter at work and Stuberville called her and everything started to fall apart in her mind. Plus, she'd gotten a good look at the child and there was no way Kirby had provided any DNA at all. Maybe Kirby saw the same thing. Maybe that's why Luke was still alive.

"Your color isn't good," Greg says. "You all right? Have you eaten today?"

"No," I say. Did I take my blood pressure meds? I take them at bedtime, which was three hours ago. I'm an in-bed-by-9-P.M. guy now. If it needs to happen after midnight, usually it means someone else is doing it for me. "I'll have Caroline fix me something."

Greg cocks his head. "Pops," he says. He stubs his cigarette out on his shoe. I see the butt of his gun in his belt. He's got a concealed carry permit. A little something I got for him if he was gonna roll with me and if he was my grandson's father. He comes over to me. "I'm going to touch your face," he says, like I might bite him. He puts the back of his hand on my cheeks, my forehead, my neck. "You're burning up. You should sit down."

A white Ford Fiesta pulls up.

The driver's door opens and a woman about my age gets out. She's got gray hair pulled back from her face and into a tight bun. Even in the darkness of the parking lot, I can see that she has shocking blue eyes, like a husky. She's pretty in a sad way, like she's been crying for twenty years, and maybe she has. She's wearing a Rolling Stones tour shirt, from when they played out here in the desert a few years ago, jeans that are too tight. Boots with fringe on them. She doesn't look like anyone's grandmother and she sure as shit hasn't been a grandmother to Luke, so I think what I'm seeing in her face, mostly, is fear.

"I'm real sorry about this," Lisbeth says. She opens the back door, unhooks Luke from his car seat and before I can even move, Greg is right there, wrenching the kid from her hands, burying his face in the boy's neck, sobbing, murmuring and then, before I can say even a single word to Lisbeth, three patrol cars come from behind the grocery store, lights and sirens waking up the dead parking lot. "Jesus," Lisbeth says, "is this necessary?"

"Be happy the news van isn't here yet," I say.

"I didn't kidnap your grandson," she says. "Jesus. I'm *helping*."

"You knew Luke wasn't your son's kid," I say. "You haven't been in his life at all. Don't give me this bullshit."

"Mr. D'Amico," she says, "we don't need cops."

"Be happy the cops are here," I say, "because without them, you'd be fucking dead."

Cruisers block Lisbeth's car. Cops come flooding out and then Lisbeth is facedown, a knee in her back, cuffs on her wrists, getting hauled up, tossed into the back of a car, door slamming, Greg still sobbing, everything moving so fast now that I don't even know where Detective Nitch was hiding when he appears before me, except it's like he's tilting to one side. I'm in a fun house. Greg is saying something but I'm not hearing him. I try to tell him to look for the meteors, point to the sky, it's been ten thousand years since the sky has looked like this, make sure the kid sees it, make sure he remembers this night . . .

I lean against my car. I'm covered in sweat. I want to take off my shoes, I'm so cold.

Detective Nitch grabs me by my wrist. I feel his thumb bury into my flesh. "Easy there, big daddy," he says, "just breathe."

Caroline says, *Not yet.*

FIRST FACE I SEE when I come to is Mad Tony. He's sitting in a chair beside my hospital bed. Caroline is behind him, staring out the window, the sun so bright I might be in Heaven, but I know Mad Tony wouldn't be there.

"Back from the dead," he says.

"What day is it?"

"Thursday."

"What day was it?"

"Tuesday."

I try to sit up, but that's not happening. "Was I shot?"

"Heart attack," Mad Tony says. "Cops saved your life."

"How about that."

Mad Tony gets up, comes back with a nurse. "Mr. D'Amico," the nurse says, "are you in pain?"

"No," I say. "Maybe a little."

The nurse nods, adjusts the bag hanging above my head. "Between one and ten," the nurse says, "where's your pain?"

"Six," I say. Caroline says, *Liar. Tell the truth. They want to help you.* "Maybe closer to eight."

"Good, good," she says. "I'll be back in just a minute with your doctor. He'll be very happy you're up. Stay right here."

Mad Tony waits for the nurse to leave then says, "You put a fright into us." He squeezes my hand. "We've been working but I don't got news."

"Diane was here," I say. "Caroline, too."

"Whatever you say," Mad Tony says, "but I've been here every day, Ceec."

"No," I say. "Diane was here." I tap my head. "I felt her with me. She's gone. You don't need to look for her."

Mad Tony says, "We've been looking for that shitbag."

"Stop."

"Stop?"

"He'll show up," I say. "He's got nowhere else to go. My guess, he tries to take me out."

"That isn't gonna happen."

"That's how a guy like him thinks."

"Cops get him first," Mad Tony says, "we'll take care of him in jail."

The doctor walks in. He's tall, silver-haired, wearing a blue shirt open at the collar. I recognize him from the billboards in town. If you're a good cardiologist in the desert, you've got a billboard. "Mr. D'Amico," he says. "I'm Dr. Hirshberg. You're a lucky man."

"I'm not that lucky," I say.

"Well," he says, "then maybe you just have good timing. In either case, let's talk about how to keep you alive."

GREG DRIVES ME HOME, Little Luke in the back in his car seat, a stuffed dinosaur on his lap. It's been a week. Diane is sitting beside Luke. She's been visiting every day.

Greg clears his throat. "Listen, I know you've got a nurse coming, but I don't feel right about it. You home alone. So, me and Luke, I'm thinking we take the guest room. Mad Tony can't be cooking meals for you. Hunters will give me time off. Please don't fight me on this."

I look back at Little Luke. Diane nods. She's always the same. About twenty-five. I guess that's where she's locked for me.

"I think that's fine."

Little Luke says, "Cat!"

"That's all he says now," Greg says. "Everything is 'Cat!'"

"Lisbeth still in jail awaiting trial?" I ask.

"Yeah," Greg says.

"We got someone take care of that?"

"That what you want?"

"That what *you* want?"

Greg thinks for a moment. "I can't be involved in this level of shit anymore, Pops." He looks up into the rearview, at his kid. "If I'm in prison, Luke has no one. So, something happens, they're gonna be looking at me straight away. Let's let the law handle it. Okay?"

"You're not worried about Kirby coming back?"

"I wish he would," Greg says. "But I'm not looking for him. And neither should you. Not in the condition you're in."

We pull up to the house. There's maybe fifty people out front. Diane. Caroline. My own father. My brother Dominic, who caught a shank at Pelican Bay. Missy Debarka, who died in a car accident when we were 17, flew out the window, but I had on a seatbelt. My cousin Andrew. My grandfather. Paul Bisco and Lloyd Mitas, AIDS back in the '90s. Carl Degollado, froze to death a thousand yards from the tram station up the mountain, back when we were just kids. Sarah Wade, who I loved before I met Caroline, and who left me for an accountant. And more. And more.

"You invite all these people?" I ask.

Greg says, "Doctor said to keep it quiet for a few days. We'll get you settled and see about getting some dinner."

We park in the garage. When I get out of the car, the fifty stand four deep on the driveway. It's about 4 P.M., the sun already buried behind Mount San Jacinto, and so I make eye contact with each of them, tell them I see them, tell them that I know what to do.

STUBERVILLE CALLS ME.

It's after ten at night. Greg and Luke are both asleep. It's June now. Three months since everything. Today it was 116 degrees outside. It's cooled down to an even 100. The night is thick with cicadas. Pallid bats fly low over the golf course, searching for mosquitos and scorpions. I'm on a chaise lounge, sipping a cocktail of ice and cranberry juice. Dr. Hirshberg told me alcohol is a no-go for another six weeks.

I could be living on my own. Could be going down to the club. Making sure everyone is collecting. Running the business. But fact is, I like having Greg and Luke in the house. Like seeing Diane in Luke's eyes, now that Diane and Caroline and most everyone else has stopped coming by. So Mad Tony brings by money, gets groceries, sits and bullshits. The end of my pain meds coincided with a bit more clarity on reality. Heart is working good now, too, my brain getting the blood it needs. My decision-making is back. I'm like the old me.

That's the problem.

The old me.

Not the young me.

Fifty-three and feeling like I'm eighty-three.

All this rage, waiting for its release, and here it comes.

"I have him," Stuberville says.

"Where?"

"He's scared."

I get up, walk to the edge of my property, turn back and stare at my house. If I didn't know, who would I think lived in that house? Would I think three generations of mobsters had lived between those walls? If I were on the fairway right now, bats overhead, and I saw myself standing *here*, a cell phone pressed to my ear, would I think the man I was viewing was a killer?

"Tell me where," I say.

"First thing," Stuberville says, "he says he buried Diane in the desert."

"Where?"

"He couldn't find it. We went out looking. He was high as shit. She's in the dirt now, Cecil, she got her burial. She's at peace. Let's handle this business and then call it."

Diane sits with her feet in the pool. She's sixteen. Before the problems. The drugs. The losers. Everything we tried to do right backfiring. So much my own fault.

She nods.

"Fine," I say.

"Two minutes," Stuberville says, "I'll be on your drive-way. He's blindfolded. I gave him about seven Xanax. He's got his sentence. That's code. However you want to do it, I support it."

MAD TONY PICKS ME up. It's before dawn. We're an hour east of Palm Springs. We've used this place before.

In the distance, Stuberville's stolen car still burns.

"Boss," Mad Tony says. "The fuck?"

"It's done," I say.

"What's done?"

"All the scales are even."

"How'd you even—" he begins, but then stops. "I guess I don't want to know." We sit there for a minute, Tony looking me over. "You lost a shoe."

I look down. Sure enough. I was wearing slippers when Stuberville called.

He gets out of the car. Walks toward the fire. Turns on the flashlight on his phone. Scans the area. Leans down, picks up a slipper. Waves it at me. Twenty minutes later, we're getting onto Interstate 10. The sun's up. I doze, wake up with Diane's voice in my ear. *You did what was right,* she says. *No more.*

I'm too old, I tell her.

You have to promise me. It ends here.

"It ends here," I say.

"There was no question," Mad Tony says. "You did what was right."

We come down the long slope of highway into the valley. The Salton Sea glimmers to the south. The desert mountains push up through the landscape like jagged glass. And so we go, faster and faster into the present, leaving it all behind, this last act, this last vengeance.

PEARL JOY

IIIII SJ Rozan

Pearl Joy had been dead a week when Chang Lo's dreams began.

The dreams weren't the first odd occurrences during those days. By the time the whispers and the pale figure started coming to disturb his sleep Chang had already been first angry, then worried, then frightened by the things that were taking place.

He hadn't bothered to hide the anger, but he'd lied about the reason and concealed the worry and the fear from Big Boss. Chang's value to Big Boss lay in his ability to provoke those sensations in others. An enforcer cowering from the ghost of a murdered whore would be useless and Chang knew what happened to people who were useless to Big Boss.

The same thing that had happened to Pearl Joy.

Chang had been there when Big Boss killed the girl. He'd been surprised not to be given the assignment, but Big Boss said there was no assignment because he hadn't meant to do it. He'd just meant to beat her, to tell her in a way she wouldn't forget that letting one of her regulars go from customer to boyfriend was a very bad idea. Boyfriends gave girls presents; they thought they had rights; sometimes they even wanted girls to go away with them. No one but Big Boss gave Big Boss's girls anything and a girl even thinking about leaving before she'd paid off her smuggling debt was an infection that could spread through the house and make all the girls more difficult to control.

He'd intended to teach Pearl Joy a lesson and at the same time make an example of her to the others. When she stopped groaning and then stopped moving, Big Boss was disgusted that the house was now one girl short but Pearl Joy, he said, had been trouble from the beginning. He'd get a replacement girl from the snakehead. Meanwhile the example he'd wanted to make of her to the rest of the house had been well and truly made. All the girls knew what had happened. The beating had taken place in the slop room. The kitchen women, Old Mi and Ugly Lu, had seen it. Big Boss hadn't hidden it and he didn't deny it.

Chang was the one to make sure the kitchen women and everyone else also knew what would happen to any girl, and to her family back in China, who said a word about it.

Big Boss considered sending Chang to go after the boyfriend, also, but the boyfriend was a drug dealer. They had friends—and enforcers—of their own. Big Boss didn't back away from a fight when it mattered, but here he just didn't care that much. Better to have Chang go to the boyfriend and say that Pearl Joy had run away, that Big Boss considered the boyfriend at least partly responsible because of the ideas he'd put in her head, and that everyone would be happier if the boyfriend took his business to another house from now on.

Chang did get the assignment of disposing of Pearl Joy's body. Four days after he'd done that, rolling the girl in a blanket and dumping her weighted form into the waters off Staten Island, the first odd thing happened to Chang. Later he came to realize that that fact—four days, the unlucky number, the homophone for "death"—had been significant in itself. At the time, after his first gasp of shocked surprise at seeing gleaming white chopsticks sticking straight up from the white porcelain bowl of perfectly mounded rice outside his bedroom door, he'd gotten angry. Vertical chopsticks in a bowl of food—an offering from the living to the deceased. Who dared to curse Chang this way, to suggest that he was already dead?

He'd grabbed up the bowl and charged down to the kitchen. The cook, Old Mi, was stirring a pot. Old Mi had once been one of Big Boss's girls. When her value to the customers decreased as she aged, Big Boss, impressed with her abilities in the kitchen, gave her the job of cook. She'd long since paid her smuggling debt and now sent money home. She could have left the house and tried her luck elsewhere, but her life would not have changed: somewhere she'd be a cook, and the house was a place she knew. She looked after the girls, giving them tea, drying their tears, applying remedies to bruises. Listening to their memories of home and their hopes for more than this.

While Old Mi stirred the pot, her assistant, Ugly Lu, unpacked a bag of vegetables she'd bought at the market. None of the girls were allowed out of the house without one of Big Boss's men, except Ugly Lu, so she could shop. Ugly Lu had gone straight from the snakehead's boat, the same one that had brought Pearl Joy, to the kitchen; and lucky she was that Big Boss had decided Old Mi needed help. Ugly Lu was young but she had a long red scar on her face and the beginnings of a hump on her back and she would never have paid off her smuggling debt if she'd had to wait for a customer to select her from among the other girls. Big Boss would have sold her to a much worse place than this and even there she'd have died before she'd earned her way out. But the snakehead claimed Ugly Lu could cook, so Big Boss took a chance.

Ugly Lu could cook. She could clean, also, and was happy to spend extra hours doing it, the more quickly to repay her debt. And one more thing: she was a fortune teller. The girls consulted her, which Chang thought absurd: their futures for the coming years were not in doubt, and better to spend time with their customers and earn their freedom faster than to waste it asking questions which had only one answer. Some of the men had also been to see her and even Big Boss had consulted her twice.

Chang hadn't. He believed in signs and omens, of course he did; only a fool ignored the spirit world, and at his peril. But Chang had no questions for Ugly Lu. He was content in the knowledge that his next years would be the same as his past ones, in his position as Enforcer Chang, Big Boss's right-hand man.

So the first strange thing, the rice bowl, only made him angry. When he burst into the kitchen with it, both women looked up and then backed away.

"Who did this?" Chang demanded.

Old Mi shook her head, eyes wide on the unlucky bowl. Ugly Lu shook her head, too, then reached out and plucked the chopsticks from the rice. Old Mi let out a breath and Chang couldn't deny feeling relieved himself. Ugly Lu spoke. "They're not ours."

"Not ours? Not whose? What aren't?"

"That bowl," said Ugly Lu. "These chopsticks. We don't use those here. In this house. Pure white porcelain? No." She looked at Old Mi, who shook her head again.

Chang stared at the bowl in his hand, at the chopsticks in Ugly Lu's. He slammed the bowl to the floor. Shards of porcelain and grains of rice flew into the air. "Clean that up and throw it all away." Chang stalked out of the kitchen, leaving the door swinging behind him.

One day later, a gift was left at the doorstep of his room, waiting when he awoke in the morning. It was beautifully wrapped—but in white paper, with white ribbon. Again, Chang flared with anger. White, the color of mourning! Who dared? He tore the paper off and opened the box.

Within lay a clock.

"Giving a clock"—the homophone for "bidding fare-well to one on a deathbed!" And the clock itself, a reminder that one's time is finite.

And this clock, face and case, was white.

Chang's fury flared, but at the center of his burning rage he felt a small cold stab of fear. He hurried from the house and tossed the clock and all its wrappings into a dumpster a block away.

Throughout the day Chang went from girl to girl, speaking to each in the voice of quiet menace that was his hallmark. He didn't expect any to confess and none did, but by night he was satisfied that whoever had been play-ing these tricks on him, for whatever reason, understood now the stakes for her if she continued. Nevertheless, that night he used cocaine and stayed awake, ready to leap upon any sound that might mean someone was placing something at his door.

There was no one, and there was nothing.

The following night Chang considered staying awake again, but he was very tired from the night before and the cocaine; and if he stayed on watch a second night he'd be giv-ing the unknown trickster a power he refused to let her have.

When he awoke in the morning he found a white-framed and white-beribboned mirror on his bureau, positioned facing the door, to most easily attract the ghosts a gift mirror will.

In his room! This trickster had been in his room! Chang strode to the door and turned the handle to yank it open.

It was still locked.

He felt the icy stab of fear again. It spread from the pit of his stomach to freeze the heat of his anger.

It wasn't a difficult lock to pick. And the house had a master key. Or maybe he'd forgotten to lock it, so tired was he when he went to bed. He told himself all these things, and immediately dismissed them. If he'd forgotten to lock it, why was it locked now? If someone had come in by either key or lock-picking, why hadn't he woken?

Chang spent the day under a cloud so dark it filled the house. Girls turned away from his glares. The other men frowned and muttered to each other. Big Boss asked Chang if something was wrong. To that Chang said no. How could he tell Big Boss that he was frightened because he thought he was being haunted?

That night he was again very tired. He made sure, though, that the door was locked before he fell into bed and into a dark, troubled sleep.

When he awoke, his fingernails had been clipped.

They were very short, very ragged. The clippings sat in a neat pile on his night table on a white—white!—square of paper.

Chang began to shake all over.

Clipping fingernails at night invites ghosts into the house. As does a gift mirror. Someone had come into his room and done this and he'd felt nothing. Someone had given him a clock, someone had left white chopsticks standing in a white bowl of rice—

Chang shook his head to clear it of an unaccustomed heaviness, of a worrisome confusion. He searched for sounds or sensations from the night before but found only whispers and shadowy forms.

He dressed and staggered to the kitchen for a cup of tea.

Old Mi and Ugly Lu looked up when he walked in. Both women's eyes widened. Old Mi immediately turned away and went back to cutting up a chicken. Ugly Lu said, "Chang Lo, do you feel well?"

"Just give me tea."

She poured a cup while he sat on a stool at the table. She watched him; when he was finished she poured him another.

"Don't you have work to do? Stop staring at me," Chang said. Ugly Lu turned and went to lift the top of a pot on the stove. She added chopped cabbage to it, stirred it, tasted the liquid from it.

"No," said Chang. "Come back here."

Ugly Lu replaced the top of the pot and returned to the table.

"Tell my fortune," Chang said.

The woman turned to Old Mi, asking permission to neglect her kitchen duties for a time. Old Mi looked scared, waved for Ugly Lu to hurry to comply with Chang's request. He might be pale and tired but he was still Enforcer Chang.

Ugly Lu wiped her hands. From a cabinet she took a book and a bucket of Kau Chim sticks. "Shake them," she told Chang.

He did, until one stick fell out onto the floor. Ugly Lu retrieved it, read it, and consulted her book. She bit her lip and she glanced at Chang.

"Well?" he said. "What is it?"

"Someone . . . " she said, then, "She's angry. Someone's angry."

"Who?"

"I don't know."

"What does she want?"

"I don't know that either. Let me read your palm—"

"No!" Chang jumped up. His chair clattered to the floor. "This is meaningless. Old women's superstition! Get back to work." He stomped from the kitchen.

That night Chang used cocaine again, and the next night, too. Nothing happened, nothing appeared, not at his door or in his room. The next night he almost did the same, but after dinner a heavy tiredness overcame him. His head was pounding. He chose to sleep.

That was the night the dreams began.

A figure in white, whispering. An icy touch on Chang's hand. "You know," she said. "You know." Then she vanished.

The next night he used cocaine but after a few hours the strange heavy exhaustion returned. He slept despite the drug.

The figure returned. Chang felt his heart pound at her icy touch but he couldn't move. "You know," she whispered. "You know, and you must tell. I'll take you with me, Chang, unless you tell." She wrapped her wintry fingers around his wrist and tugged gently. Terror surged in him. She let him go. "I'll take you with me. To hell, Chang. I'll take you to hell." Her wild laugh was soft, but the quiet just made it more frightening. Then she was gone.

In the morning Chang forced himself out of a heavy slumber and down to the kitchen. "My palm," he said to Ugly Lu. "Read my palm."

Ugly Lu glanced at Old Mi, then hurried to comply. She took Chang's hand in her own, traced its lines with her finger. "Oh," she said, then even more quietly, "Oh."

"What is it?" Chang snapped.

The woman let out a long sigh. Without looking into Chang's eyes she said, "It is . . . it's Pearl Joy."

"Pearl Joy? What about her?"

After a moment: "Will you do the Kau Chim sticks again?"

"The sticks? Why?

"I can't be sure. From your palm."

"Sure of what?"

Now she did look into his eyes. "I can't be sure of what she wants."

Cold fear flooded Chang's heart. He was struck dumb. When Ugly Lu brought the Kau Chim bucket he took it and shook the sticks. She picked up the one that fell out, read it, consulted her book; she read the stick a second time, and the book again, also. "Chang Lo . . . " she began, then stopped.

"What? What does she want?" He tried not to show his mounting dread.

Ugly Lu spoke slowly, making every word clear. "She says you know what happened to her. You were there and you saw. She says you must tell."

"Tell? Tell what happened to Pearl Joy? I can't do that. I'll be killed." So great was Chang's terror that he forgot to appear unconcerned, forgot to try and save face in front of the kitchen women.

"Chang Lo," said Ugly Lu, "no matter what you do in this moment, one day you'll die. Pearl Joy wants her killer brought to justice. If you don't do as she asks, she'll be waiting for you in hell."

"No," Chang whispered. "She won't be waiting. She'll take me there. She'll drag me off. But I can't. I can't tell." Chang rushed from the kitchen, leaving Ugly Lu and Old Mi staring after him.

It was three days before Chang gave in, three nights of whispers and glacial touches, heavy limbs and exhaustion and stabbing morning headaches. On the third night, when the ghost of Pearl Joy brushed Chang's lips with her own icy mouth, Chang screamed. Pearl Joy laughed and pointed a long white finger at him. "Tomorrow night," she said. "Tell my story, or I'll be back tomorrow night and we'll ride to hell together."

In the morning Chang stumbled to the bathroom to be sick. After staring at his reflection, he thought about killing himself. Suicide would save him from having to betray Big Boss. But it wouldn't save him from Pearl Joy. She'd be waiting on the other side, angry, vindictive, and immortal.

And Big Boss—this was all his fault, wasn't it? It was he who'd killed Pearl Joy. Chang had asked her why she wasn't haunting Big Boss, why she was coming to Chang instead. She'd just laughed, a horrible cackle. But three times in the past seven years Chang had killed for Big Boss, and no ghosts had ever come to him. Now Big Boss had done it himself and Pearl Joy was going to come tonight to drag Chang off to hell.

When Chang left the house for the last time he didn't go to the nearby precinct. If Big Boss got word of what he was doing before he'd done it, it was possible he'd be killed before he'd told the story. That, he knew, would not satisfy Pearl Joy any more than his suicide would have. He glanced at the house, then headed uptown, to a randomly chosen precinct in another neighborhood.

Chang never went back to the house; he was put into protective custody as soon as he told the police who he was and what he'd come to say. He never saw another ghost as long as he lived, which was quite a long time, though most of that time was spent in prison—a different prison from the one to which Big Boss was sent, after the trial.

And because he never went back, there were other things Chang never saw. He didn't see the look that passed between Old Mi and Ugly Lu when he left the house that last morning. He missed the pile of white paper and white ribbon, bundled together with the flowing white fabric that made Ugly Lu look so like a ghost when she wore it. He was not aware of Ugly Lu thrusting deep into the center of that parcel what was left of the heroin and the hallucinogens she'd gotten from Pearl Joy's drug-dealer boyfriend. He'd been grimly happy to help when Ugly Lu explained her plan, and she'd only needed the tiniest amount of each drug to dissolve in water and sprinkle in Chang's rice bowl at night. Chang didn't see Ugly Lu stuff the bundle into a garbage sack, or take it with her when she left the house to do the shopping, or toss it into a dumpster a block away. He didn't know how carefully she cleaned his room when she returned, making sure to scrub away all signs of drips from the ice cubes she'd used to keep her hands and her lips so cold. She made his bed as though she expected him to return and she conscientiously locked up with the master key Big Boss had given her after her first year in the house. Big Boss said there was no reason she shouldn't have a key. She wouldn't dare steal from any of the rooms. It would be too obvious who had done it, and Big Boss was sure Ugly Lu knew just how good she had it here.

Chang was totally unaware of the smiles on the faces of Old Mi and Ugly Lu, who didn't think they had it so very good and felt they could have it much better, as, before sunrise the following day, they slipped out of the house together. Old Mi took nothing except family photos and what money she had. Ugly Lu had no money. She took only her Kim Chau sticks and her book.

As for Big Boss, he didn't know they were gone until the police, who arrived just after daybreak, had rousted all the girls and the men. Big Boss couldn't account to himself for the absence of Old Mi or Ugly Lu, or for Chang's; but he didn't focus on them. By then, he had much bigger problems.

EDITORS

||||||||||||

Gary Phillips has published novels, comics, novellas, short stories and edited or co-edited several anthologies, including the Anthony-winning *The Obama Inheritance: Fifteen Stories of Conspiracy Noir. Violent Spring,* his debut effort more than a quarter century ago, was named in 2020 one of the essential crime novels of Los Angeles. He is also a story editor on *Snowfall,* an FX show about crack and the CIA in 1980s South Central, where he grew up.

Gar Anthony Haywood is the Shamus and Anthony Award–winning author of fourteen novels, including the Aaron Gunner private eye series and Joe and Dottie Loudermilk mysteries. His short fiction has been included in the *Best American Mystery Stories* anthologies and he has written for network television and both the *New York Times* and *Los Angeles Times.* He and his wife, Donna, make their home in Denver, Colorado.

|CONTRIBUTORS
IIIIIIIIIIIIIIIIIIIIIIIIIIII

Scott Adlerberg is the author of the novels *Spiders and Flies, Jungle Horses, Graveyard Love,* and *Jack Waters.* He has written many short stories and contributes pieces regularly to sites such as *Criminal Element,* CrimeReads, and *Mystery Tribune.* Every summer, he hosts the Word for Word Reel Talks film commentary series in Bryant Park in Manhattan. He was born in New York City and lives in Brooklyn.

Cara Black is the author of twenty books in the New York Times bestselling Aimée Leduc series as well as the thriller *Three Hours in Paris.* She has received multiple nominations for the Anthony and Macavity Awards, and her books have been translated into German, Norwegian, Japanese, French, Spanish, Italian, and Hebrew. She lives in San Francisco with her husband and son and visits Paris frequently.

Christopher Chambers is a Washington, DC native. He is the author of the crime novels *Sympathy for the Devil* and *A Prayer for Deliverance*. His pulp repertoire includes *Rocket Crockett and the Shanghai She Devil*, and *Black Pulp* I & II. He co-edited the *The Darker Mask*. His noir detective novel *Scavenger* debuted in 2020. His short stories "I, Shuri" and "In the Matter of Maybell and Bobby Jefferson" appear in *The Black Panther: Tales of Wakanda* and *Midnight Hour*, respectively.

Sarah M. Chen has published a children's book and numerous short stories, one of which won a Derringer Award. Her noir novella, *Cleaning Up Finn*, was an Anthony finalist and IPPY Award winner. She was a co-editor for several anthologies, including the latest from Sisters in Crime/LA, *Avenging Angelenos*. She's written for the *Los Angeles Review of Books*, *Hapa Mag*, and *Wellbeing*, among others. Follow her on Twitter at @sarahmchen.

Aaron Philip Clark is a novelist and screenwriter from Los Ageles. His crime thriller *Under Color of Law*, featuring Detective Trevor Finnegan, is a Thriller Award finalist and the 2021 Book Pipeline Adaptation grand-prize winner. *Blue Like Me*, the second novel in his Trevor Finnegan series, will be published in November 2022. To learn more, please visit www.AaronPhilipClark.com and follow him on Twitter @_Writemeaworld.

Teresa Dovalpage was born in Havana, Cuba. She earned her BA in English literature and an MA in Spanish literature at the University of Havana, and her PhD in Latin American literature at the University of New Mexico. She is the author of thirteen other works of fiction and three plays, and is the winner of the Rincón de la Victoria Award and a finalist for the Herralde Award. She lives in New Mexico.

Tod Goldberg is the *New York Times* bestselling author of over a dozen books, including *The Low Desert, Gangsterland,* a finalist for the Hammett Prize, *Gangster Nation,* and *Living Dead Girl,* a finalist for the *Los Angeles Times* Book Prize. He lives in Indio, CA where he directs the Low Residency MFA in Creative Writing & Writing for the Performing Arts at the University of California, Riverside.

Darrell James is the author of the award-winning and multi-nominated Del Shannon series to include: *Nazareth Child,* winner of the Left Coast Crime Eureka Award for Best First Novel; *Sonora Crossing,* and his most recent, *Purgatory Key.* In addition, his more than forty short stories appear in various mystery anthologies, including the story *Even a Blind Man* that appears in the Lee Child anthology, *Vengeance.* You can find Darrell at: www.darrelljames.com.

Richie Narvaez is the author of *Roach-killer and Other Stories*, *Hipster Death Rattle*, and *Noiryorican*. His YA historical novel, *Holly Hernandez and the Death of Disco*, won an Agatha Award and an Anthony Award. He lives in the Bronx.

SJ Rozan is author of eighteen novels and over eighty short stories, and editor of three anthologies. She has won multiple awards, including the Edgar, Shamus, Anthony, Nero, Macavity; Japanese Maltese Falcon; and the Private Eye Writers of America Life Achievement Award. She'll be teaching this summer at the Art Workshop International in Assisi, Italy. Her latest book is *Family Business,* and her website is www.sjrozan.net.

Alex Segura is an acclaimed, award-winning writer of novels, comic books, short stories, and podcasts. He is the author of the noir novel *Secret Identity*, *Star Wars Poe Dameron: Free Fall,* and the Pete Fernandez Mystery series (including the Anthony Award–nominated crime novels *Dangerous Ends*, *Blackout*, and *Miami Midnight*). He has also written numerous short stories, comics, and a fictional podcast.

Attorney and award-winning author **Pamela Samuels Young** has penned more than a dozen books, most of them fast-paced legal thrillers that tackle important social issues. Her thriller *Anybody's Daughter* won the NAACP Image Award for Outstanding Fiction. The dearth of women and people of color depicted as characters in the mystery genre prompted Pamela to write her first novel while still practicing law. To read excerpts of her books, visit Pamela's website at www.pamelasamuelsyoung.com.